FATE

FALLS

HARD

LELIA A PIET

FATE FALLS HARD

LELIA A PIET

Origins First Press

Library of Congress Control Number: 2023912714

ISBN: 979-8-9882545-0-8 (paperback)

ISBN: 979-8-9882545-1-5 (ebook)

Cover designed by Miblart.

Published by Origins First Press, West Palm Beach, Florida 33401.

AIYANNA

APRIL 1958

Today should be one of the happiest days of my life. Instead, I steel myself against the growing angst and ferocious pain ravaging my body. My people have always flaunted their ability to endure, survive, carry on in the most adverse of times. I don't feel strong. I don't have the energy to fight the pain, to argue with Wacquin, to battle The Community, to stave off the fear. Wacquin claims I have nothing to fear. The Community is behind me—the faith of its people and the wisdom of the elders will pull me through. Women throughout history have bore babies without medical facilities, he says.

"Breathe in the life force around you," Wacquin instructs, the light from the fire burning across the room haloing him. "Envision our beautiful little babies."

Though Wacquin isn't my legal spouse, I love him all the same and can't imagine my life without him. Yet, I do. We may be 'coupled,' but I cannot raise my babies in The Community, under the scrutiny and guidance of the elders, deep inside these woods, no modern comforts of electricity, of plumbing, of running water. Another contraction seizes the bottom half of my body. A scream escapes. I clamp my lips together under my teeth, but the mistake has been made.

"Hush, love. Breathe. Inhale the energy around you. Surround our babies with peace. The elders assure, it won't be much longer. Our girls will be here soon."

In my mind, I bring forth an image of the two, Ama and Leoti, hoping the prophecy of the elders holds true. At four months, the elders informed me I would have twins, and soon after I felt the kicks of four little feet. Later in the pregnancy, their visions foretold the gender of the babies.

"Wacquin, please, I need a doctor. The girls. What if something goes wrong?" I ask, struggling to mask the grimace tugging across my face.

"Aiyanna, the elders have seen the birth, they've seen the children, all is well. We have nothing to fear," he says calmly, bracing my contracting abdomen between his large, strong hands.

The peace Wacquin promises swims in his dark eyes. I want nothing more than to share his confidence, to trust him. But I've done that before. I left my people, my family, my land because I believed in him, believed all he told me of The Community. Desperate to exit my ancestors and their bitterness over actions against them moons and moons ago, I put my faith in Wacquin. Over time, it has become clear Wacquin will never love me as I do him. Wacquin's allegiance to The Community is strong, stronger than his devotion to me, and I do not harbor the conviction for this place as Wacquin does. I want my girls to grow up in the modern world, go to regular schools, have friends they can play, skip, and sing along with.

The bottom half of my body feels as if it is being wrenched apart. The heat, the pain. My screams fill the small room.

"Please, Wacquin. Please, help me."

"It's almost over, my love." Wacquin presses a wet, cool cloth to my forehead while brushing the hair from my face. I breathe in the scent of the spiritual wash, a mixture of bay and olive leaves steeped in salt.

Under the flickering candlelight, I watch him. How can I be so conflicted? When I first met this man, I believed him to be a gift from God. The color of his skin never mattered to me. All I saw was a good, kind, gentle, and loving man. Wacquin told me of the group he had formed, where people existed in peace and as one with nature. Aside from the bitterness and loathing I observed each day, it didn't sound that far off from my own upbringing. Anxious to escape the reservation on which I had lived my whole life, as well as the condemnation of my family for loving a man of a different race, I eagerly accepted his invitation to be part of The Community. But there are two sides to this group, and I cannot practice their peaceful ways when it means I must condone the evil acts accompanying this lifestyle. My people were healers who condemned witches and their heinous activities. Not everyone in The Community holds such power, only the elders. Some of the elders are healers, while others are conjurers. According to Wacquin, all healing and conjuring work must be performed with a pure heart—each spell must be justified, he explained. Having witnessed some questionable instances, however, I can't help but wonder where the line of justification is drawn, and I will not subject my girls to such actions and proclaim them acceptable.

"You know we don't have to move far, Wacquin." Though it's a tired plea, a lost battle, I have to try again every time I pose it. "We can settle in the next town, and you can still be near The Community. Waynesville is just over the ridge, and the girls would have a normal life. We could find a small house, nothing too large. It would be our little family."

"No, Aiyanna. You know I cannot do that. The Community needs me."

"I need you, Wacquin. The girls need you."

"Aiyanna, you are a beautiful Cherokee woman. I am a black man. The common world does not hold a place for us, only bias. Here, in The Community, we are accepted. Wanted. Loved."

"And surrounded by the workings of evil." The words slip from my tongue.

Shaking his head, Wacquin lowers his gaze. He lifts himself

from the chair beside my bed and walks to the dresser near the door.

"Please don't leave," I plead.

"I could ask the same of you, but I won't." Wacquin returns to my side with a fresh cloth. He rubs it over the length of my right arm, then reaches across me to repeat the process on my left.

"Wacquin, I can't stay here."

I watch him refold the cloth and place it on the bedside table. "And you know the rules of The Community. The members in this place live peacefully, giving love and accepting love as we choose. We each have a responsibility to seek our own personal enlightenment, and while there may be members who are wiser than others, here, we are all equal."

Wacquin looks down, laces his fingers, and looks back to me, ache etching the corners of his eyes and mouth. "Our coupling in The Community may not be considered marriage by modern society, but it is a solid bond. Still, no member of The Community is expected to sacrifice their happiness for another, Aiyanna. Each member is free to live by the means that makes the individual happy."

"You make me happy, Wacquin."

"As you do me, Aiyanna. I will not force you to live a life you do not want, but the world you wish to be a part of holds no place for me."

I search for a retort but cannot think through the pain ripping through the lower half of my body. I howl without reserve for the pain, for the frustration, for the agony I understand I will endure in the days to follow. Wacquin will not choose our children or me over The Community.

Cool air of the April evening rushes into the room as the door swings open. Elder Dena, who has watched over me throughout the last long months of my pregnancy, lifts the sheet from my bottom half. Through tears and sweat and exertion, I look to her for relief, for hope.

"It's time, my girl. The little ones are ready."

* * *

I WAKE WITH A START, a chill coursing through me, prickling my skin. Hands fly to my stomach, feeling for the little, hard, round bodies. They're gone. Pushing to a sitting position, I take in the room. All of the candles have been extinguished. Light from the fire burning inside the fireplace now serves illumination duty for the small space. The chair Wacquin occupied earlier is empty, no babies sleep close by.

"Wacquin," I call out. "Dena?" The only response I receive is from the crackling fire and the wind outside the cabin.

I swing my legs to the side of the bed, use my arms to push to a standing position. Light-headed and faint, I fall back to the edge of the mattress, willing myself steady. I close my eyes and take a moment to cease the spinning motion of my head. Taking a deep breath, I try again, slower.

The door swings open, hinges squealing under the force. Elder Dena rushes across the room, taking me by the shoulders, easing me back into the bed.

"Where are the babies? Are they okay? They're girls? Where's Wacquin?"

The elder hurries away without an answer. I watch as Dena struggles against the wind to close out the night sky beyond the door.

Dena crosses back to the bedside, tugging the blankets, tucking them tightly underneath me. "The girls are perfect. Wacquin is with them, as is Elder Rey."

"I want to see my babies. Take me to see them." I wrestle to release myself from the confines of the bedding.

"Wacquin will be in very soon to introduce you. We wanted to make sure you got some rest. You lost consciousness during the last push."

"I don't remember," I tell her, allowing her to settle me back against the pillows. "And they're okay? Healthy?"

"All fingers and toes accounted for. Beautiful complexions, a gorgeous blend of you and Wacquin. They're identical," she croons.

I smile, allowing air into my lungs again. "Please. Will you tell Wacquin to bring them now? I need to see them. I want to meet my girls," I say to her, and then, "Ama and Leoti." I smooth the sheet over my legs, a sense of accomplishment swirled with an overwhelming ache to hold them fills me.

The door opens. Wacquin enters the room, cradling a small angel in one arm. He looks at me, his eyes bright with tears. I sit up, arms reaching out, anxious with anticipation.

Wacquin walks toward me, carefully passing over the precious bundle. I take her into my arms, eyes never leaving the sleeping ball of perfection. She is the two of us, our own little creation. I run one hand over her small head covered in fine jet-black hair, touch my finger to her tiny nose. I've never felt more in love than at this very moment.

I look back to Wacquin watching us. "Which one is she? Number one or two?"

"Two," he whispers.

"Leoti," I sigh. "It's so wonderful to meet you, my love." I look back to Wacquin. "Where's Ama? She's okay, isn't she? Dena said they were both okay." I look around the room for Dena to confer, but she must have slipped out.

"Nothing to worry over. Ama is perfect. Just like Leoti," Wacquin answers, watching our daughter sleep.

I ease Leoti onto my chest. "I want to see her. You'll go get Ama?"

Pulling the chair closer, Wacquin lowers himself to sit beside the bed. He runs a finger over the back of sleeping Leoti. He looks at me, a smile stretching across his face. "Ama is marked, Aiyanna."

"What? What do you mean she's marked?" I hold tighter to the child in my arms.

"On her cheek. Ama's right cheek has the large red mark."

"I don't understand." I shake my head at him. "Did I do

something wrong during the birth? Will it heal?"

"No. You did everything just right. It's a birthmark."

"Will she grow out of it? What do the elders say? We should take her to a doctor, Wacquin." I carefully scoot myself up in the bed so as not to disturb Leoti, readying to get Ama and take her over the ridge to Waynesville to find a proper doctor.

"It may get smaller; it may not. There is nothing wrong with her. In fact, she couldn't be more right. It's the mark of greatness, Aiyanna."

"Greatness?" I don't understand. If I could just see her. "Please, Wacquin, bring her to me."

He lowers his head. "I can't."

"What? Bring me my baby, Wacquin." I pull Leoti to rest on my other shoulder, easing her away from the tightness building in my chest, away from her father.

"Aiyanna." Wacquin raises his gaze. "She's an identical twin with the mark of greatness. Ama has to be trained; there are procedures."

"And what the hell is that supposed to mean?" What is wrong with him? Why is he doing this? "She's my child. I am her mother. I have to take care of her, feed her." My voice betrays me, showing the terror burning from deep within my body.

Wacquin moves his hands to rest on his knees, elbows out, squaring off his torso. "That's not possible."

"Wacquin, the baby has to eat. I need to see her. She's only an infant."

"Ama must receive a special diet for the first twenty-four days of her life. I'm sorry, Aiyanna, but you won't be able to see her or nurse her until that time period is up."

"No. No. NO. That is not happening. You will bring me my child. I will not allow this." My voice escalates with frustration and panic. Leoti stirs. A low whimper builds to a wail. I place her to my breast, stroke my finger along her cheek as I have been taught by the other mothers in The Community. She quickly latches on and begins to suck. I cannot even allow myself a congratulatory moment at the first momentous feat, not with Ama's well-being at stake.

"Ama must be trained, Aiyanna. She is a special gift from The Great Provider—an identical twin born with the marking. Ama has the potential to be a two-headed worker. She will one day become a sage and skilled elder."

"No. She absolutely will not. We're leaving. I'm taking the girls away from here. I will not bring them up in The Community, and I most certainly will not allow Ama to become a two-headed worker, a healer maybe but never a conjurer. My child will not be a witch. You can stay with your beloved people, or you can come with your daughters and me. The choice is yours. I've made my decision."

"Conjurers are not witches, Aiyanna. Their abilities are used for the betterment of others."

"I know what conjurers are capable of, Wacquin, and Ama will not be a conjurer, for the betterment of others or for casting evil."

Wacquin sits back in his chair, folding arms across his chest. "I told you I would not ask you to sacrifice your happiness for my own. You are free to leave The Community. I do not wish it so, but Leoti is free to go with you. Ama, however, will not leave here; she must stay with me."

I can no longer hold back the tears welling in my eyes. Defying me, they streak my face, boldly displaying my weakness. I lay my head back against the pillows, stare at the ceiling, will some reasonable solution forward, but exhaustion envelopes me suffocating any sensibility and rational thought.

"If you live in Waynesville," Wacquin continues as I turn my head to him, waiting for him to end this nightmare, "I can bring her to see you. She will always know you are her mother, but if you fight this, Aiyanna, The Community will fight back. Ama will never know you or Leoti."

"Wacquin, please. These are my children," I beg.

"No, Aiyanna. They are our children."

AUGUST 2017

While I may not cling to the faith God exists, one thing is certain—someone is definitely watching over me. Less than two weeks ago, I had accepted the unwelcome fact I would be living with my Aunt Letty and Uncle Shu in the only town I'd ever scribbled at the end of my address. My plan was to substitute teach through this year as a way to get my foot into the doors of an elementary school. But someone or something had other plans for me.

Through the windshield of my car, my focus holds on the facade of Patrick Schelly Elementary. The opportunity could not be more perfect. A new start, in a new town, a new-ish school. No old ghosts looming behind every street sign or sneaking up behind me. No whispers or averted gazes at the local grocery store.

I twist the rearview mirror to check my makeup. The brown eyes boring back at me are familiar, but I still struggle to recognize the reflection in front of me. "You need to be more confident. You belong here," I tell the mirrored image. "You're the teacher this time around, not the parent."

I pull my phone from the cup holder in the center console to find another text message from my aunt. Letty wishes me luck. Asks me to call her soon. I shrug off the guilt she's sprung and slip the phone into my handbag. Other than my internship last spring, I've little idea what to expect on my first day and do not need the distraction of bygones.

The principal gave me no instructions or insights other than to report for teacher workdays on August seventeenth at eight AM. According to the 2017-2018 school calendar I found on the internet, I have seven days to prepare a classroom for my first group of students.

The heat and humidity of August are the first to greet me as I lock up the car. Traveling the sidewalk are others who appear to be teachers heading for the front door of the school. I fall into cadence with them, pretend to be one of them. *You are one of them*. Squaring off my shoulders, I pull open the heavy door.

Inside the front lobby, colleagues embrace one another, exchange pleasantries about their summer breaks. Peering around the clusters, I spot an easel farther down the hall. "Welcome Back Teachers." Everyone seems to be making their way toward the sign. I follow the pack to where several women are perched behind a row of tables outside the entrance to the school's cafeteria. An older woman with dark hair and cat-eye glasses waves me in her direction.

"Hello there, dear. I don't recognize you. You must be one of our new teachers this year. What's your name?"

How many of us are new to the school, I wonder, but rather than answer her question with one of my own, I simply state, "Merel Sowanoke."

"Oh my, that's going to be a mouthful for some of these little ones," she absently replies, shuffling through a stack of name badges.

"I don't plan on using it. I'm going to have the children call me Ms. S."

She locates my name badge inspecting it as she stands to go through a stack of manila file folders. Glancing up at me over her glasses, she nods, offering, "That's a good idea."

"My son had a teacher years ago who had a name that started

with an S. It was also a difficult name to pronounce, so she had her students call her Ms. S." The admission is out of my mouth before I can yank it back. The long, dark hair clings to the base of my neck. I should have pulled it up, tried for a more tailored look. I run a palm under it, wipe the sweat pooling at the collar of my blouse then switch my handbag to hang on the opposite shoulder. Idle hands move to tuck the hair behind my ears. The inevitable inquiry looms.

"That's nice. Did your son go to school around here?"

"No. I've recently relocated. Last week, actually. I haven't even had time to completely unpack yet." *You must stop rambling.* I fold my arms across the middle of my body, immediately thinking it better to pull them back to my sides.

"I know it's in here somewhere," the woman mutters, flipping the folders back and forth. "Okay, here we are. I think I've found everything now. Your class roster is in the folder along with a schedule of all the in-service sessions for the week and a welcome back letter from the PTA." The woman opens the folder, viewing the contents, then closes it to look back at me over the glasses resting on the tip of her nose. "You're the new second-grade teacher," she states as if I didn't know already. "That's such a fun age. Wait a minute. You're..." She lets the thought trail as she looks back inside the folder. "Why, yes, you are. You're Dorothy Conners's new teammate. Well, I'm so glad to meet you." She offers a smile but no documents, holding them securely to her chest. "I'm Hazel McPherson. I'll be your EA. We're the educational assistants," she says, swinging an arm out to indicate the women seated alongside her. "And I'm assigned to you and Dorothy this school year." Her eyes wander over my shoulder. "Look a here! There's Dorothy now. Dorothy," she shouts over the crowd around the table, waving the file folder over my head to get the attention of a petite, trim, older woman. The woman rushes over to stand beside me, her agility belying the creases etching her features. The grey ponytail she's pulled tight to sit high on the back of her head swishes to and fro as she reaches over the table, embracing Hazel McPherson. I edge back, waiting for the women to catch up on the events of their summers, holding to the hope Hazel intends to relinquish my folder soon.

From behind me, I hear someone call my name and twist to see Principal Garber marching toward me. She's no less intimidating today than the day she interviewed me for the position. My hands go back to my hair, pulling it from behind my ears, smoothing it flat. I step forward as she nears, reaching out to accept her handshake.

"Welcome, Merel. We're so glad to have you here at Schelly Elementary."

"Thank you. I'm happy to be here."

The woman looks me over, frowning. Careful not to break eye contact, I run my fingers along the buttons of my blouse, checking they are secure, straight.

"You don't have your paperwork, Ms. Sowanoke?"

Hazel pipes in. "I've got it right here, Jeanine." She waves the folder as evidence of her claim, finally passing it over to me.

"Hello, Dorothy. Have you met your new teammate yet?" Leaving no pause for Dorothy's response, Principal Garber continues, performing the introductions, efficiently moving us on from the sign-in table and ushering us swiftly inside the cafeteria. "Help yourselves to this lovely breakfast the PTA has laid out. We'll be starting soon," Principal Garber informs, turning her attention from me to Dorothy. "You'll get Merel settled in? Show her around?"

"Of course, Jeanine," Dorothy says.

The buzz of multiple conversations amplified in the white cinder block space draws my attention, my head swiveling to take it all in. Stainless steel serving fixtures line the far end of the room. Colorful murals of happy children adorn the two walls on each side enclosed by floor-to-ceiling glass windows at the back of the room. Outside the window is a small fenced in playground.

"So this must be quite the whirlwind for you." Dorothy takes hold of my elbow, leading me to a buffet table set up in front of the cafeteria line. "It's only been a couple of weeks since we found out we needed a new second grade teacher." Dorothy hands me a paper plate then takes one for herself.

"Well, yes," I begin, unsure of how much to say, but decide to take the opportunity to find out more about how I got this job. "About a week and a half ago Principal Garber called me in for the interview and offered me the position immediately. Do you know what happened to the last teacher?"

"I do. Betty McGuffey is one of my oldest friends. She's taught all her life. Betty woke up one morning same as usual and, by midday, had suffered a series of mini-strokes leading up to the big one that has left her debilitated. Poor thing can do nothing for herself right now. In fact, Betty may not be able to look after herself for the rest of her life. The doctors are hopeful, though."

"Oh. That's terrible." We work our way along the brunch layout.

"Betty was born to teach, and goodness, what a pack rat. It's going to take you some time to sort through her classroom. No telling what you'll find in there," Dorothy sorts through a platter of bagels, settling on one with raisins. "There's a little bit of every-thing here." She eyes my empty plate. "Aren't you eating, Merel? Nothing catching your fancy?"

"Maybe some fruit. I don't know if my stomach can handle much more than that this morning. Nerves. First day jitters, I guess."

"Well, that's silly. There's nothing to be nervous about, 'cept maybe what you're going to find in Betty's file cabinets." Dorothy gives my arm a reassuring pat, then turns back to the platter. "Here." She plops a plain bagel on my plate. "Come on. Let's go have a look at our rosters."

We settle ourselves at the end of a long cafeteria table, the attached seats made to accommodate smaller bodies. Dorothy informs me we need to save a couple of places for the rest of our second-grade team. "There are four of us," she explains. "Ben and

Alicia are probably still working on their classrooms. They'll be in soon."

"They've already started putting their rooms together?" I push my plate forward to lay out the file folder.

"Oh, yes. Most of us do. I finished mine off last week. There are so many meetings and in-service sessions we have to attend during these scheduled work days, it's hard to get your classroom put together if you don't do it over the summer during your free time."

"Guess unpacking my apartment is going to have to wait," I say, perusing the calendar of meetings scheduled for the next seven days.

"You're new to the area then?" Dorothy chomps off a chunk of bagel, jaws popping in protest.

I nod in response while trying to make sense of the Teacher's Duties schedule.

Dorothy points to my name on the list. "That's good," she says, dabbing the corners of her mouth with a napkin. "You'd much rather have morning bus duty than afternoon. You may have to get here a bit earlier than usual, but the mornings promptly end with the first bell at 7:35 AM. In the afternoons, you never know what will happen or how long you're going to get stuck. And you never want car duty, no matter what time it is."

I look at her in question.

"Parents. No parents involved with bus duty."

I nod.

"I take it you haven't taught before?"

The words on the paper in front of me begin to blur as I consider the complications, the additional inquiries of the truth. "Actually, this is my first year. I only received my degree in April."

"From where 'bouts?"

"UNC Asheville."

"Pretty area," Dorothy says, studying my face. Noting the furrow in her brow, I answer her obvious question. "I always wanted to be a teacher but got a late start. Life happens, right?"

"Indeed it does," she replies. Dorothy's gaze drops to my left hand.

"My son is grown, and I'm divorced," I lie before she can ask.

I've found that the lie doesn't prompt the questions the truth dredges up, and I can't deal with my past or any more truths today.

* * *

ALICIA HARGROVE and Ben Roberts must be at least ten years my junior, but each has five-plus years teaching experience under their belts. I like them immediately and appreciate their light-hearted and eager attitudes. It helps, too, that they aren't full of questions about who I am, where I came from, and why I'm suddenly here.

Having finished introductions, Alicia and Ben pull out their student rosters and begin to compare. I follow suit, looking over the list of names I need to memorize.

"Yes! I have Jenny Amhurst." Ben fist pumps the air, a toothy grin stretching across his face.

"No," Alicia exclaims. "I wanted her." Alicia looks at me to explain. "Jenny's mom is PTA president. She has two older children in the upper-grade levels. She's the best room parent ever." Alicia punches Ben's arm. "I'm so jealous. We should plan co-class parties this year."

"Nope. Fend for yourself," Ben teases her.

Dorothy looks over my shoulder to view my roster. "Luke Kelser," she reads. "Alicia, isn't that the little boy you held back last year?"

"Oh, precious little Luke. You're going to love that child," Alicia says to me. "He's such a sweetheart."

"Why did you hold him back?" I ask.

"His mom and I agreed it would be the best thing for him. Luke has an August birthday, so even though he was technically old enough to enroll in Kindergarten when he started school,

Luke has always been the youngest and smallest of his classmates. We both decided that having another year in second grade would give Luke time to mature and grasp some of the concepts he struggled with last year."

I nod, watching as Dorothy runs her finger down the list of names in front of me. Her finger stops. "She has Jack," Dorothy tells the pair sitting across from us, shaking her head at the revelation.

Ben looks at Dorothy, then Alicia. "I thought he was moving."

"Me too," Alicia agrees.

"Evidently, the threat didn't hold up," Dorothy says, adding, "Let's just hope his mother has finally decided to get that child some help."

"What's wrong with Jack?" I ask the team.

Alicia leans across the table and lowers her voice. "His past teachers have dubbed him 'Jumping Jack' because if he's not jumping, then he's got you jumping."

"Nonsense," Dorothy says. "Each child responds differently to different teachers. Merel could be just what Jack needs. And besides, Merel has experience with boys. Right, Merel?" Dorothy looks at Ben and Alicia. "Merel raised a boy."

ESME

AUGUST

"We can't stay long, Jay."

"Why not?"

I roll my neck from side to side, shift my eyes upward for a brief second. *Please, God, give me the strength to get through the evening ahead.*

"You're always harping at me to go outside and play," Jay goads when I don't reply.

Using the rearview mirror, I look at him in the backseat of the car. "Because tonight is Meet the Teacher night at your school." His eyes bore back at me, daring me to break the gaze. "Remember, I told you last week all the teachers had gone back to school and you would be going soon too?" I draw my eyes away and stare out the windshield, waiting for the light to change. "Aren't you excited to meet your new teacher?"

"No, Esme." Dripping with sarcasm and disdain, Jay draws out the retort. When did... no, where did he learn to do that?

"Jay, please don't call me that."

"That's your name, isn't it?"

"Yes, but it's not polite for a little boy to call his mother by her name." Though I've tried to curb it, I hear the exasperation in my tone.

I steal a quick glance at the mirror to check if he's noticed my impatience. Jay's cold glare catches my eye.

"Why not?" I ask, trying to turn the conversation back to the event later tonight.

"Why not, what?" Jay's voice escalates with each spoken word.

"Why aren't you excited about going back to school? And, there's no need to shout."

I take another approach, hoping to break his mood. "I wonder if any of your friends will be in your new class. Maybe Kelvin or Alex?"

"I don't like them anymore. They call me names. They're stupid." Jay's foot makes a repetitive connection with the back of the passenger seat in front of him.

"Jay. Stop kicking." I draw air in through my nose, expanding my chest. *Patience, Esme.* "You guys were best buds last year." Immediately, I regret having given the statement a voice. Neither of the boys' mothers has called about playdates this summer. I should have recognized the slight before now, reached out to the women to arrange a time for the boys to get together, for Jay to keep some connection to his classmates. This summer has gotten away from me. With Amanda quitting the daycare at the end of the last school year and my promotion to director, I've not had the time to devote to Jay that a good mother would.

Jay's sneakered toe continues to make contact with the seat in front of him. Ignoring the action this time, I reassure him. "You guys will work out your differences."

We arrive at the park. I maneuver into the empty parking lot, choosing the space closest to the gated entrance. Jay unbuckles himself and throws open the door before I can cut the ignition.

"Jay," I yell to him as he tears off, toward the swings.

I grab my purse from the passenger seat and lock up the car. The heat of the late August afternoon rises from the black pavement. I hurry through the gate and along the path, anxious to find a bench under the shade of a tree. Settling into the coolest spot I can find, I see my son yank and twist the swings rather than use them as intended.

"Jay Duncan! Stop that! If you're going to swing, then do so." The heat and humidity fuel my aggravation. It's really too hot to be at a playground. Due to advisory warnings from the local meteorologists, we didn't let our kids at the daycare go outside today, so Jay has been cooped up all day. I'm hoping this little excursion will work off some of Jay's aggression, especially since we are scheduled to go to the school in less than two hours. I roll my neck side to side again, attempting to dissolve some of the tension that's been building over tonight's meet and greet. Jay must be feeling it too, I decide, watching him as he furiously pushes the merry-go-round with no intentions of jumping on.

Looking away, I bite down on the chastising reprimand and dig through my bag to find my cell phone. I text Kirby, reminding him of the meeting tonight. The prompt reply from my husband lets me know he will be home in time to go with us; he's looking forward to it. *At least one of us is excited about tonight.* The truth, of course, is that when Jay begins the school year, it frees up the time I spend with him. And while I find the fact appealing, (though I feel so guilty for even thinking it) the thought of going through another year bombarded by teacher emails and conferences with the principal regarding my son's antics coils my stomach into knots.

I toss the phone inside the bag and pull out my bible to read over the scripture for next week's bible study group. The bookmark is missing. I dig through the contents of my oversized purse to search for the notepad where I've scribbled the verses, laying aside my First Baptist Church fan. At the bottom of my bag, I discover the bookmark ripped to shreds. *Jay. Well, at least he left my bible intact.* I collect the pieces and stand to walk to the nearest trash can.

From the other side of the park, a little boy who looks to be Jay's age runs in the direction of the swings. I search the area for Jay and see he has spied the child as well. Scoping the playground for the child's guardian, I see a woman outside the gate entrance pacing, hands flying. Closer inspection reveals she uses headphones attached to a phone in her back pocket. I swivel my gaze back to the children then settle back onto the bench. One of us needs to pay attention to what is going on I decide, dropping the bible back into my bag and saving the scripture for a time I can properly concentrate.

I pick up the fan, swish through the warm, muggy air, and watch as Jay approaches the boy. Jay hops onto the leather seat of the swing next to the child. I let out the breath trapped in my lungs as I see him use the equipment in the manner intended and swing alongside the boy. The two pump in unison, maintaining a reasonable height. Jay tends to make every activity a competition. It is nice to see him simply enjoy another child's company.

I shift my focus back to the boy's mother and see her walk toward her car. The woman holds to the door handle, raising her voice to the person at the other end of her conversation. I can't make out what she says, but it is obviously not a polite chit-chat. She opens the door and slams it shut, closing herself inside the car. I hear the crank of the engine. She carries on the exchange inside the vehicle (no doubt under cool air) leaving me to guard over the children.

Behold, children are a heritage from the Lord. Blessed is the man who fills his quiver with them. The verse from Psalms is one I recite regularly.

Perspiration pools at the base of my head. I locate the clip I saw earlier in my bag and pull the hair up off the back of my neck.

The boys have struck up their own conversation and now take turns plunging down the slide. I flap the fan once more, check the time, and decide to ring Mama, knowing she's closed the bakery for the day and is probably heading home.

"Leoti Shulman here," she answers after two rings.

"Mama, there's no need for you to announce yourself to me, you know."

"Sorry, sweetie. I guess I'm still in work mode. How are you? I hear kids. You still at work?"

"No, I'm at the playground with Jay."

"Good Lord. It's too hot to be outside. You'll have a heat stroke."

"Jay needed to work off some anxiety. We're not staying long. We have to be at the school soon for Meet the Teacher night."

"Already. Good grief, where has this summer gone? I thought you were just getting started on vacation bible school."

"That was last month, Mama."

"Well, it's hard to keep up with you when you don't answer your phone, Esme."

"I know. I'm sorry, Mama. Work has been wild, and we've had one function after another with the church lately."

I register the huff she lets out and work the fan in my other hand harder, searching my mind for an uplifting bible verse, chomping back the retort on my tongue.

"Speaking of unanswered phone calls, I called you this past Saturday to invite y'all for Sunday lunch. Your daddy'd love to see you all, Esme."

"I found the message Sunday right before service began and meant to call you back," I reply, not bothering to add more. Sidestepping the well-worn argument about how much time I spend with my church family, I change the topic. "How's Daddy feeling? His new medication working?"

"It seems to be. The doctor says he needs less stress in his life, but you know your daddy. He says he'll rest when he retires," she says with a weary sigh. "How's Jay? You say he's starting school soon?"

"He is, tomorrow, in fact. I'd like to say he's excited, but it's hard to tell with Jay."

"I know, honey. It'll get easier. Just give it some time. Is Kirby still driving the Asheville route?"

"Asheville is where he picks up now. Kirby's new route is Bristol, Lexington, Bowling Green, then down to Nashville and Chattanooga. He's been running it twice a week for the last two months."

"I hate thinking of him being on the road like that all the time."

Kirby's job driving for one of the local trucking companies is not one I particularly care for either. I can't count the number of horrific scenarios that run through my head, the number of prayers I've said begging God to keep him safe. But this is what Kirby has done all our married years. "It's not too bad. He's only gone two nights a week right now." In years past, Kirby was often on the road for two months at a time.

"Well, that's better than it used to be, I guess."

"Listen, Mama, I've gotta run. I need to round up Jay and head home so I can get him presentable to meet his teacher."

"Okay. I'll let you go. Don't be a stranger."

"We'll talk again soon. Promise."

"Wait. Esme. Y'all come to dinner this Sunday?"

"I will do my best to be there, Mama. Tell Daddy I said hi."

I push the button to end the call, looking up to see the boys take turns spinning one another on the merry-go-round. I hate to pull Jay away, but we do need to be getting home. Kirby should be arriving home any minute now.

"Jay," I yell across the playground. The little boy whirling Jay on the round structure looks my way, but Jay neglects to acknowledge me. "Jay," I call again.

The boy stops his efforts. Jay jumps off the platform, running toward the climbing equipment. "We need to go soon," I call, deciding to allow a few more minutes of play.

While the kids go about their final games, I think to work on my to-do list. Because the beginning of the school year starts midweek, my whole schedule has been thrown out of whack. From my bag, I pull out the notepad, turning to the list of chores I began Monday. Shoot. I forgot to throw the laundry into the dryer yesterday before work. *Where is my mind?* That load will have to be rewashed; no doubt it has soured in this heat. I need to go through the school supply list with Jay tonight and make sure his backpack is loaded and ready for school tomorrow. Lunch? To the list, I add the reminder to load money into Jay's lunch ticket account.

I look up to check on the boys. Like monkeys at the zoo, they're dangling from the bars of the climbing apparatus. Jay hurries to catch the boy, who effortlessly swings from one arm to the next, making his way to the other side of the structure. Jay seemingly yields the contest and turns to retreat to the opposite side. The two reach their platforms and call out to one another.

The phone in my purse chirps with a text notification. I bring up the message from Kirby letting me know he is at home, asking if there is anything I would like him to prepare for dinner. I message back that we will have to take care of dinner after the school event; we'll be home soon.

The noise of a car door slamming in the distance startles me, draws my attention to the parking lot. The boy's mother runs, screaming out her child's name. I swivel to look in the direction of the boys. Jay and the child hang in the middle of the climbing bars, the two facing off. Jay kicks with all his force at the boy in front of him.

"Jay! Stop it! Stop that right now!" I scream, throwing the phone aside as I, too, run in their direction.

"Albie," the boy's mother cries.

Albie clamps both hands to the bar above him. Jay swings himself back and forth, gaining momentum, using both feet to kick Albie's midsection.

I reach the climbing structure before Albie's mother, positioning myself underneath Jay, grabbing one of Jay's legs. He flails the other leg, continuing to make connection with Albie's stomach.

"Jay, stop that this instant!" I try to get hold of the other leg. Jay delivers another kick causing Albie to lose his grip on the bar. Albie falls with a thud to the ground. I manage to get both of my arms wrapped around Jay's lower body and pull him down to the ground, away from the boy who wails for his mother. She arrives by his side, kneeling, crying, trying to make sense of Albie's garbled words. The woman checks over her son as I hold firmly to Jay, keeping him back.

"What is wrong with you?" She screams at us. Her terror transfers to the little boy, who howls in pain and fright. Blood spills from his mouth. She turns her attention back to the child, trying to comfort him, asking Albie where he hurts.

I don't know where to begin with my son. "Jay?" I grab him by the shoulders, twisting him to face me. "Why would you do such a thing?"

"I kicked him." Jay jerks from my hold. His eyes, void of any emotion, pierce mine.

"Why, Jay? Why did you do that?" My own tears fall, in fear for the child, in compassion for his mother, in frustration with my son.

"I didn't want to play with him anymore," he states, his tone matter-of-fact.

Leaning over her child, the woman cries, "I can't get the blood to stop. Something is wrong with his tongue."

"The hospital is only a couple of blocks away, the emergency room," I offer.

"Keep that monster away from my son," she says through tears, struggling to cradle, to lift the boy from the ground.

"I'll help you get him to the car," I say to her, then turn to Jay. "You. Go sit on that bench and don't move," I command.

This time, thankfully, Jay complies, stuffing his hands into the pockets of his shorts, toeing the ground as he heads toward the bench.

As we approach the woman's car, I hear the purr of the engine. I run ahead to open the back car door and find it locked. I try the driver's door. It, too, is locked.

The woman's eyes widen. "Oh my god, I locked the keys inside?"

"I'll take you. I'll get you to the hospital," I offer, worrying for her son, the blood running over his lips, soaking the front of his shirt. "My car is right over there. Let me grab my bag. I'll be right back."

* * *

IN THE WAITING area of the emergency room, I think to call Kirby, let him know what is going on.

"Stay here," I tell Jay. "I'm going to call your dad." Unfazed by the announcement, Jay continues to stare blankly at the television screen hanging in the corner of the room. I walk through the doors of the waiting area into the hallway, standing at the window so I can keep an eye on Jay while I talk to Kirby.

"Hey," Kirby answers immediately. "You guys almost home? Is there something you want me to pull out for Jay to wear tonight?"

"We're not going to make it." I fill him in on the incident.

"Jay is okay, though, right?"

"Jay doesn't have a scratch on him, Kirby. He went wild on that poor child. When Albie fell, he bit into his tongue—deep; there was so much blood."

"Did Jay say why he did it?"

"Because he didn't want to play with the boy anymore." I watch Jay impassively focusing on the TV. "What are we going to do with him, Kirby? I don't know what gets into him."

Kirby holds in silence, no doubt trying to make sense of our son's latest unprincipled action.

"I'm waiting for her husband to arrive," I tell Kirby. "He has a forty-five-minute drive to get here and then has to go by the park first to turn off the ignition of her car. She has no purse, no phone, no insurance information. I can't leave her stranded."

"All right, you take care of everything there, and I'll start dinner. We can talk to Jay together when you two get home." Kirby pauses, then asks, "Did Jay say he was sorry for doing what he did? He needs to apologize, to the boy, to the mother."

"Oh, we've had that conversation, or rather I've had it. The only thing Jay had to offer was that he was bored; he wanted to go home. I tried to get him to pray with me, but he wouldn't even take my hand. He has no remorse, Kirby. He just sits there, eyeing me with that searing glare."

MARCH 1979

eoti steers the old Ford alongside the road leading to the cemetery, creeping to a stop, pushing the gearshift into park. I pluck a bag of supplies from the backseat, then yank the handle to push open the passenger side door. Stepping into the frigid night air, I wait for Leoti, use the light of the full moon to examine the trees that are eager to bud as they wait for the last of winter to make its exit. Anxious to get on with the activity, I walk ahead while Leoti gathers her things. Behind me, I hear the door slam, her footfalls nearing.

"Are you sure about this, Ama?" Leoti asks in an exaggerated whisper.

"Of course." I keep my focus on the gates of the cemetery. "I've helped the elders perform this spell a hundred times." I exhale, watching the misty cloud of air escape into the night, then add, "At least. Will you keep up? You're poking, Leoti."

"I am not. You don't have to be so bossy," she says, finally falling into pace beside me.

"We're doing this for you."

"I asked for a baby, Ama, not a midnight field trip to the graveyard." Leoti grabs my arm, tugging me to a halt, holds tight to my hand. "Maybe we should wait, think about this some more."

I twist to face her, my identical twin, but prettier than me, softer, more feminine. "You want to wait? That'll be another month gone. This has to be done on the night of a full moon." I throw my free hand to the sky in gesture, then fling it down to rest on my hip. "Besides, Rubin is out of town tonight, not breathing down my neck and watching my every move. I know you love him, but your husband is a pain in my ass. Don't be a chicken shit, Leoti. Let's just get this done."

Leoti drops her eyes as she releases her hold on me.

"Look, we get the dirt, and then I can do the work, and the next thing you know, you're picking out baby names." I take her hand this time, for her reassurance, to calm her fears. "What have you done to your hair? It looks different."

Leoti smiles. "I feathered it. You don't like it? I like it." She pulls her hand free and runs her fingers over the wings framing each side of her face. "You should do something new with yours instead of that bone straight, part down the middle look."

Leoti reaches for my hair. I slap her hand away. "No." Anticipating her next words, I add, "And no. Makeup is out of the question."

Leoti works her face into a pout. I turn to look at the old iron gate standing sentry in the distance, locking in the dead.

"Where's the spray?"

Leoti tucks the stems of the bundle of flowers under her arm and digs into the bag hanging from her shoulder. "It's in here somewhere. Ah, here." She hands over the bottle of spiritual wash. I move to stand behind my sister. Starting at the back of her head, I spray the prepared water—back to front, head to toe.

"I didn't realize I was going to be taking a cold shower," Leoti exclaims, punctuating her displeasure with an overly dramatized shiver.

"Here." I hand over the bottle. "Do me and be thorough. I don't want anything latching on and following me home."

"What? What's gonna latch on? Like bugs?" She squeals.

"No, like unwanted spirits."

Leoti sprays me down and moves to shove the bottle back into her bag. "Don't put that too far away," I tell her, making my way to the entrance. "We need it for the headstone."

"The headstone?"

"Yeah, we have to clean it with the wash."

"Latching spirits. Cleaning the graveyard in the middle of the night. I'm beginning to wonder what I've gotten myself into."

"Where are the coins?" I stop, turn, hold out my hand.

Leoti hands over the bundle of flowers for me to hold, then pulls the bag from her shoulder and searches deep inside it.

"Did you really need to bring these tonight?"

Digging to the bottom of the bag, she absently replies, "If I am coming to see Mama, I'm bringing her flowers, especially if I'm taking dirt from her grave. Here." She hands over the coins, and I pass the flowers back to her.

At the gate, I bend to lay three of the coins down in offer and repeat the phrase I've been taught by the elders. "Heneni. Ditlida hihu isti."

"What are you saying?"

"I'm asking the spirit keeper for permission to enter the graveyard."

"Well, what did it say?"

"Shhh." I pause, look to the moon, wait to feel the responding energy. A wave of peace flows through me. "Heneni. Tsugjali di ha uya."

"Now what?" Leoti demands.

"We're good. I was giving thanks to the spirit keeper. Let's go."

I lead Leoti along the path we've grown accustomed to taking over the last two years. Approaching Mama's headstone, the old familiar tension builds in my chest. I work to ease it away for the sake of Leoti, for the success of the spell to come.

As she has always been able to do, Leoti reads my mood. "I

wouldn't ask you to do this if I didn't want it so badly. Ama, you know that, right?"

"I know."

"It's just, you know, Mama never wanted you doing this stuff, and I feel like I'm being disrespectful to her by asking you to do this now." Leoti's nervous chatter clangs on. "And using her grave... I don't know; it just doesn't feel right."

Stopping to stand at our mother's gravestone, I turn to my sister. "You're going to need to set yourself right with this, Leoti. It won't work unless you do."

"And how do I do that, knowing how Mama felt about this stuff?"

"You're going to have to talk to her, explain how important this is to you, to Rubin."

"Rubin doesn't even know we're here. And I don't think he'd be comfortable with this voodoo shmudoo if he did know."

"It's not voodoo. It's a simple conjure spell for the greater good of both of you. Think of all the stress that will be off y'all once you're pregnant."

I place my bag on the ground and reach out for Leoti's bag. I pull out the spiritual wash and a cloth then begin the work of cleaning Mama's headstone.

"Wegwo di nede uya."

"I know this one," Leoti says, a beaming smile across her unscarred face. "Love be with you."

"Yes, dingbat." I roll my eyes. "Papa says it every time he sees you and leaves you. Now start talking. Explain away."

Folding arms across my chest, I wait. Leoti falls to rest on her knees beside Mama's grave. She inhales deeply and begins.

"Hey, Mama. We came to see you, Ama and me. I miss you so much, so very much.

"Our birthday is coming up next month. Twenty-one. Gosh, I feel like we're getting so old, but not old enough not to need our mother. Since I know better than to think I can wish you back, there's only one other wish I'll make when I blow out the candles on my cake this year—the same one I've had since Rubin and I married three years ago. I want a baby. I want to be a mama. I want to be just like you, but I can't seem to get pregnant, no matter how hard Rubin and I try."

"I doubt she wants to hear about your sex life, Leoti."

She huffs, looking up at me. "I'm not telling her about my love life, Ama." Leoti swipes at her cheeks. "Let me do this my way. Please."

I throw my hands up and take a step back to let Leoti continue.

"I know you always wanted Ama to have the upbringing I did, that you didn't want her growing up in The Community and being subjected to the teachings of the elders. Ama and I both understand that. But she did, and she's okay. Everything turned out just fine. Really. That's why I have to ask you, Mama, to let her do this for me. I don't mean to disrespect you in any way, but Ama has the ability to help me get pregnant. It's just so awful; month after month and no baby.

"I know you had your doubts about Rubin—about Rubin being so much older than me, that I was too young to get married —but we're doing great, Mama. Rubin's law practice is going strong, and I'm running your bakery. Our lives are only missing one thing."

Leoti continues her rambling as I take another step back from the gravesite. I don't belong here. I love my sister, and I'd do anything for her. Leoti is the most important person in my life, next to Papa. I know Leoti as well as I know myself. She's my other half. But this need she has for a child I cannot comprehend. Nor can I understand the bond she has with Mama. Leoti and I may use the same term of endearment for our mother, but she wasn't my mama. She was Leoti's. I knew how Mama felt about me every time I looked into her eyes. Leoti was our mother's child, and I belonged to Papa.

I jerk out of my musings to hear Leoti continue.

"Here's the thing. We need a bit of your dirt for Ama's spell.

She has all the other herbs and roots she needs, but now she has to get some graveyard dirt. And well, you're family. The spell will be so much stronger with your dirt, especially since you're our mama. I don't want you rolling over in your grave about this, though. I really, just really want your blessing is all. I love you, Mama."

Leoti lifts onto her knees, bending from the waist to kiss Mama's headstone. She pushes herself to stand and looks at me. "Okay, now what?"

I hold out the spade and container.

* * *

LEOTI TIGHTENS her grip on the steering wheel, concentrating on the road ahead. She's got something she wants to say. I can tell by the way Leoti bites her lower lip and twists her face she's trying to make up her mind as to whether or not she does.

"All right, whatever it is, go on and spit it out."

"What?" Leoti asks, glancing over at me and then back to the road.

"Is this about the dirt?"

"No." Leoti keeps her gaze forward. "I know Mama wants me to be happy and that she's glad she can help."

"Good, I'm *glad* you're feeling better, but I know you got something working in that head of yours, so whatever it is, get it over with."

"Fine. I was wondering if you ever get mad at Daddy for not letting you see Mama. I mean, I could tell you were uncomfortable back there at the cemetery when I was talking to Mama."

Sometimes it escapes me that my sister can read me as well as I can her. I make a note to practice masking.

"What are you talking about? Papa brought me to see you two all the time, practically every single weekend." It was a well-worn routine. Papa and I spent the week in The Community, and unless it was a ceremonial weekend, we stayed Saturday and most of Sunday with Leoti and Mama in Waynesville.

"Yeah, but Daddy didn't let you spend time alone with her."

"Well, Mama didn't let Daddy spend time alone with you either. And y'all never came to stay with us."

"I think she was afraid."

"Mama? Afraid of what?"

"Afraid Daddy would take me away from her like he took you away. She cried every single time you two left."

"Mama made her choice, Leoti. Papa wanted her to stay, to live in The Community with us, but she didn't want to. We've both heard the stories. They made it work." I fold my arms over my chest. "And for the record, Daddy didn't take me away from her."

Leoti flips the blinker on the car to make the right-hand turn onto Humming Bird Lane. She maneuvers the car into the third driveway on the left and inches under the attached carport. Leoti looks over at me as she cuts the engine and asks, "Where'd you tell Daddy you were tonight, anyway?"

"I told him Rubin is out of town, and you were scared to stay by yourself."

"I am not."

"Well, I couldn't tell him what we were planning on doing, Leoti. I'm not supposed to be doing this stuff on my own yet."

"Well, how long do you have to train? Good grief, you've been an apprentice almost twenty-one years. You practically have elder status already. And you're marked. Wait. Are you telling me this isn't going to work? That we've gathered all this mess for nothing?"

"No. I know what I'm doing. Like I said, I've assisted others on this same spell more times than I can count. Being an elder has nothing to do with the effectiveness of a spell." And besides, I think to myself, I'm a long way off from elder status. I have years and years left of training, and I might add, by elders who didn't have to put in the amount of time to gain their status that I have to. Sometimes I wonder if being an elder is really worth it, but I don't dare tell Leoti. She might blab my misgivings to Papa, and I couldn't bear the hurt it would cause him.

Satisfied with my response, she tilts her head and grins. "So, how are we doing this?"

MEREL

AUGUST

Rising out of a squatting position, I release the little girl from my embrace. "I can't wait to see you bright and early tomorrow morning, Libby."

"Me too, Ms. S. I'm so excited to be in second grade. I can't believe how old I'm getting."

Libby's mom and I share a conspiratorial laugh as I walk them to the door where we say our final goodbyes. I stand in the doorway, watching them walk hand in hand down the corridor, all the while repeating to myself Libby, Libby, Libby.

The crowded hallways of earlier have thinned. Only a few parents and students loiter during the final minutes of the meet and greet. Absently observing them engage with one another, my mind busily scrolls through all the children I met tonight. The sudden weight of a hand lands on my shoulder from behind, startling me out of my thoughts. I spin around, yanking myself from the hold.

"Oh, Dorothy. You scared me," I admit. "I keep forgetting the office connects our classrooms."

"You haven't spent much time in there yet," my teammate states.

It's true. I've been so focused on getting the classroom set up for the children, I've given little thought to organizing my half of the office.

I follow Dorothy as she ambles in the direction of the pupils' desks, expecting her to pull out one of the small chairs and take a seat. She looks tired. We're all exhausted. It's been a long seven days. Instead, Dorothy remains standing, her gaze roving my classroom walls.

My eyes sweep along with hers. In the short time I've had to put the room together—broken by faculty meetings, in-service training, and curriculum coaching—I've managed to create a stimulating and fun environment for my future students.

The white cinder block walls of the room dressed in bright posters and teaching tools are accented in red and yellow. My desk is situated in the far corner of the room at an angle, so all student desks, as well as the classroom door, are in my line of sight. Two large windows break up the wall at the back of the room. Navy blue valences hang atop the school issued teal blinds that I draped with long chiffon scarves: one red and one yellow. Arranged in the center of the room are the student desks in groupings to form mini-tables around the orange reading rug at the front of the room. I've sectioned off areas for the computer lab, the library, and the game center along the perimeter of the space. Set up off the side of the room's storage cubby is the horseshoe table I plan to use for small reading groups.

"Your room looks great. You've put in a lot of work these past few days. Betty wouldn't even recognize it," Dorothy claims, taking in the word wall on her left.

"How is she?" I inquire about the woman whose place I have assumed. "Did she get moved to the rehabilitation center?"

"Yes. Poor thing. I haven't had a chance to visit her since we started back to school. I'm going this weekend to see how she's getting along," Dorothy says with a weary sigh. She turns her head to look back at me. "Mind if I take a couple of pictures, show Betty what you've done to the room? Might help to raise her spirits."

"Of course, please, take as many as you like." I feel bad about having taken the woman's classroom, a classroom she clearly had no desire to relinquish. And I do hope she makes a complete recovery, but I can't help wondering how long I will have to live in Betty's shadow. The past seven days, each introduction amongst my coworkers has been prefaced with 'the woman who took Betty's place.' I certainly can't blame Betty for the others' actions, but I'm ready to be my own person. Not someone's mother, or somebody's wife, and definitely not the teacher who replaced beloved Betty.

Dorothy breaks through my thoughts. "How'd it go tonight? You meet all your new kiddos."

"I need to check my roster to be certain, but I think I came close." I head to my desk at the back of the room to grab the roster of students. "How 'bout you? All of yours show?"

"All but two. I knew they weren't going to make it, though, because their parents contacted me ahead of time."

Checking off Libby's name, I look at the list and find one name without a checkmark. "I met all but one of mine," I report. "Jack was a no-show. Do you think Ben and Alicia were right? Do you think Jack's family moved?"

"You might have an easier year if that's the case, but just because the family didn't show tonight doesn't mean much. And besides that, you'd much rather start off with a full class than have a new student placed later in the school year."

"Really?"

"New students tend to disrupt the flow you get into with your class. Breaks the routine."

I lay aside the list, nodding. "That makes sense." In the past few days, I've come to hang heavily on Dorothy's advice, soaking up her years of acquired knowledge, heeding her guidance.

Dorothy heads toward the library corner, inspecting the cataloging system I've established. "I like this, Merel. I may have to do something like this next year."

I welcome her compliment with a smile and ask, "Have you taught other grade levels?"

"K through six, thirty-eight years, I've tried them all." Dorothy replaces a thin novel back into the slot she extracted it from.

I lean against the edge of my desk, watching Dorothy as she aims the camera on her cell phone at the library corner and clicks. She inspects the image then tucks the device into her pocket.

"Which grade level did you like teaching best?"

"Second," she says without thought. "Once I got to second grade, I knew this was where I wanted to stay. They're sweet at this age, eager to please, can button their own britches, and not quite at the eye-rolling stage yet."

Memories of my years as the parent of an elementary-aged child filter in. "Come to think of it, second grade may have been the best school year for my son."

"Which year would you say was the worst?" Dorothy asks.

"Pardon?"

"You just said second grade was probably your son's best school year. Which do you think was his worst?"

Had I really given voice to the thought?

"I don't know about that one." I shrug, bending over my desk to arrange and straighten the papers on top of it. "I guess middle school was pretty tough," I offer, realizing the question requires more than a simple feigning of ignorance.

"Yep, middle school age is hard on everyone: parents, teachers, and the students."

"Mmm," I reply, continuing the unnecessary shuffling of papers. Heat creeps up my neck, flushing my face. Although I don't look up, I can feel Dorothy's scrutiny.

"Where is your son now? Is he in college?"

"Uh, no. He's in the military," I place a colorful paperweight atop the stack of papers and look at Dorothy. "The Marines."

"That's a hard branch," she claims, studying me.

"Yes, it is." I nod in agreement, folding my arms across my chest.

"You must stay on the edge of your seat with worry."

"I just try and stay busy. He's an adult and dead set on doing things his way."

"You poor thing. No wonder you're working so hard. Does he at least check in with you, keep you up to date?"

"I don't hear from him very often." I sigh heavily and add, "It's not something I like to talk about," hoping to end this topic of inquiry.

"I guess not." The pity I read in her eyes lets me know I've succeeded in squelching the conversation.

"All right, Ms. S., I'm going to mosey on home. Big day tomorrow. You about ready to call it a night?" Dorothy moves slowly through the room.

"I have a few things left I want to do before I leave. I'll see you in the morning."

Dorothy disappears into the office, connecting our classrooms. I hear her open the closet behind her office desk then retrieve her purse.

I pull out the top drawer of the filing cabinet behind my classroom desk, locate the students' morning assignments, and push the drawer shut. From the bottom drawer, I grab the bundle of pencils I sharpened earlier in the day and busy myself with setting up the students' desks. As I place the assignment and a pencil at each spot, I check the name badges on the appointed seats, digging deep into recall for the faces that go with the name. I'm halfway through the chore when Dorothy pops her head out from our office to find me tapping a pencil to my chin, attempting to surface the features of Winston Duffin.

"Hey, before I forget, I saw Tony."

My eyes squint in confusion.

"The custodian," Dorothy reminds.

"Oh, right. Tony. Custodian."

"I told him about our office doors locking us inside when we close them. He said he'd try and get around to fixing them for us this week. That poor man's got so much on his plate right now, it may be a while before he can take care of them. I'm going to close my classroom off from the office before I leave. Be careful about closing yourself in there. You're liable to be sleeping on the office floor tonight," she warns.

"Thanks for the reminder. That does sound like something I would do."

We call goodnight to one another as Dorothy turns to walk back through the office and closes the door leading into her classroom. Following her path to the office, I pull my purse from the closet on my side of the room. I place it on the floor in front of the door as a reminder not to lock myself inside for the night, then return to finish my task of setting up the desks.

Desks readied for students, I walk to the dry erase board and pen instructions for the students to follow once they have taken their seats in the morning. As I finish up, I remember I still need to check that the cubby area is ready to receive the children's backpacks and that each has all the proper textbooks I need to issue the students stacked under the respective numbered slots.

Satisfied the cubby is in order, I move to the sink, pulling a fresh bottle of hand sanitizer from the cabinet below. I place it on the countertop and recall Dorothy's warning to prepare for all the supplies that will be piling through the door tomorrow—to be sure I have a place ready to stack them. I check the cabinets above the hand washing station, rearranging objects inside the space to make room for the school supply checklist items.

Tasks complete, I clasp my hands in front of me, surveying my room, giddy with the anticipation of being the second-grade teacher for twenty-one eager little learners.

At the sound of my classroom door opening, I swing around. The heel of my shoe catches on the reading rug. I stumble into a student desk, quickly righting myself to greet my principal, who is inquiring if I am okay.

"Yes, thank you, Principal Garber. You caught me off guard. I didn't realize anyone was still here." Knots of tension furl at the base of my neck.

"And that is exactly why I'm here. Everyone has gone home for the evening, and you should do the same, Ms. Sowanoke. That morning bell will be ringing before you know it."

I straighten my spine, lift my neck, and nod. "Yes, I am getting my things together now. I just had a few last-minute details I needed to attend to before class tomorrow." Given my height at five foot ten, I've got an easy six inches on the intimidating woman, but I could never match the intensity of her gaze.

To Principal Garber's credit, however, I've never been comfortable with anyone who holds a position of authority. I'm surprised she even offered me the job after my botched interview. I did nothing but stammer through my answers, trying to recall the last bit of information I had given her without relaying too much about myself personally. When she made the offer at the conclusion of her interrogation, I wanted to hug her but could bring myself to give nothing more than a head nod and a stumbled thank you. I am more than aware the last-minute loss of tenured staff is the only reason I received the position. Nevertheless, I owe the woman a great debt for her part in granting me the opportunity to start anew, and I've no intentions of letting her down.

"Okay, then," she says, turning, heading back towards the door, "Tony has strict instructions to lock up the building in thirty minutes."

"Tony. The custodian."

Principal Garber holds the door handle as she looks over her shoulder. "Yes, Tony, the custodian," she affirms. "Good night, Ms. Sowanoke. Or should I say, Ms. S.?" She asks, eyeing the colorful magnets I have arranged on the side of my desk.

"I hope that's okay with you." My hands fly through the air as I explain. "I figure it will be easier for the children to say." I rein in my arms, holding them firm and awkward against the sides of my thighs.

Principal Garber gives a curt nod and exits the classroom.

Eyes circle to the ceiling, shoulders slouch, the pressure of the confrontation over, I take a deep breath. It is time for me to get home. I still need to decide what to wear for my first day and then locate it in the boxes yet to be unpacked.

* * *

I STEP inside the office that connects my classroom to Dorothy's, careful not to close the door behind me. The desk we split runs along one side of the tight, confined space. Above the desk, bookshelves rise to the low ceilings, packed to the rim with teaching manuals, old educational resources, and yellowing magazines I've had no opportunity to peruse, much less organize. Two compact closets line the back wall of the office, Dorothy's on her side and another allotted for my things on the other. To this point, the closet has been the only area I've been able to clear out. I may have been successful in erasing Betty from my classroom, but my predecessor has a strong representation in the tiny shared workspace.

I shake off Betty's ghostly presence and set about gathering my things, shoving all I need to take home into a big canvas bag. My mind races with all I still need to do tonight while my body moans in protest. Noise from the hallway jolts my attention. I lean around the office threshold, listening, waiting to hear more.

Outside my classroom door, the sound of a child's laugh echoes through the darkened hallway. I leave the office and walk to the door, eyes fixed on the small rectangular window. Turning the handle, I pull the door open. The light from my classroom spills into the hallway, a gleaming spotlight on the freshly waxed floors just outside my door. I look across the hall at the teaching suite of Ben and Ashley, the only other second grade teachers. The windows of their doors appear to be a dark pair of ominous eyes watching me in the dim lighting. I scope the long corridor, looking as far as I can see in one direction and then the other. Now a full two hours after the scheduled reception with parents and students, the school is eerily quiet, empty. As Principal Garber reported, everyone else seems to have left for the evening. I shrug off my unease deciding I am tired; I've only imagined the noise.

I take a step back inside my room, pushing the door closed. Before the latch catches, I hear it again—a giggle rolling the length of the long hallway. I step outside of my room and let the door close behind me. Small footfalls sound in the distance, traveling in the direction of the gym. *Is there a student roaming the school, perhaps looking for a way out?* In search, I leave the narrow beam of light coming from my door's small window.

The cinderblock walls reverberate the clacking of my heels striking the smooth tiled floors. Counting my steps along the trek, I halt at twenty, listening. No longer can I hear the sound of padded feet.

The sour smell of bleach lingers in the stale air assaulting my nose while my eyes strain to focus in the dim light of the emergency illumination. I scan the corridor in front and behind me. A peal of laughter cuts through the silence. The noise seems to be behind me now.

I turn to retrace my steps through the hall. Ahead, I see the light from my classroom and move toward the beacon. Reaching my room, I place my hand on the handle, eyes searching up and down the deserted hall, swallowed in silence once more. I shake my head, twist the doorknob, and push the heavy door open. Farther down the hallway, a door slams. Footsteps tear down the corridor, laughter trailing. I turn quickly and catch a glimpse of a small body running in the distance.

That is not a shadow or a trick of my mind. Under Principal Garber's orders, Tony will be locking up the school at any moment. I rush down the hallway, desperate to find the child who will be trapped inside the school if I do not do something. *Where are the child's parents?* Pushing my luck in the heels, I step up my pace, slide on the polished floors. The giggle continues, goading, daring.

The clicking of my shoes makes it impossible to determine how to follow, where to go. I stop to listen for the direction in which the child has run but am offered only silence. So much time spent within my classroom, I'm still not completely familiar with the layout of the school and am unable to ascertain my whereabouts in the building. I look behind me, at the route I have run. There was a hallway I made a righthand turn into I'm sure, but now I do not see it in the poorly lit corridor.

A loud crash from somewhere just ahead breaks the stillness. From deep inside my chest, pounding responds, halting the last breath I managed to inhale. Hesitantly, I twist in the direction of the noise, pushing the air out of my lungs, bringing in a shallow replacement. Reluctant to take action, I force my legs to move toward the sound, careful to control the clacking of my heels on the smooth, slick floor.

"Come and get me," a tiny voice challenges.

I spin to locate the source and lose my balance. Falling to the cold floor, I catch myself, wrists taking the full weight of my upper body. Lowering onto my knees to alleviate the pressure, I hold, wait, catch my breath. The old familiar compression seizes my chest, threatening to pull me back to a place I fought to leave behind. *You will not go there.* I won't give myself over again. I push to stand, bracing in a wide stance, squaring my shoulders.

"Who's there?" I call out. The words bounce off the walls. The pounding in my chest quickens. Sweat trickles along the back of my neck. Rapid and shallow breaths wrestle the tension washing over my extremities.

A muffled whisper answers, the words indecipherable. Reaching down, I slip off my heels, leave them, and step toward the voice. I turn the next corner of the hallway. The whisper grows louder. I can almost make out the words. Cocking my head sideways and leaning my upper body forward, I hear the word 'something' but can't catch any of the other ramblings. Easing further ahead—determined to find the source of the sounds, set on coming to the aid of the child, resolute in my intent to prove this is not in my head—the words become clearer.

"Come closer," the whisper directs.

I follow the voice. A young boy, I think. Ahead, I see an open door on my left. The voice takes on a singsong tone. I stop to listen, to decipher the message.

"I know something you don't know."

Anger and frustration push out the fear and apprehension. My mothering instincts return. "And I know you will be locked inside this building for the night if you don't come out immediately."

Picking up pace, ready to end this game of hide 'n seek, I move toward the door that appears to be propped open. I reach the open door positioning myself at the threshold to look inside. The room is dark. I reach forward, groping at the air, finding the doorframe, and bracing my hands on each side of the threshold.

A jolt of fear singes the center of my body as I hear the ringing noise of a wooden handle—maybe a broom or a mop—falling against the tile floors and bouncing. I twist inside the doorway, trying to determine where the racket has come from but see nothing.

A rush of air races past me. Something brushes the underside of my outstretched arm. I spin to find the source, arms grasping at the shadow. A forceful push rams my midsection and sends me stumbling. I fall to the floor as the door slams, closing me inside the pitch-black room.

Using my hands, I climb up the door, feeling for the knob to pull myself upright. I find the lever and yank for my freedom, but it is locked. The smells of cleaning chemicals flood my nostrils, sending waves of nausea rolling through my stomach. My throat constricts, closing off my airway. Hands to my neck, I work my fingers in a massaging method to aid in swallowing the excess saliva pooling in my mouth, fighting off the choking sensation. Sweat forms over my brow in reaction to the whirling motion inside my head, cheeks warm and wet with the tears leaking from the corners of my eyes. I haven't had one in a while, but I know what this is, and I am well-practiced in how to control it. I must get a hold of myself. *I can do this.* I've done it a hundred times before.

Slowly, I turn to lean my body against the door. Although it's dark, I close my eyes and focus on drawing air into my lungs; one slow pull in, then out, then another, and another. Breathing under control, I bring forth the image of a wide open field, the sun high above, a beautiful tree in the distance. My heart rate begins to slow. The tension gradually releases its grip on my body. I open my eyes to the blackened room, careful and conscious of my breathing. Wiping away the moisture from the sides of my face, I announce, "I am in control."

There must be a light in here somewhere. I turn and run my hand over the door and to the side, along the wall, searching. Locating the switch, I flip on the light to take in my surroundings. The custodian closet.

Keys jangle outside the door. Stepping aside, I grab a broom propped in the corner to shield myself and wait for the door to open.

Tony jumps as he takes sight of me, a startled grunt escaping his throat. I let out the breath in my chest and lower the broom.

"Ms. S?" The older man questions. "What are you doing in here?" A puzzled look crossing his face, Tony runs a calloused hand over his receding hairline then brings it to rest on his hip.

"I thought I heard a child," I start, setting the broom back in its place, then push the hair away from my eyes. "I..." I begin and stop, unsure of how much I want to reveal. "I followed the noise through the hallways and then got trapped in your closet." My fingers fumble the hem of my blouse that has come untucked.

"No kids left in the building." Tony uses his middle finger to push the glasses up the bridge of his nose. "I just did my final walk through. Saw the light on in your classroom, though. Went in to tell ya I was locking up but couldn't find ya." Tony clips a keyring onto his belt, pushes the door toward the hallway, and stoops to prop it open. He moves to the other side of the open door and leans down. As he stands, Tony holds out my pumps. "These your shoes? I found them in the middle of the hallway."

I step forward to take them from him. "Yes, thank you," I say, bending to slip them onto my bare feet. "I'll just grab the bags from my room and be out of your way." I edge around him and into the hallway.

Feeling the heat of his gaze as I walk away, I drop my hands to the side of my body, pull my shoulders straight, and turn the corner.

AUGUST

From a dead sleep, I bolt upright. A blaring noise blasts through the stillness of the night. I look around the dark room, disoriented, reaching to the bedside table, searching for my phone. I tap the bright orange button, extinguishing the noise of the alarm and view the screen to learn it is only two AM. Plopping back on my pillow, I hold the phone above my face to check the alarm settings. My standard five-thirty wake-up alert has been changed. I work backward in my mind, scrolling through the last events I can recall.

Jay used my phone in the emergency room to play games yesterday. I should have made him sit there and think on his actions. But instead of creating a scene, I gave in to Jay's demands while we waited for the child he battered to have his tongue stitched back together. That poor child. That poor mother. No matter how I phrased my numerous apologies, the words fell short. How can I make amends for my child's horrific behavior? Make allowances for my inadequacies as a parent?

I needed Kirby tonight to calm me, to talk with Jay, to have the only other person in the world who understands what we go through with Jay help me sort this out. But before we ever left the hospital, Kirby had been called back to work to cover a sick driver's route—a shipment with a delivery deadline. We can't very well put Kirby's job in jeopardy simply because I wish to be consoled.

The sun had long set by the time Jay and I finally left the hospital. Our path home took us by Jay's school. There were a few cars parked outside, still some lights left on inside the building. On impulse, I whipped into the parking lot, ordered Jay out of the car, and marched him to the school's front entrance before I could think twice about what I was doing. As uncomfortable as I always feel in the presence of Jay's school principal, I was willing to sweat through the encounter if it meant Jay might get a better start on this school term than years past.

The unlocked school doors and the light from the principal's office gave me hope that just maybe, we'd get lucky and have an opportunity to meet Jay's teacher before the first day of school. Given his prior experiences inside the office, Jay insisted on staying outside in the waiting area.

Despite a good amount of certainty about the reception I would receive, I mustered the courage to knock on the principal's door. As soon as I made that first rap, I regretted my actions. What excuse was I going to give for not attending the regularly scheduled program? That due to the conduct of my problematic son, we'd been held up in the emergency room waiting to be sure the latest child to suffer at Jay's hand wouldn't lose his tongue? I couldn't lie. I already have enough to atone for without adding another transgression to the list for which I ask God's forgiveness. But I was trying to be the unconditional advocate my son deserved.

I needn't have worried about an excuse as I was immediately, and rather brusquely, informed we were too late for the meet and greet and too early for the morning bell. In the end, I got no further than being offered the name of Jay's new teacher—information we had already learned from the letter we received two weeks ago.

Wide awake and mind racing, I throw my legs over the edge of the bed. I make my way to the kitchen for a drink of water, easing down the hallway, careful not to creak the loose floorboards. Any bit of noise drags Jay out of sleep.

I pull a glass from the cabinet and fill it from the tap. Sipping my water, I pad to the window overlooking our little backyard, chainlink fence wrapping the perimeter. The tiny play set in the far left corner is weathering. Kirby and I have discussed donating it to another young couple at church once their baby is born. Jay has outgrown the structure, and we have no plans for more children, though we did give it serious consideration early in our marriage.

Kirby and I married immediately after we finished high school. I crossed the graduation stage carrying the secret we had yet to share with anyone. Mama and Daddy were somewhat disappointed when they learned of my pregnancy and the news I wouldn't be attending college anytime soon, but they accepted what was done was done. On the other hand, Kirby's parents were downright furious with their son and saw me as the evil temptress who had lured their only child to sin. 'A roll on the dark side,' I believe, is how they put it.

Kirby's family would have nothing to do with him. Kirby was the son of a preacher and had shamed his father's good name. To this day, Kirby's parents have yet to forgive their son or reach out to meet their only grandchild.

Before Jay was born, Kirby and I lived with my parents. Kirby went to trucking school at a local transport company and was hired upon completion of the coursework. Once Kirby had six months under his belt driving a rig, we had enough resources to establish our own little family home.

We've resided in our small two-bedroom house (built years before both of our parents were born) since Kirby and I moved out of my parents' home. We believed at the time the rental was only temporary until we became more established. After Jay's second birthday, Kirby and I tossed around the idea of moving, assuming in the near future, we would try again for another baby.

But Kirby and I were both so young, we reluctantly took my parents' advice to wait until we were more settled. With each passing anniversary, it became clearer we had more than either of us could handle just trying to raise Jay. Now, I can't possibly imagine bringing another child into this world when I am unable to properly parent the one I have.

Motherhood has not proven to be what I conceptualized during the long months of watching my belly grow. Sure, I've bandaged the boo-boos, read the bedtime stories, and held long conversations on park benches with other mothers. But I thought I'd be closer to my son, and Jay never lets me near him. I don't wipe away tears, coddle him after a bad dream, or snuggle up in front of a movie. From the moment Jay learned to walk, he's traveled a path away from me, never toward.

As I swallow the last of my water, I decide to check in on Jay before heading back to bed. I travel back down the hallway past the bedroom Kirby and I share, to the last door on the left.

I twist the knob of Jay's bedroom door, opening it just a crack to peek through, enough to see Jay's bed. Covers thrown back, fitted sheet rumpled, Jay is not in bed. I push the door open to step inside, looking around the room. No light shines in the play tent set up in the corner. Still, I move to check it anyway, hoping he fell asleep inside. The tent is empty.

Jay's last sleepwalking episode was a couple of years ago, but given the stress of a new school year, it is possible the condition has returned. The pediatrician informed us most children grow out of the disorder, and because Jay hasn't had an episode in so long, Kirby and I determined those worrisome nights were over.

I head back through the door and down the hall toward the bathroom, mindful not to make noise or flip on lights that might startle Jay awake. Kirby and I have each been victims of Jay's attacks when he's awoken suddenly. The nightlight I keep in the bathroom illuminates the room enough for me to see Jay is not at the toilet. I ease back the shower curtain to check the bathtub, a usual spot for Jay's night walks. Not tonight.

Moving back into the hallway, I rule out the kitchen and the backyard as I was just there and head toward the living room. The sofa vacant, no sign of Jay sleeping in the middle of the room's floor, I check the coat closet. Kneeling, using my hands, I carefully grope at the floor for his sleeping form. No Jay. I stand, close the closet door, and think to check the deadbolt on the front door; the thought of him wandering the streets accelerates my heartbeat.

Finding the door securely latched, I exhale and think. The only one other place he could be is the basement. We only use the space for storage, though we have talked about setting up our family room down there. The unfinished space already has a fireplace and has been plumbed out for another bathroom. Our landlord offered to finish off the area, hanging sheetrock, laying carpet, installing the bathroom fixtures. I like the idea of having a bit more room for the three of us to spread out. Maybe set up part of the area as a home office instead of the cramped corner in the kitchen we now use. All we had to agree on was a slight rent increase and to oversee the construction work. But finding the time to supervise the project has kept us from undertaking the venture.

The door to the basement is off the kitchen. I'm positive the door was closed when I went for water earlier but head to check the downstairs room for Jay. It is the only possible place left to look. In the kitchen, I retrieve the flashlight from the cabinet beneath the sink. Worry settles into my bones as I think of Jay, glassy-eyed and semi-conscious, traversing the steep stairwell in the dark. I pull out the flashlight and click the button to find the light doesn't illuminate. I beat the handle against the palm of my other hand. The batteries are dead.

Setting aside the flashlight, I hurry to the door leading to the basement, hoping Jay hasn't hurt himself. *What will I do if I find him in a heap at the bottom of the stairs? Where else do I look if he isn't there?* Maybe it hasn't happened in our town, but children have been abducted from their own bedrooms while parents sleep in the next room. *Who would I call first? Kirby, the police, my parents?* I draw a deep breath to settle my nerves. I'm sure everything is fine.

Above all else, I must not startle him if he's sleepwalking, as much for his safety as for mine. Jay was much younger and smaller when he attacked me last, leaving me to sport a black eye and a sprained wrist.

The basement door hinges groan; I cringe. A glowing light filters up the staircase. Smoke tickles my nose. Covering my mouth, I fight the urge to sneeze. I hold to the handrail and ease down the stairs. The light grows brighter the farther I descend. Turning the corner, I view the source. Flames dance inside the fireplace at the far end of the room. Jay sits with his legs crossed underneath him, staring into the fire.

The scene brings back unsettling memories of my childhood nightmares when a figure I called the shadow woman haunted my dreams. *It's not her; it's Jay.* I shake them away and pad lightly to stand behind him, whispering his name. Jay's gaze remains focused on the fire. He reaches in front of him and tosses something into the flames.

The doctor explained to us when Jay first started these nighttime jaunts it is common for sleepwalkers to carry-out regular tasks from memory. But we've never allowed Jay to start a fire and have adamantly warned him about the dangers of playing with fire. I look over his head to see a pile of tinker toys in front of him, the container cast aside. The classic wooden, five hundred piece set was a gift from my parents a few years back when Jay began showing interest in building things with his other toys.

I bend, holding my hair back as I lean over his shoulder. "Jay," I whisper.

Jay slowly turns his head, meeting my eyes. He's conscious, coherent, fully awake, the glassy look I remember from his previous sleepwalking episodes, absent. Capturing the hue of the fire, Jay's green eyes appear orange; the effect is disturbing and alarming. The stone-cold glare he delivers chills me despite the heat from the fire on the warm August night.

I stand upright, taking a step away from him. "Jay, what are you doing?"

"I wasn't sleepy." Jay tosses another piece of the set into the fireplace.

The smell of the burning toys catches in the back of my throat. I cough into the crook of my elbow.

"Jay, stop." I grab his hand before he can toss another piece into the flames.

Jay jerks his hand from my grip, hurling the piece into the fire. I step in front of him, scooping the toys away from his reach, pitching them into the discarded container. "How many times have we talked about playing with fire? You could have burned the house down."

Jay slaps at my hand, fills his fists with toys, heaves them into the fire.

"Jay, I said stop it. Stop it right now."

He bolts up, stomping off to the other side of the room, screaming, "I hate you. I hate you. You trash bag whore." He flings the wooden block in his hand. I feel the edge of the cube pierce the back of my head.

The abusive actions, the hate rhetoric, I've learned to expect from my son, but the name calling is new territory. I don't even know where his knowledge of such a word comes from, certainly not our home.

My throat tightens. I force air through my mouth, pushing the sob into my lungs. "Jay," I pause to gather my composure. "Calm down. You know we don't say things like that to people. It's..." Before I get the rest of my sentence out, Jay's rants begin again.

"Shut up. Leave me the hell alone."

I walk toward him, reaching out to take his hand.

"Get away from me. Are you stupid? I said leave me alone," he yells. I take his hand, but Jay yanks it away. "Don't touch me. I don't want to be touched. Stupid bitch." Spit flies from his mouth, spatters my arm.

I take a step back. "It's time for bed." I look away, folding my arms across my body, letting him know I've no intentions of trying to touch him again. I give him a moment, then return my gaze to meet his eyes. A fixed, calculated leer has replaced the hatred I viewed only seconds ago. Prickles rise along the flesh of my bare arms.

Turning away to finish picking up the toys, I hear Jay take himself up the stairs and slam the basement door.

MEREL

AUGUST

I unlock the door of my classroom, pushing it open then reaching inside, fumbling for the light switch. The fluorescent bulbs buzz to life, spotlighting all my hard work. I take a moment to let my pride swell and the significance of this day settle. Opening the door to our shared office, I find Dorothy sitting at her side of the desk.

"Good morning, good morning," she calls out, spunky and cheerful in her bright yellow dress, hair pulled into the high ponytail she's worn each day I've known her. Sporting a statement necklace and a wide cuff bracelet, her outfit is perfectly accessorized. I peek down at the bland and boring black and white (my signature colors) ensemble I wear, not even remembering the act of getting dressed this morning, sighing in relief that I've managed to slip into a pair of matching shoes.

"Good morning," I reply, closing my side of the office to open the closet door, placing my bags on the shelf inside the space.

"Uh-oh," Dorothy mumbles as she watches me.

"What?" I reach around the back of my neck, checking my blouse isn't on inside out.

"You closed your door."

"Huh?" The inquiry comes out a bit gruffly.

56

"You closed your door and locked yourself out of your classroom."

"Oh, for Pete's sake." My shoulders drop in defeat. "So far, this day is not going according to plan, and it's only six AM." I exit out Dorothy's office door, then her classroom door, enter my classroom, and open the office door once more.

"I take it you didn't sleep very well last night," Dorothy states. "First day jitters?"

"I guess so. That and the fact I stayed longer than I should have after the meet and greet. I was so worked up when I got home, it took forever to get to sleep."

Being locked inside the custodian closet last night shook me up more than I'd like to admit, but I have no intention of filling Dorothy in on the mishap. Hopefully, Tony will keep quiet about the incident. I hate to think of the after-hours escapade getting back to Principal Garber. I'm not sure how I could possibly explain running through the empty, dark hallways, chasing a phantom child to a woman whose confidence I desperately need. Lying in bed, tossing and turning into the wee hours of the morning, I went over and over the details. And though Tony claims no one was in the school at the late hour, I'm more convinced now than when I ran through the hallway; there was someone in the school. The noises were real. The shove to my midsection was not something I imagined, and someone did slam the door closed locking me inside the custodian closet.

"The first day of school does that to teachers and students. We're all so anxious about starting the school year, there's not a lot of rest for any of us the night before the first day," Dorothy says, watching me shuffle through my lesson planner.

I nod to acknowledge I've heard her and continue to look for the notes I made on the students and their parents last night. Flipping back and forth through the notebook, my frustration grows. *Where is that piece of paper?*

Dorothy reaches to lay her hand on my arm. "Hey, you're going to do great. Take a deep breath, center yourself. The last thing you want to convey to those kiddos, and most especially to their parents, is a lack of confidence in yourself."

"You're right. I know you're right," I say, then add, "I've read that," more for myself than for Dorothy's sake.

"Say, did you give any more thought to the idea of taking a first day of school picture?" Dorothy asks.

The outside of Dorothy's office door is papered with beginning and end of year class comparison pictures snapped throughout her years of teaching. The difference in the students' appearances from the beginning to the end of the school year is amazing. I love the idea. I would love it more if I didn't know it was a ritual she and Betty shared. Nevertheless, I want to start my own collection of photographs.

"Yes, I did, and I absolutely adore the idea. So, when do we do it?"

"We need to get it done before lunch. Otherwise, it will be far too hot to have the children outside. Recess is one thing, but when you attempt to get twenty-plus seven-year-olds to stand still and pose in this heat, it's another story altogether. We'll take them to the courtyard at ten-thirty."

"Ten-thirty," I repeat, writing the note into my planner for the day, trying to quash the vision of Dorothy and Betty marching their students to the courtyard year after year at precisely ten-thirty.

"There's doughnuts and coffee in the break room. Might be a good idea to get some caffeine and sugar into your system before the little ones arrive. Come with me?"

"I'm not hungry, but I could use some coffee," I tell her, closing up my planner. While I may not have slept much last night, the truth is I've barely slept in the past month. The job search, the move, setting up my classroom—all have taken a toll. The lack of rest is starting to catch up with me physically and mentally, but I don't have time to relax now or in the near foreseeable future.

I push myself to stand and follow Dorothy out her office door.

* * *

STANDING at the horseshoe reading table, I look out over the twenty seated children. Heads bent, intently working to finish their first assignment. The buzz of collective anxiety cuts the silence. A smile stretches across my face, witnessing their tenacity in completing the simple work I've assigned. Truthfully, the project is more about establishing a routine and to find out about who they are rather than what they know. This first week of school, I plan to focus on getting the children into a comfortable, structured schedule while gaining their trust and getting to know them.

My eyes move to the one empty desk. The same child who was a no show at last night's meet and greet has yet to arrive for day one of the school year. The clock on the far side of the room ticks forward. Twenty-two minutes since the morning bell rang and no sign of Jack. I look back to the table beside me, piled high with school supplies. The chore of packing them away into the cabinets I cleared last night will be a task I take on after the students have left this afternoon.

I walk to my desk, double-checking my planner for the next activity. The door to the classroom bursts open, pulling the students' attention away from their assignment. I follow their gazes. A woman, arms loaded with bags from the local superstore, tugs a little boy through the door. I cross the room to introduce myself, anxious to finally meet the infamous Jack.

"Good morning." I reach to shake the woman's hand. She ignores the gesture, instead pushing the bags into my offered palm then pulling the child in front of her. I quickly move to place the bags onto the reading table so I can better address my newest student.

Turning back to the pair, I bend to greet the boy. "Hello, you must be Jack." As did his mother, the boy disregards me. His head turned, he takes in the likes of his classmates.

"No," his guardian brusquely informs me.

I stand to address the woman. "I apologize. There is only one child on my roster marked as not present. I assumed this must be Jack."

"Yes. I mean no," the woman stammers. She keeps a firm grasp on the boy's shoulders, sighs heavily, then adds, "This is Jack, and I'm his mom."

I wait for her to offer her name but do not receive the information. Breaking the awkward silence, I move ahead with my introduction. "It's nice to meet you both." I keep my focus on the woman, giving the child a moment to warm up to me. "I'm Ms. S."

"Whew, that's a relief. We were worried about how to pronounce your name." She removes a hand from the boy's shoulders, placing it protectively on the top of his head, ruffling his hair. Jack shakes his head, jerking away from his mother's grip. Breaking from our eye contact, the woman's empty hands move to adjust her handbag, holding tight to the strap over her shoulder.

"I thought Sowanoke might be too much for the children. Ms. S. is how I've asked them to address me." I look down at Jack, who has yet to acknowledge me then back to his mother. "I was worried when I didn't meet you all last night at the meet and greet that you may have moved out of the district."

"We tried to make it last night. I had pressing obligations to deal with, however. We did come by after I finished, but most everyone was gone."

"Well, you're here now, and that's what counts." I offer a polite smile, wondering if all the rumors I've heard from the other teachers about Jack's mother are more than just unverified suppositions. Noting the mother has yet to provide a reason for the tardiness of her child this morning, I determine to set forward my expectations for prompt arrival. "I'm sure the first day of school traffic was madness. Hopefully, the traffic pattern will be ironed out by the end of the week so all students are in their classrooms by the 7:40 bell each morning."

The woman studies me with an expression I can't quite read. I break my gaze with her to check the students seated at their desks. Several have finished the assignment and are waiting for further instructions. I need to get this woman on her way so I can attend my class.

"Speaking of transportation, how will Jack be getting home today? Car rider, bus rider, daycare?" I ask, retrieving the clipboard with my afternoon transportation list, locating Jack's name to record the information.

"I'm NOT Jack." The harsh announcement lands all eyes in the room on the boy who claims not to be Jack though his mother only moments earlier confirmed him to indeed be Jack.

For the first time, I see the face of the boy. His square jaw, his sandy blond hair, his eyes locking on mine. The haughty green stare so cold, so hateful, so familiar, I barely stifle the shudder vibrating my chest, choke down the yelp in the back of my throat.

The mother shakes her son. "Don't yell at your teacher. It's just a misunderstanding. Look, you've upset her." The woman looks at me. "He doesn't want to be called Jack anymore," she explains.

"I see." The only words I think to reply spill forth as I work to regain composure.

The woman continues in a low whisper. "He says there was a bad nickname for him going around last year and insists he not be called Jack anymore." She squeezes the boy's shoulders, pushing him slightly forward. "Please. Call him Jay."

* * *

HOW I'VE MANAGED to make it through the last two hours following the exit of Jay's mother is nothing short of miraculous. I can't take my eyes off Jay. I can't stand to look at Jay. My heart stops, then revs. Back and forth, and back and forth, it's gone. It doesn't help the way he stares back at me, something in his eyes so knowing, so sinister. For the sake of the students, I have to get control of myself.

A glance at the clock lets me know I have just enough time to instruct the students on how I expect them to line up at the door then take a quick restroom break before heading out to meet Dorothy and her class in the courtyard. I stand at the front of the room, calling the attention of my students. As I explain the procedures for how we will complete the activities, a thumping noise breaks my train of thought. The racket persists, finally requiring me to address the nuisance. Jay sits at the grouping of six desks arranged to make a table on the far edge of the reading carpet. He uses his foot to kick at the corner leg of the desk, his intensity growing with each kick.

"Jay, please do not kick your desk," I say, making sure to curb any irritation so as not to alarm the children.

Jay continues to kick as he throws out a curt, "Why?"

"Because you might miss the desk and accidentally kick someone at your table."

"I never miss."

"Jay, it's disruptive. Other children cannot concentrate on what I'm saying while you're making the noise."

He bangs his elbows onto the desktop dropping his chin to rest in his palm. "Whatever."

I ignore the remark and finish my instructions. We play the quiet game to determine which table group will line up first at the door.

Earlier in the morning, we discussed classroom jobs. From my pre-made cards, I pulled random names, assigning the children their first roles, all of which will rotate next week. Jay happens to be this week's door holder. Before the first table is called to line up, I instruct Jay to take his place at the door.

The students file out of the classroom and stop at the directed point along the wall to wait while everyone exits the room before we move down the hallway. All goes well until Jay realizes he will be the last one in the line.

"I don't like being the last one in line," he yells, his voice booming through the narrow passage.

I walk to the end of the line. "Jay," I say, my voice low. "We don't yell in the hallway. It disturbs the other classrooms."

"I don't want to be the last person in line." He looks up at me, his green eyes piercing mine.

I stare at his defiant face, his icy glare. For a moment, I lose time, forget that behind me, a line of anxious students awaits my next instruction.

"Being the door holder is a very important job, Jay. It's actually two jobs. First, you hold the door, and then when all the other students have gone through that door, you take your place at the end of the line. Your next very important job is to be the caboose. Do you know what a caboose is?"

"Yes, it's the butt end of the train."

I let his comment meant to startle me slide. "The caboose makes sure everyone else stays in line and doesn't leave the line. It would be terrible if someone got out of line and we lost them. Right?"

I hold Jay's unblinking stare.

"If you don't want to be the door holder and the caboose, I can give the very important job to someone else. Would you like me to do that?"

"No, I'll do it," he finally concedes.

"Good, because I think you're just the right person for the job."

I walk back to the middle of the line, letting the students know we are now ready to make our way down the hall to the bathrooms.

I wait as five boys and five girls at a time take turns in the restrooms, ushering in another child as one exits. When each child has had a turn in the restrooms, we make our way along the hallway to the door exiting to the courtyard.

Traveling the short pathway to our meeting point, I am again grateful for Dorothy's wisdom. She was right to suggest getting the project completed in the early morning hours. The air, heavy and dense, humidity levels well into the high eighties, compound the late August temperature. We arrive to find Dorothy and her group already lined up for their class photograph. The students flap their hands back and forth in front of their reddening faces. I instruct my students to wait as Dorothy takes her place for the picture. Using her digital camera, I snap several photos, inspecting each one as I shoot it to be certain there will be a good picture she can use for her door.

Our students switch places. Dorothy moves her group to the benches as I position my class for our photo—making three lines, stair-stepping the children according to height so all their precious faces will be seen. Dorothy lifts the camera in front of her, focusing in on our gang, commanding us all to smile on the word 'cheese.' Dorothy snaps a few photos, examines her work, and declares she thinks we need a couple more.

Giving us time to rest our cheeks, Dorothy turns to address a little girl from her class. The children begin to fidget, antsy under the heat of the sun. In an effort to curb their escalating restlessness, I reach my hands high above my head and wave them back and forth, instructing the students to do the same. "Pretend you're an inflatable tube guy—like the ones at car dealerships," I command. The antic proves two-fold as it calms my group and entertains Dorothy's class. Giggles abound. As Dorothy indicates she's ready to finish the pictures, I pronounce, "All right, now we're smiling statues again."

Dorothy aims the camera and spouts the magic word, her eyes growing big, mouth flying wide. A loud shriek slices through the thick air. Olivia, a blonde, blue-eyed, little girl, screams from the second row. I turn to witness what the commotion is about and see Olivia holding onto the back of her head, fat tears rolling over her cheeks.

Rushing over to find out what happened, I bend to view

Olivia at eye level. "Sweetie, what's wrong?" I ask her as Dorothy hurries to my side. Dorothy's students observe the action from the benches, some standing to get a better view.

Olivia's wails prevent her from relaying the issue. The children in my class gather closer around, curious about Olivia's distress.

Dorothy looks down to where I now kneel in front of the distraught child. "I saw her head snap all the way back. It looked like someone pulled her hair."

"Olivia, honey," I pull her into a hug making every effort to soothe her, attempting to coax answers from her. Olivia is flanked by two boys. My eyes travel left where Turner stands, looking incredulously at Olivia. I look to Olivia's left, where I positioned Jay only minutes earlier. Unlike Turner, Jay watches the scene with an impassive gaze, unmoved by his classmate's apparent anguish.

I stand, moving to face Jay, preparing the series of questions to get to the bottom of what has happened to Olivia. Jay holds his arms at the sides of his body, lifting his chin to look up at me. His face is that of a cherub, a sprinkle of freckles over his nose and full cheeks. But under Jay's long, feminine lashes, his green eyes are unsettling, something menacing lurking behind them. Despite the heat, a shiver rises the length of my spine, crawling the back of my neck. I lose sense of what is going on around me. Pulling away from his fixed look, my eyes drop to his hands. He holds a fist full of long blonde hair.

"Jay, did you pull Olivia's hair?" I ask though the answer is obvious.

"Yes," he states matter-of-factly.

"Why?"

"Because I wanted to know what her scream sounded like," he voices even and flat.

I turn, searching for Dorothy. She has rallied both classes into straight lines as she holds onto Olivia's hand. I take hold of Jay's hand as he flings away the strands of hair from the fingers of his free hand. Marching him to where Dorothy and Olivia stand, I order him to apologize to the little girl. With minimal, if any, sincerity, Jay tells Olivia he is sorry he pulled her hair then moves to take his place at the end of the line. I reach for Olivia, who releases Dorothy's hand to take mine.

Following the pathway, Dorothy and I walk side by side to lead our students through the courtyard and inside the building.

As we reach the doors, she leans toward me, whispering, "He might have changed his name, but his attitude is still just as hateful."

AMA

OCTOBER 1979

"Ama, you got something stuck in your craw?" Leoti asks. "We don't have to do this right now, you know."

Sitting at the small breakfast table in Leoti's kitchen, I ignore my sister and lay out the white cloth on the table in front of me, smoothing it flat, brushing it clean. On the stool next to me, I unfold the apron, organizing the items necessary to perform the ritual according to the order of their use.

"I'm serious, Ama. Something's got you in a mood. Just tell me."

"I can't concentrate with you gnawing at me, Leoti. Hand me that candle."

"Which one? Red, white, or black?"

"The white one first." I take the candle from Leoti and place it in the center of the cloth, then hold out my hand. "Now the red one, then the black."

Out of the corner of my eye, I see my sister watching me. Shadows of curiosity and doubt streak her features. If we're going to get any answers from this reading, Leoti is going to have to be rid of the skepticism she harbors.

I understand her lack of confidence in me, given that for the last six months, I've executed every fertility spell I can think of, and yet, Leoti stands across from me, rail thin and barren. Even I'm starting to have doubts about my abilities. But I have promised her we'll get some answers if we do this reading, and so, I intend to do this letter perfect.

I place the red candle to the left of the white one, the black candle an equal distance on the right. The three pillars form a straight line across the center of the table. I turn to the small stool set up on my left and double-check the tools. Leoti stands in front of her kitchen sink, silently observing, arms folded across the middle of her body. She brings a hand to her mouth and begins chewing at the cuticle of her thumb.

I halt the setup process. "Leoti, please. You're making me nervous."

Turning my attention to the window, I look out at the back-yard, waiting for Leoti to calm down, taking the moment to garner some faith in myself. I concentrate on the energy force outside of the window. The trees sway with the breeze that ushers in the cooler fall air. Drawing in a deep breath, I close my eyes and imagine the energy of the landscape entering my body, coursing through my veins. I open my eyes to find Leoti seated across the table from me.

"I'm sorry, Ama. It's not you. I'm just anxious all the time lately. I'm beginning to think I'll never get pregnant," Leoti puffs her cheeks and releases her frustrations into the tiny room's air supply.

"You've got to stop thinking that way. All this negativity...." I stop short, knowing the next words out of my mouth won't help the situation either. "Come on. Let's go sit outdoors and clear our minds for a few minutes."

Leoti and I stand and walk the short distance from her kitchen to the front porch. I head to the hanging swing and sit. Leoti plops down next to me. We use our feet to rock the swing to and fro, quiet with our thoughts.

"How's Daddy doing?" Leoti breaks the reverie.

"Ornery," I relay without giving thought to my answer. I

shouldn't have said that to Leoti. Now she is going to want to know why, and the truth is I can't tell her. It would hurt her feelings to know Papa thinks I am spending too much time with my sister—too much time with commoners, as we call them. But Leoti isn't a commoner, and I said as much to Papa. Of course, Papa considers anybody who doesn't live in The Community and practice our way of life a commoner. Leoti's different; she's my other half. Yes, her husband Rubin is inarguably a commoner, but Leoti was born in The Community. Although she may not practice our doctrine, Leoti understands us and knows our way of life.

"What's making him ornery?" Leoti asks.

Using my arms to brace myself, I lean over the swing, stopping our rhythm, and look at my feet—look anywhere but at my sister. From behind the screen door, the phone rings. Leoti stands and hurries inside to answer the call, leaving me to mull over my argument with Papa this morning.

Our father was not happy when I told him I planned on coming to see Leoti today. It's not that he doesn't love Leoti; he just doesn't approve of the way she lives. Papa wouldn't feel the way he does if it weren't for Mama's decision. If she had chosen to stay inside The Community after our birth, Leoti wouldn't want to live as a commoner; she might even be an apprentice as I am. We could have been elders together one day. She would have only had to train as one worker and would, therefore, be an elder long before me, though. Because I've been marked, I have to train as both a healer and a conjurer. I shake my head to drive away the bitterness in my thoughts.

Looking through the window, I see Leoti with the receiver to her ear, twirling the phone cord. It's obvious from the way she holds herself Rubin is the voice on the other end. No one can claim she doesn't love that man. Sometimes I wonder what it must be like to live as Leoti does: without all the expectations of the ever-watching elders, free to love whomever she wishes, free to make her own decisions as to how she spends her days.

Papa doesn't come right out and say he doesn't want me

spending so much time with Leoti. Instead, he claims I spend too much time in the city, that all my time spent outside The Community hinders my training. I have years and years of training left before I attain the title of chief elder. I hardly think one afternoon with my sister will make much of a difference. If I didn't have this damn muscadine stain on my cheek, the so-called mark of greatness, I would be an elder by my thirtieth birthday; though, I don't know which worker I would rather be, and it's not as if the choice would be mine. The elders make that decision before a child is even old enough to know he or she has been chosen. I enjoy learning the skills of both a healer and a conjurer, and both are equally rewarding. Working with the two different sets of elders to hone my crafts, however, provides double the opportunity for their discernment.

Papa has been receiving their shaded glances for much longer than I have, though. The elders did not agree with his decision to allow Mama and Leoti to leave The Community, and they certainly didn't approve of all the weekends he took me to stay with them. But Papa is our leader and founder. How could they buck his resolve? Not that Papa doesn't respect the opinions of The Community's members. After all, the philosophy behind our way of life is to give and receive love, to accept all others' differences. We are all equal. We are each seeking our own personal enlightenment. So who is to say that spending time with my sister is not advancing my spiritual awareness?

No one in The Community lives above another—even the elders. We all work together to live off the land in unity with one another. Everyone has a job that contributes to the good of The Community. In addition to apprenticeship duties, my daily responsibility is to drive workers to the odd jobs they perform in nearby towns in order to make money for The Community. Papa and the elders agreed that because I have spent so much time among the commoners due to my dual upbringing, I am the best one to carry out the necessary chore, that the commoners will view me with more neutrality.

The screen door squeaks open. Leoti looks across the way, waving to her neighbor. "Hey there, Mr. Thompson. You feeling better today?"

I watch their exchange and wonder how it is that we both have exactly the same features, yet people view us both so differently. People seem intimidated by me, whereas Leoti is seen as unassuming, open, and kind.

Leoti finishes her conversation with Mr. Thompson and moves to rejoin me on the swing. "That was Rubin. He'll be leaving Asheville in about an hour."

"We don't have much time then. We better get to it."

"You didn't tell me why Daddy is so ornery. What's up? Y'all have a fight?"

"I'm just tired of being the one who makes all the spiritual water." Leoti nods her understanding. She's heard the same rant many times. "And the dressing oil. I should be spending more time learning from the elders instead of prepping their supplies."

"Is that why you walked this afternoon? Because Daddy got mad and didn't let you take the van?"

Papa thinks I've heeded his wisdom. After our words, I told him I needed to go for a walk to clear my head. A half-truth but still a lie in the eyes of The Community.

"No," I lie for the second time today. "I just felt like walking."

* * *

I STAND in front of the table studying the candle set up.

"Did you get a photograph of yourself?"

"Oh, I forgot. Be right back."

Leoti rushes out of the room. I move to sit behind the table and turn to the stool where I've laid out the tools. I find the nail, pick up the white candle, and begin to carve.

"Okay, I got one," Leoti says as she returns. "What are you doing to that candle?"

"Carving your name into it," I tell her, never taking my eyes away from the task at hand.

"That nail is all rusty; your hands are going to be a mess. Let me get you another one. Rubin has some in his tool chest." Leoti turns to leave the room once more.

"No thanks," I stop her. "The rust helps relay a better view of the reading. It's more powerful."

Leoti looks doubtful.

"I know what I'm doing."

Leoti concedes, taking her seat across the table from me, waiting patiently, intently watching as I use the prepared oil on the candles, then lift them one by one and whisper the sacred chants over the top of each pillar.

"And this is going to get us answers, right? We're going to find out why I'm not getting pregnant. Will you be able to tell me what I need to do to get pregnant?" Leoti babbles, twisting her hands in her lap.

"Leoti, please. You have got to remain calm. You're going to scare off the spirits."

"Well, who's here? Is Mama going to be here?"

"Leoti."

I reach across the table and take the photograph she retrieved. Glancing at it as I lay it in front of the center candle, I note it was taken this past summer when she and Rubin took their beach vacation. I want to lose myself for a few minutes, imagine it's me in the picture, standing at the edge of the ocean. I quickly release the daydream, knowing I will never see the ocean, only ever live it through my sister's experiences.

I reach for the pouch inside the apron and pull out my bone collection.

"Oh, my god. Ama. What are those?"

"What do they look like? They're bones, Leoti."

"I'm not an idiot; I know they're bones. Why do we need bones? And what kind of bones are they? Did you kill something to do this reading? I don't want any part of you killing things for my benefit, Ama."

"Relax. They're 'possum bones, and no, I didn't kill it. I found them in the woods. They've been treated and spiritualized especially for readings."

Leoti's posture eases. She slumps back into her chair, clasping her hands in her lap as she sighs heavily.

"Are you ready?" I ask her.

"Yes, let's get on with it." Leoti straightens her spine, pulls her shoulders back.

I take the lighter from the apron and touch the flame to each of the three wicks, left to right, then close my eyes and whisper the chant, calling upon our ancestors for their help and insight. At the conclusion, I pick up the bones and hold them out toward Leoti.

"Say your name three times, then blow three short breaths over the bones. And don't ask why, just do it."

Leoti does as instructed. I draw my hands and the bones back toward me, then drop them carefully onto the tabletop. We sit in silence as I put together the message relayed before me. I stare at the bones, laid out in no particular order, though a clear message is present. Leoti is not going to be happy with the reading.

I furrow my brow, drawing my eyes to squint as if in concentration, trying to buy some more time before I tell my sister she is perfectly capable of bearing children. It's Rubin who is sterile.

Leoti will not interrupt the reading. She knows not to break in on the visions until the reader is ready to speak. I continue to study the bones, looking for something more positive to convey to my sister. The candles flicker brighter, tugging my attention from the bones to the flames. My spirit guide makes her presence known to me. She has more information to add to the message of the bones.

How can that be? I silently ask my spirit guide.

A rush of air enters through the open window. The gust

blows through, catching the screen door, causing it to open and slam, extinguishing the flames of the candles.

I receive no answer, for my guide is gone as quickly as she came through.

Leoti looks at me with expectant anxiety.

"The message was clear. I saw a beautiful little girl."

ESME

OCTOBER

At the entrance of the First Baptist Childcare Center, I stand, awaiting the arrival of the daycare's transport van. Our program has twelve school-aged children whose parents need assistance in the three-hour window between the last school bell of the day and the end of their workday. I am no exception. Jay is in that van, and I dread to learn what new episode my son will have to report. *Let me rephrase that—what new episode will I read about in Jay's daily behavior report from his teacher?* Not that Jay ever denies responsibility for the misdeeds, but he's certainly never forthright with the information.

It started day one. Day one of the school year and we were already receiving communication from Jay's teacher about 'an incident' he perpetuated. Since then, it's been one 'incident' after another. Bouts in the lunchroom. Brawls at recess. Classmates' snacks gone missing from backpacks (the very same kind of snack Jay just happened to bring for himself that day.) Little girls having their hair pulled. Little boys being pinched. Tripping, pushing, punching, stomping, kicking, poking. October twenty-eighth—*we're only two months into the school year.*

The principal intervened early this year. Three weeks into the school year, I was approached about Jay's aggressive behavior. Last year, it was proposed Jay see the school's behavioral intervention specialist. When I expressed concern that Jay would be missing instruction time in the classroom, thereby falling further behind his classmates, the principal let the suggestion fade. However, it was then 'gently' suggested that perhaps we consult our pediatrician regarding Jay's behavior. Although ADHD was never uttered, Kirby and I both understood the heavy undertones of the recommendation. Caring for children on a daily basis who have been diagnosed with the disorder, witnessing firsthand the side effects of the medications administered, knowing what labels can do to children, I was reluctant to heed such advice. Kirby, however, felt differently. After much discussion, we decided it couldn't hurt to see the doctor, gain some insight into our son's behavior.

At the conclusion of testing, the only knowledge we gleaned was that our health insurance was minimal, and Jay's IQ tested borderline genius. He was not, as the school so readily (yet vaguely) implied, living with ADHD. And so, when we were called in the first weeks of this school year to speak with the principal, I believed I had no other choice than to concede and allowed Jay to see the behavioral intervention specialist twice a week.

I have followed, to the letter, every last suggestion the behavioral intervention specialist has proposed thus far, and none of them seem to be making any difference in Jay's behavior. Rewards are not worthy. Consequences are simply inconsequential. And Jay is now visiting the woman's office three times (more often if there is an 'incident') a week, leaving me to assist Jay with the makeup work he misses during class instruction hours. To make matters worse, Kirby's routes have changed—so many of his fellow drivers have been laid off, Kirby is on the road more often than not. The situation is becoming more than I can handle. But, as Kirby tenderly reminds me, God doesn't give us more than we can handle. I know he is right.

All I can do is pray. And pray I do. Every morning, standing under the warm spray of the shower, I ask God to be guided through his hands on the best way to raise my son, to foster him into manhood, for strength and wisdom—but not patience, never patience.

For years I did pray for patience. Then, one wise parishioner from our church explained to me that when one prays for patience, God will present situations to test patience so to strengthen the virtue. I've endured enough afflictions of that particular prayer.

Now, when I catch myself lapsing on the lesson, I quickly recall Romans 12:12: 'Rejoice in hope, be patient in tribulation, be constant in prayer.' But I'm struggling with rejoicing in hope. Hope is positive, and my only expectations for Jay these days are negative. Though I hope for the best, I expect the worst of my son. *What kind of mother does that make me? What kind of mother doesn't believe in the goodness of her child?* I have to be a better parent. There must be something I can do better, or not do, or something I'm not doing at all that I should be doing.

The sixteen-seat van rounds the corner onto Houghflin Street and pulls to a stop in front of the daycare. I walk to greet the children as they pile off the van, eager for their after-school snacks and playtime. Jay is the last one off of the van.

"Hey, sweetie. How was your day?" I wrap my arms around him, trying to physically transfer my love, hoping Jay will feel it spread through him. But as is typical with Jay, he just stands, arms at his sides, no emotion on his face, and endures my embrace.

Jay's arms fly out to the sides of his body, breaking from my hold. "What's for snack?"

"Fruit cups and chocolate chip cookies," I relay. "Sounds yummy, huh?" I prod, brushing the blond hair away from his eyes.

Jay slaps my hand away. "I don't like fruit cups."

I clasp the stinging hand with the other in front of my body, meet his fixed look, offer a reassuring smile. "Well, you don't have to eat the fruit. You can just have the cookie, but you should try some of the fruit." I search his eyes for some indication he might give a bit of thought to what I'm saying, for some flicker of emotion... any emotion.

Jay turns and walks ahead, leaving me to watch as he enters the door and tosses his backpack to the middle of the passageway. The tension of the moment over, I follow him inside, pick up the discarded school bag, and hang it on an empty hook—next to where all the other children hung their backpacks.

* * *

KIRBY DOESN'T ANSWER his phone. I can only assume he arrived late for his delivery this afternoon and is now unloading. Jay enters the kitchen as I relay to Kirby's voicemail that Jay and I are home and settling in for the night.

"Mom, I've decided what I want to be for Halloween this year," he announces without considering he might be interrupting me on the phone.

A weary sigh escapes as I press the button on my phone to end the call. *How am I going to address this statement without spurring an argument?* "We bought your costume last week. Remember, Jay?"

"Yeah, but I don't want to be a cowboy anymore. They're dumb and boring. I'm going to be a clown."

I bend to retrieve a pot from under the cabinet, take it to the sink, and begin filling it with water.

"Did you hear me? A clown."

"I guess clowns are fun," I say, placing the pot on the stovetop, closing my eyes. *'Rejoice in hope, be patient in tribulation.'*

I turn and use my arms to brace myself on the countertop as I lean forward. Across the counter, Jay swivels the barstool back and forth, the motion constant and wearing on the structure of the secondhand stool. "Halloween is only three days away. Are you sure you want to change your costume this close to the holiday?"

"I don't want to be a stupid cowboy. I already told you that."

Moving to the pantry, I open the enclosure, searching the shelves for macaroni—the only meal Jay has informed he will eat tonight.

"And cowboys aren't scary. Halloween's about scary stuff," Jay insists, the stool under him groaning louder with the force of each rotation.

Macaroni in hand, I shake it in Jay's direction. Plotting my next move, careful to choose the right words, I move back to the counter. "Clowns aren't scary. They're happy and funny," I add, hoping to find fault in his argument, some way for him to yield and believe it his choice.

"Yes, they are. Lots of people are scared of clowns." Jay jumps from the stool and runs to the living room. The television roars to life.

Elbows propped on the countertop, I let my head fall into open palms, trying to recall where I put the receipt for the cowboy costume. I can return it tomorrow after work, give Jay a bit more time to make up his mind fully. I lift my head and see Jay's backpack where he tossed it onto the kitchen table earlier.

"Jay, do you have homework?" I call to the other room.
"No."
The water rolls to a boil, splashing from the pot to the stove's eye and sizzling. I dump the box of macaroni, adjust the heat of the burner, and head to the kitchen table to go through Jay's backpack.

A sticky note is affixed to the science book I pull from the bag. The message states Jay needs to use pages fifty-six through sixty-one to complete the assignment he missed during his session with the behavior intervention specialist today. Underneath the book is the dreaded behavior folder.

At the beginning of the year, Jay's teacher informed the

students' parents the blue folders would be sent home on Fridays to report on the children's conduct for the week. It started with emails from Jay's teacher. Every time an 'incident' occurred, the details would arrive via digital communication. I didn't know how to respond other than, 'I will speak to Jay about this.' How many times could I return the same message? Finally, I just quit responding. Now, Jay's behavior folder is sent home daily for my signature, and if he doesn't return it the next morning, another mark goes on the record. I understand the school wants him to accept responsibility for his conduct, but the process clearly isn't working.

Slowly, I lift the cover of the folder to read about today's issues, hoping for a better report. *Yes, rejoicing in hope, preparing to be patient in tribulation.* Inside the front flap of the folder, drawing immediate attention, is a picture. I study the grainy resolution of an image printed on multi-purpose copy paper. A little girl poses for the photo, her hair chopped short and uneven to her ear on the left side of her head. A long, brown pigtail falls across her right shoulder, her eyes wide with fear. The knot in my stomach swells, muscles slacken, lethargy settles into my limbs. That poor little girl. I can not bear the thoughts hurtling through my mind. How? Why? Who? And yet, I know the answers before I even seek them out. My eyes travel to the right side of the folder where the details of the 'incident' have been posted.

Due to the heavy rain, our area received yesterday, the school playground was flooded. Therefore, we were unable to take the children outdoors for recess this afternoon and had to hold the activity inside the classroom. The students were permitted to play games, use computers, read, draw, or assemble puzzles during this time. Jay spent his recess with a group playing a board game. They wanted to spread out in the cubby area to do so (which I've always permitted in the past but will be reconsidering moving forward.) During the game (from what I gathered among the children present), an altercation erupted between Jay and the little girl pictured on the left side of the folder. One of the students reported that Jay was mad about having to follow the rules of the game. Another stated Jay quit the game and left the area but returned after a few minutes. None of the children observed the scissors Jay was holding until he cut off the little girl's right pigtail.

Jay's scissors are now in my possession. He will be permitted to use them only as required for supervised class activities. I will return them to you at the end of the school year.

The principal and behavior intervention specialist, as well as the girl's parents, have been informed. Please sign below that you have read and are aware of this latest incident.

Warm wetness streaks my face. Lifting my chin to the ceiling, I beg for strength, for mercy. *Where do I begin with this? How do I deal with my son, Lord?* I cannot ignore this, overlook it. A confrontation is sure to ensue when I question Jay about the photo, the note.

"Mom," Jay calls from the other room. "What's that smell?"

I rush from the table to the stovetop. The macaroni has boiled dry, burning and sticking to the bottom of the pot.

* * *

Dinner is behind us. Homework is done. Bath time is complete. Only one task remains before bed. The last thing I want to do is set Jay off before bedtime, and yet, I've waited until that very moment to have this conversation.

Pajamaed and clean, Jay enters the kitchen.

"Did you remember to hang your towel?" I start.

"Yeah." He walks to the bookshelf in the corner. The goldfish he won at the fair last weekend swims inside the fishbowl that sets on top of the shelf. "I'm going to feed him," Jay announces.

"Okay, not too much, though. If you overfeed him, he'll die."

"No, he won't. He'll just get fat."

"He won't be able to eat it all, and the excess food will contaminate his water, Jay."

I turn away to retrieve his backpack. I pull the behavior folder from the bag and lay it on the table. Unable to look at the photo I know waits inside, I leave the blue folder closed.

I tap the folder and ask, "You want to tell me what happened at school today?"

"It was boring," he replies without bothering to look up from the bowl where he watches the fish swim.

"Tell me about indoor recess." I hold onto the back of the dining chair pushed under the table, conscious of keeping my body language open and accepting.

"I played a game with some kids." Jay takes the tiny fish net from beside the bowl and dips it into the water.

"Which game was it?"

"I don't know. Just some stupid game, with some stupid rules." He swishes the water in the bowl with the net. The fish darts around the foreign object intruding the space.

"You're going to scare the fish."

"Fish don't get scared. Only people and animals get scared."

"Do you think you scared that little girl today when you cut her hair?"

"Yep," he says flatly.

"Why would you want to scare her?"

"She's bossy. She's always telling everyone what to do." A bored undertone laces Jay's words as he continues to focus on the fish, refusing to meet my eyes.

"That doesn't mean she deserves to be scared."

Water sloshes out of the bowl, spilling onto the top of the bookshelf. "Jay, stop that. You're getting water everywhere."

I walk to the sink and take a paper towel from the roll, then move to clean up the mess. Jay yanks the net from the bowl, swinging it back and forth through the air. Water droplets dot the floor.

"Jay, give me the net." I hold my hand out in demand. He slams the net into my open palm, the wire handle cutting into my skin with the force of the action. The sting brings tears to my eyes.

I ignore the pain, determined not to draw attention away from the conversation. "Did you apologize to the girl for cutting her hair?"

Jay meets my gaze. "Yeah. The teacher made me say sorry."

"And were you? Were you sorry for what you did?"

"No," he states, unblinkingly. The one-word reply spoken, his lips resume the straight, thin line crossing his set jaw.

"Why not? What you did to that girl was terrible. Can you imagine how sad she must feel to have lost her hair?"

"She didn't lose all of it. She only lost one side."

My grip on the net tightens in frustration. "And now, her mother has to cut the other side to match. How would you feel if someone shaved half of your head?"

His tone flat, Jay answers, "Nobody's going to touch me."

"And why not? What makes it okay for you to touch some-one, cut their hair, but not okay for them to touch you?" I ask, words stumbling out, unable to manage my growing exasperation or the tone of my voice.

"Because I'd cut them first."

I watch him, waiting, searching his face for some sign of compassion, of goodness, but all I find is indifference.

"It's time for bed. You need to go say your prayers and ask God to forgive you for what you did."

"I didn't cut God's hair," Jay mouths, exiting the room. "God, you're so dumb sometimes," he yells back.

"Jay, do not take the Lord's name in vain." I raise my voice in return.

The breath I draw expands my lungs to capacity. Releasing the pressure from my chest, I exhale, swatting furiously at the air with the net, then fling it to the table.

I turn, grab my purse from the kitchen counter, and dig for a pen. Flipping open the folder, averting my eyes from the picture, I scribble my signature at the bottom of the teacher's notice and slam the folder shut. I grab Jay's backpack and stuff his book, homework, and behavior folder inside the bag, then move to hang it on the hook beside the back door.

Turning away from the door, I move to the bookshelf, looking down into the fishbowl. The goldfish floats lifelessly along the surface of the water.

MEREL

OCTOBER

*E*xhaustion settling into my bones after another long day of work, I maneuver my car to make the turn onto the street that runs behind my apartment building. Immediately, I note something is off. The naked trees lining the roadway, their skeletons rising into the dull, gray sky, loom over the oddly empty street. On most days, it's a five-minute struggle—reverse, forward, reverse, forward—to fit my car into one of the coveted compact parallel spots.

My unit has dual entrances, a perk most other renters in the building don't have. While upper floor units have balconies, those of us who have ground level units in the apartment complex have porches that serve as a second entrance. The exit to the street makes the living arrangement feel more like a traditional house than an apartment complex. I appreciate the ability to step straight outside rather than use the inside entryway, which requires traversing long, tight corridors.

I pull easily into the spot sectioned off directly outside my unit's door and slip the transmission into park. Only one other car is visible, parked farther down the road. I scope the sidewalks, looking for a jogger, a dog walker, some sign of life.

"Maybe I missed a memo?"

Catching sight of myself in the rearview mirror, I rub at the dark smudges under my eyes, the attempt futile. "You have got to get more sleep. That or find a make-up tutorial. You're going to scare the students if these circles around your eyes get any darker."

"Ah, but it is Halloween. I fit right in," I answer my reflection, a creepy inflection lacing my voice.

"And I've got to quit talking to myself."

But then again, who else am I going to talk to if not myself? The only human contact I have is inside the walls of the school. It's probably time for me to make some friends, but with the schedule I am keeping at work, the idea of finding the time for camaraderie is a daydream at best. Perhaps now that the first school quarter is complete, things will slow down, get easier. I'm establishing a routine, at least.

Yesterday marked the end of the first nine weeks and ushered in the pressing matter of completing the children's assessments. My first grading period is over. Three more to go, and I will complete my first year as a teacher. There'll be a new roster, new challenges. First year behind me, hopefully, all will be less challenging and no more Jay—or Jack, or whatever he chooses to call himself.

"How can I already be looking to next year when I'm barely getting through this one?"

I grab the door handle and push, eager to be free of the confined space. Outside the car, I check again for by-passers. All I notice is a charge in the air, a raw, cold undercurrent of energy tingling my skin as daylight quickly slips away. I retrieve the bags of schoolwork I've brought home to complete before tomorrow's morning bell and lock up the vehicle then make the trek to my apartment.

I insert my key into the lock on the door and grab the orange envelope addressed RESIDENT, wedged into the doorframe.

My eye catches sight of a small brown box left atop the cafe table in the right corner of the porch. I don't recall ordering anything online. Maybe Letty sent another of her care packages, her sights set on being the perfect aunt who wants to be more, who longs to play a more significant role in my life. I wish I could return her kind deeds, share the details of my life she desires. But I can't, not yet.

I place the envelope in clenched teeth, heave the work bags onto each shoulder, and move to pick up the package. Noting the lack of heft, I search for the sender's name and address but find no information. Shaking the box to listen for hints as to its contents produces little in the way of clues either. I place the parcel under my arm, dropping my keys to the concrete in the process, then awkwardly stoop to snatch them up. My eyes take in the pumpkin I set out at the beginning of the fall season, now softening.

"Well, now I have an excuse not to carve you." I stand upright and open the door, stepping through the threshold.

Dead-bolting the door behind me, I turn to take in the small space—living room flowing through to the kitchen, the bedroom off to the left. Everything is as it was when I headed out to work this morning, a wreck. I wasn't always a bad housekeeper. In another life, I would have cringed to have thought about leaving my living space in such a mess. But it seems pointless to keep everything in its proper place now that I'm single. Why bother to make the bed when I'm too tired to turn it down at night? Who cares if I leave a few dirty dishes in the sink? What does it matter that I didn't put away the cereal box after a hurried breakfast? There's no one for me to answer to and no one who visits. My students wouldn't believe this is my home, the teacher they've affectionately dubbed their "neat-freak school mom."

Bags sliding down both arms, I release everything in my hold onto the kitchen countertop. I grab a paring knife from the utensil drawer, slitting through the packing tape sealing the top of the cardboard box. I lay the knife aside and open the flaps. White tissue paper fills the space. Lifting away the paper, I find a hand-made doll at the bottom of the box.

It's the doll from my childhood. The one that lay on my bed awaiting my arrival home from school each afternoon. I'd almost forgotten about it. I pluck it from the box, run my fingers over the light brown felt, recall the long hours I spent playing with the doll.

"A gift from someone special," I remember being told. But from who? I'm sure it must have been someone I knew at the time, but I was so young, I don't even remember when I received it.

Cross stitches in dark brown thread along the outer edges of the doll's form hold the soft stuffing inside and give it the appearance of a gingerbread boy. The same dark brown thread stretches across the bottom of the head, marking the mouth of the doll. Strange—I never thought about how its lips appear to be sewn together, giving him the eerie look I now see. His black button eyes, sewn on with cream thread shape the Xs of his pupils. A twine bowtie accessorizes his neck. I thought I'd lost the tie. I remember thinking at the time his head would fall off without the tie to secure it. Someone must have replaced it. The red heart attached to the right side of his body adds just a pop of interesting color. How many times did I place my finger on that heart and tell him, I love you too, Poppy? That's what I called him, Poppy. Can it be this is the same doll? He doesn't look worn from years of play. This doll appears newly formed, but yet just the same in every detail.

Letty must have found him in my things I left behind. Or one just like him, perhaps? I check inside the box, rifling through the tissue paper for a note but find nothing. I study the label. All block letters clearly, severely stating my name and address. The script is not from Letty's hand. More confounding is the lack of a postmark or label from a shipping company.

"How did you find me here, Poppy?"

I pull Poppy to my chest, gripping him tighter, memories resurfacing. Seeping, rising, flooding every recess of my mind. The walls around me begin to spin with the thoughts swirling, swishing inside my head. The room darkens. Heat flushes the length of my body. I drop Poppy and grab the countertop to balance myself. As I practice the mindful breathing activity I've grown to rely on, I feel my body temperature return to normal, dizziness subsiding, and finally light fills the space again.

Hands shaking, I push away Poppy, the unwanted recall of a life that is no longer mine. There is no room for the past. Not now. Not again. Forward, present, future only.

My eyes catch sight of the orange envelope. I reach to check its contents, wary of what I might find.

Reminder: Due to scheduled road closures, all vehicles must be moved off St. Albans Drive by midnight. Any vehicle parked along the street will be towed at the owner's expense. Please use the parking garage located above Harris Teeter until further notice.

Great, just one more thing to do tonight. That activity will have to wait, given that costumed children will be ringing my doorbell in an hour, looking for sugary treats I don't have. Throwing my head back, I look at the ceiling with dread, the trudge to the grocery store unavoidable.

Halloween is not my favorite holiday. As a matter of fact, it's probably my least favorite. Holidays, in general, are difficult to get through, but there is something about this day that makes me overly anxious.

There was a time I meticulously plotted the days until each holiday celebration: planning the meals, decorating the house, selecting festive attire for all of us. I wanted to make every occasion as special as possible for my family, desperate to give my son the wonderful childhood memories I experienced throughout my youth. Now, a single woman nearing middle age, exhausted by lack of sleep and overwhelmed by a new career, I have absolutely no desire to participate. Day's end cannot come soon enough.

Taking a quick inventory of what I have on hand, I scan cabinets, check the fridge, the freezer. Old Mother Hubbard has nothing on me except perhaps a dog for companionship. The milk in the refrigerator has expired. I dump the remaining contents into the sink—what I should have done this morning when I made the discovery, but instead chased handfuls of dry cereal with black coffee. A shake of the cereal box reveals it is almost empty. Shoving the remaining contents of the cereal box into the cabinet next to a half-eaten jar of peanut butter and an unopened bottle of ketchup, I reach to grab my purse from the counter before heading back out the door and locking up.

* * *

THE LOCAL HARRIS TEETER is only steps from my apartment. Holed underneath the enclosed parking garage of our housing complex, the convenience of the grocery store is the main reason for my lack of stocked food items. Most nights, after a long day, I can easily pop in for whatever strikes my fancy at the moment. Not that any food has been of major interest to me lately. I seem to have lost all appetite for anything but work. In spite of that fact, the grocer's location is my favorite perk of the living arrangement, especially given I had no idea about what I was looking for when I searched out my new home.

I can count the number of times I've moved in my life on one hand. When this teaching opportunity was offered, I didn't hesitate to accept. It was my chance to escape the people and the memories, everything and everyone that had caused me pain for so many years.

Draped with the urgency of having only two weeks to relocate after securing employment, in addition to my inexperience with the task, the only consideration I gave to the decision was proximity to my workplace. I certainly never contemplated the complications and inconveniences of residing in one of the same neighborhoods the school children and their parents went about daily routines. And while I might like the location of my apartment, each trip outside of my complex is an opportunity for a meetup. The students treat each chance encounter as if they've come upon a celebrity. The students' parents, on the other hand, consider it a prime opportunity for a parent-teacher conference.

Now, every time I leave the safe space of my small abode, I do so on high alert.

Normally, by the time I make it to the grocery store after working late, I manage to miss the regular shopping hours when others take on the chore, thereby dodging the chance of inadvertently bumping into my students and their parents. But given the insistent press to prepare for the night of frolic, I'm in primetime shopping hours.

Descending the steep concrete staircase (as if I've willed it), I run smack dab into Ava and her mother on their mid-ascent.

"Ms. S," Ava exclaims, wrapping my waist with her tiny arms. Using one hand to steady myself with the handrail, I embrace her small frame with the other.

"Hello there, Ava," I return in measure. "Look how pretty you are!"

Ava releases me from her hold and twirls in her princess costume, almost losing her footing on the narrow steps as she proudly shows off her attire for the evening. Ava's mother and I grab her at the same moment to keep her from falling.

"Be careful, sweet girl," I tell her, releasing my hold when I'm sure she's stable.

Ava's mother tightens her grip on the girl. "Ava, honey, you have to be careful," she chides her daughter, then looks at me. "She's so excited."

"I see that. Ava, you make a beautiful princess." The smile she returns floods my chest with warmth.

"What are you going to be for Halloween, Ms. S?"

"I am going to stay home and hand out candy for ghouls and goblins. Maybe, I'll see you again," I say, straightening the crown atop her head.

Ava's mom is in a hurry to get home and prepare dinner before the trick-or-treating hour begins, rushing her daughter along as she bids me a good evening. I've been spared. I wave them off and continue down the stairwell.

Inside the grocer, I grab a green basket from the stack at the entrance and take a few steps farther into the store, trying to recall what I came for besides candy. Scanning the aisles to jog my memory, I see they are overrun with children barely able to contain their excitement over the night ahead. The drudgery of having to rise for each ding-dong of the doorbell, putting on the smiling face, fawning over the children in costume spurs dread for the long evening ahead.

Drawing in a deep breath, I pull my shoulders back and forge ahead with the chore at hand. I take on the produce section first at the front of the store and then work my way through the aisles, searching for items that spark any hint of appeal on my waning appetite.

I check the contents of the basket dangling from the crook of my arm. Fruit, bread, lunch meat, cereal, and nuts are all I've managed to collect, and not likely going to win over any trick-or-treaters. I turn to make my way to the candy aisle.

As I look over the selection of individually packaged goodies, my legs suddenly give way underneath me. The sudden pain springs tears to my eyes. The basket drops to the floor, contents spread out before me. Palms pressed to the smooth, cold tile, I right myself intent on learning what has happened. I push upright and turn to view the grocery cart that has hit me from behind. Two small hands grip the cart, Jay's vacant, cool stare over the handle at the other end of the metal basket takes in his target.

"Hey, Ms. S."

"Hello, Jay." The greeting is anything but pleasant as I pluck my groceries from the floor, chucking them back into the basket. "You should be more careful when you're pushing the grocery cart. You could hurt someone with that."

Jay replies with silence and his cold, green glare. "Where's your mom, Jay?" I've never met Jay's father, and there has been no mention of the man by Jay or his mother. Standing to full height, I place the basket back over my arm, waiting.

"She's around here somewhere," Jay answers, clearly unbothered by her whereabouts. Most children are frightened at Jay's age when they are alone in a big store, unable to locate a guardian. But then again, Jay is not like most kids.

I look up and down the aisle, not particularly thrilled with the thought of a confrontation with Jay's mom in the middle of the neighborhood Harris Teeter. More than anything, I want to grab my candy and get home before dark. But leaving one of my students alone in the middle of the grocery store wouldn't be professional or considerate. I would most definitely help my other students locate their parents, and so I must do the same for Jay.

"Well, why don't we go find her? It must be scary to be in this big store all alone."

"I'm not scared." His response is without inflection, monotone.

Frustration kinks at the back of my neck. "Nevertheless, I'm sure your mother is worried about you. Come on," I instruct and begin to step forward, then think better of the action and move to walk alongside Jay.

Before we make the turn at the end of the aisle, I spot her, hands full, eyes wildly searching the area. She spies us, rushing to where we stand, my hand firmly holding to the end of the cart to prevent Jay from ramming another unsuspecting shopper.

"There you are. I've been looking all over for you. I told you to stay right behind me," she scolds. "Hello, Ms. S," Jay's mother addresses me, her tone unsure. Her eyes move to the basket on my arm. "Stocking up for the evening?" She asks.

"I am." I release my hold on the cart, stepping away from Jay. "I didn't want to leave Jay unescorted, but now that we've found you, I should be getting home."

The woman loosens her hold on the items she carries, dropping them into the cart with a thud. "Us too. Big night ahead," she says, inspecting the contents of her cart, asking Jay, "Did we get everything you wanted, sweetie?"

"Yeah," he answers, jerking the cart forward, causing her to take a step back so to save her big toe from the wheels of the metal buggy. It is obvious who has the upper hand in this mother/son relationship.

Is this woman oblivious to her son's horrendous behavior, or does she merely choose not to address it? Incident report after incident report has gone home for her signature, and while they've all been signed by her hand, there's yet to be any correspondence as to how she is handling the issues from her end. I feel the judgment radiating in my gaze. Hoping to conceal my doubts about her parenting abilities, I work to erase the look from my face and suddenly feel pity for the woman pour over me. What must she be dealing with day after day with that child?

The mantra I practice as I enter the school doors each morning runs through my head, treat Jay as you do all your other students, prompting me to ask Jay about his intentions for the night. "What are you going to be for Halloween, Jay?"

He shrugs. "I don't know."

"Jay has a couple of costumes to pick from at home. He hasn't made up his mind just yet," his mother offers in explanation.

"Oh." I remove the basket from my arm and hold it in front of me with both hands. "Well then, sounds like we all have things we need to do," I announce, preparing my departure. "I better be on my way."

I take a step away, heading toward the front of the store. Attempting to maintain my mantra, I twist to look over my shoulder at the pair. "Happy trick-or-treating, Jay."

His mother smiles proudly, running a hand over the top of Jay's head. He shakes her away.

"I know where you live," Jay states, no intonation, no emotion in his claim.

I search his face trying to determine if he's making simple conversation or a threat. But the voice, the one that lives deep in the recesses of my memory, whispers to me.

"You know what he means."

* * *

I TOSS the fork to the tray of the microwaved dinner, pushing away the remainder of my meal. I place the stack of graded papers I've finished into my school bag and note the doorbell hasn't rung for well over an hour. It seems the night of frolic has ended.

I walk to peek through the closed blinds covering my window. No sign of little trick-or-treaters roaming the sidewalks, I flip off my porch light and move back to the countertop. Clearing away the mess of my dinner, I spy the orange envelope. Shit. I completely forgot about moving my car. A check of the digital clock on the microwave tells me it is a quarter till eleven; I hadn't realized it was so late. I slip on my tennis shoes, grab my keys, and head out the door.

Making the dash to my car, I regret not throwing on a jacket. The night heavy with the threat of a solid frost tomorrow morning, cuts through the lightweight fabric of my t-shirt. I don't bother to run back inside, though, as the trek from the garage to my apartment is a labyrinth of long, warm hallways.

I could park in the garage on a regular basis. I have an assigned space, but the garage is a further walk than the street front. Not to mention the fire alarm in the garage is faulty and is forever triggering car theft alarms.

A short drive up the street, one right and two left turns, and I ease into the parking garage. The first two levels are open for public parking, customers shopping at Harris Teeter, patrons of the many restaurants and shops lining the plaza, while the upper two levels are assigned parking spaces for those of us who live in the attached apartment complex. I pull into my designated space, located midway between the third and fourth levels. This particular spot has the longest walking distance to the elevator—another reason I prefer parking on the street.

I lock up the car and begin the slog to the elevator, anxious to reach the warmth of a heated hallway. The squeal of tires making a tight turn on one of the lower decks reverberates through the concrete structure. Picking up my pace, I wrap my arms around the middle of my body, rubbing my arms for warmth. Without warning, the high pitch of the wailing fire alarm startles me. I place my hands over my ears to muffle the noise. The garage lights darken. Using the flashing warning signals from the fire alarms, I jog to the elevator.

Outside the sliding steel doors, I push the down arrow. The button doesn't illuminate. I look above the door to see which floor the elevator car is on, but it, too, is dark. Damn. The alarm has locked the elevator service. I don't park in the garage often and have always used the elevator to get to the ground floor. Where are the stairs? I search my surroundings. The staccato flash of the lights hinders my attempt to locate the stairwell. I walk toward the far wall scoping the perimeter for an exit sign.

Mercifully, the noise of the alarm quietens. The emergency flashers of the fire alarm cease, throwing the surroundings into a dark gulf. At this point, I can't see my hand outstretched in front of me. I halt, willing the lighting system to kick back on.

The chill of the night creeps deeper, making its way into my bones. The darkness is unsettling, the silence unnerving. No engines hum, no car doors slam, no voices in the distance. I feel the blood pumping harder through my veins, hear the quickening thump in my chest.

Turning, twisting,—straining to see behind me, to the sides, to the front—waiting, hoping my eyes will adjust to the dark. If only I had thought to grab my phone, I would have my flashlight app. Which direction did I come from? Disoriented, confused, I don't even know where to find my car at this point.

With my sight gone, my hearing heightens. In the distance, an odd repetitive noise travels through the darkness, reaching my ears. Careful not to move, I listen, decipher. The sound of clunky heeled shoes hitting the concrete. My sense of direction can't pick up where the noise is coming from. The clunking grows louder, nearer. Do I call out, let whoever else is in the garage know I am here? Maybe I should position myself behind a parked car, wait to see which direction the person heads. Follow their footsteps?

If only I could see something, anything.

I close my eyes, counting the sound of the slow and measured steps. Clunk. Clunk. At ten, I open my eyes. My vision slowly begins to focus. In the distance, I think I make out a form. Tall, clad in black, hooded. And flowing? Is that a cape? The image invokes a memory. A disturbing, recurring nightmare from my past, the monster who came for me night after night, relentless.

No. It can't be.

Hand to my mouth, I stifle the scream building at the back of my throat and realize I've forgotten to breathe. I inhale through my nose and turn, walking quickly in the opposite direction. I scan the perimeter, searching frantically for the exit, the door to the stairwell.

Smoke. I smell smoke. Is something burning? Eyes welling, the sting of warm tears sear my cheeks.

Behind me. Clunk. Clunk. Clunk. I turn to look over my shoulder. The figure is closer, nearing, the pace quickening. I break into a run. My momentum fueled by the downward grade of the garage floor. I'm headed down the ramp. If I keep going, I can run the ramp out of the garage. I don't need a stairwell.

The smoke grows thicker, choking out the air. I continue to run, pumping my arms, willing my legs to go faster. Around the turns of the garage, downward toward the cold night air, the lamplit street comes into view.

A large group of people mill about, laughing as they exit the tavern across the way. Up and down the street, I look for the red engine, firefighters in gear readying to put out the blaze, clear away the smoke. But all is calm. I turn to peer back inside the entrance of the garage. Beams of light bounce off the glossy paint of the cars parked inside. The scent of smoke extinguished. The cloaked figure gone.

* * *

I LAY IN BED, staring into the dark, unwilling to close my eyes. My body longs for sleep, yet my mind won't allow it. The doll has rattled me. The holiday has unnerved me. That is all. And yes, while admittedly, the memories have been seeping in since the first days of school, they now flood my head. I no longer wish to dwell on a life long gone. But the triggers are everywhere I turn.

Sleep was my reprieve in the past, drifting me away to a deep, dark, dreamless void. Trying to find my way back to the nothingness is useless anymore. It's his eyes I see behind the closed lids of my own. The icy glare full of hate and spite and malice, freezing me with fear.

It seems impossible to think I'll ever be able to move beyond my history. I thought I had. I believed the trunk containing that part of my life had been shut, locked tight, tossed into some never-ending body of water to float away. Now, miles from my former existence, it seems to have searched me out, followed me here, slipping into my dreams, taking my sleep, chipping away at my sanity, stealing my peace.

"Please, leave me alone," I beg in the stillness surrounding me. But the grip is tight, pressing onto my core, suffocating.

I throw off the sheet, turn on the light, and grab the work I brought home to finish.

AMA

NOVEMBER 1979

The Community workers have been dropped at their destinations, leaving me two hours to burn before the designated pick-up time. I drive along Main Street and ease the van into one of Waynesville's downtown angled parking spaces. Yanni's Bakery is a good half mile south, but I don't care to walk, and if someone reports to Papa of seeing The Community's van, I can claim to be making the mail drop at the post office.

Outside the brick facade, I look through the window. The red and white gingham cafe curtains pulled open reveal display cabinets full of baked goods ready to be boxed up and sent out with patrons. Except for Leoti, however, the shop is empty. My sister stands behind the counter, back to the window, giving her full attention to the cake in front of her. Though Leoti is doing her best, the bakery hasn't been the same since Mama died.

Mama's will stated both Leoti and I were to have ownership of the business. I didn't want it, and Mama knew that, but it was her last and final attempt in trying to pull me out of The Community. I was not about to give in to her wishes. I promptly signed away my half to Leoti. Rubin being a lawyer, was able to take care of the paperwork; all I had to do was scribble my name on the document. Leoti heatedly objected to the action. She envisioned us working side by side, continuing our mother's legacy. My obligations had long been determined for me, though. And what did I know about baking anyway? But after Papa's big announcement last night, I'm beginning to wonder if I acted rashly.

The bell over the door of the bakery tinkles with the announcement of my arrival. Leoti turns in response to see who has entered the storefront.

"Oh, hey. Give me just a second. I need to finish this cake for Mrs. Whitmore," she says, twisting back to the task.

Shaking off my coat, I hang it on one of the hooks near the door. Sugary smells fill my nostrils, flooding my mind with recall of days gone by. How many Saturdays did I sit in this place while our mother finished up her work week and Papa took care of the 'fix it' list Mama compiled for him? Leoti never minded spending our time here, and I didn't either if I had Leoti's attention. My weekends with Mama and Leoti were times I looked forward to all the week long, planning what Leoti and I would do, trying to remember all the things I wanted to tell her that had happened while we were apart. But more often than not, on those busy Saturday afternoons, my sister lent her hand to our mother, leaving me to pass the hours alone or in Papa's company while Mama and Leoti worked. Mama never failed to ask me to join them behind the counter, and I never failed to say no. Weekends were my time with Leoti; Mama had Leoti to herself all week.

Hopping onto a stool behind the cash register, I sit and watch Leoti scoop a glob of frosting from the mixing bowl, then plop it atop the center of the cake. Leoti grabs the offset spatula, dragging it over the thick buttercream, her steady hand working to apply a generous layer to the top. The frosting oozes down the edges. Leoti angles her spatula, spinning the cake turntable in a continuous motion, pushing the icing down the sides and smoothing. Leoti tosses her frosting knife into the bowl, reaches for the bench scraper, and sets to work on polishing the surfaces. The process is mesmerizing, soothing, tranquil. The tension in my body slowly releases.

"Would you say you like what you do?"

"Yes," Leoti replies without thought. "Why would you ask me such a question?"

Leoti puts so much love into her work. And while I enjoy learning my crafts, the mundane tasks of preparing oils and waters for the elders are growing tiresome.

"I just wondered if it ever got tedious, monotonous, you know."

Leoti spies a section of the chocolate cake showing through her white icing. She stops the rotation and adds another dollop of frosting, then begins the spinning process once more, talking while she works. "When customers walk out of here, they're excited. Wide grins on their faces like they've snagged the blue ribbon for having the biggest pig at the county fair. It feels good making people happy, giving them something to smile about, something to look forward to savoring."

Leoti takes a step back to inspect her work, spinning the turntable to view all angles. Satisfied, she lays the scraper aside and brushes her hands together, dusting away excess powdered sugar. I bounce off the stool and head to the bowl of frosting, pull out the spatula and run my tongue over the too.

"Ama," Leoti scolds.

"Yum," I say, eyes wide, licking the frosting with exaggeration. "It's delicious," I continue the taunt, trying to make her smile. My sister looks thinner than I've ever seen her. Makeup does little to conceal the dark circles under her eyes.

"We're not children anymore, Ama. I have a business to run. Nobody wants to see your nasty tongue all over my decorating tools. And don't even think about sticking that spatula back in there. I need the rest of that frosting to pipe the cake."

"There's not a soul around to watch me." I continue to clean away the buttercream and wave the spatula in front of her scowl.

Leoti snatches the bowl away before I can scoop another

round of buttercream. "Yes, I know. It seems to be a problem if one wants to sell baked goods. I need customers."

Safeguarding it, Leoti clings to the bowl as she moves to the sink at the back of the shop. She places the bowl on the nearby counter and opens the cabinet above the sink, rummaging through the contents.

"And what do I owe the pleasure of your visit today? I wasn't expecting you," Leoti says, digging out her piping tools.

"I had a worker drop off in town this morning and have a couple of hours to kill. Figured maybe you could use a hand. I know how busy the holiday season is."

"I wish I needed it. I can't figure out why business is so slow this year, and I could really use the distraction of staying busy right now." Leoti lays out three piping tips and bags on the countertop, tapping her chin in concentration. She takes away one of the design tips and chooses another to replace it.

"You and Rubin okay?"

"We're fine," she relays, pushing the tips inside the bags. "Trying harder than ever to get pregnant, but no matter how often we try, it just won't happen."

"Eww, please, Leoti. I don't want to know."

"Why do you act like sex is a cardinal sin? Everybody does it, except maybe you."

I watch her fill each bag a quarter full with the frosting, laying them in a neat row to the side of the cake.

"I don't think it's bad. Some things should stay private, that's all."

"Maybe after you lose your virginity, you'll want to talk about it then."

I move to toss the knife into the sink, then head to one of the two small cafe tables across from the display cases. I pull out a chair and sit, unwilling to continue the conversation about my lack of experience.

"You know there's this cute fellow Rubin's been recruiting to work with him." Leoti raises her voice to carry across the bakery, making certain I hear her. "His name is James. He's a few years older than us, clean-cut, professional, and such a gentleman. He would be perfect for you, Ama," she claims, squeezing the bag, working the frosting into the piping tip she prepares to use.

"I can't date anyone, Leoti."

Leoti drops the bag to the work surface and brings both hands to her hips. "Why? Because he's not from The Community? You might like socializing outside of the group, Ama. You might find you enjoy living like us commoners."

I didn't come to visit Leoti today to have this conversation. I came to do her a favor. I know she's trying to get her mind off getting pregnant. Leoti is putting every ounce of her energy into this bakery, trying to bring back business, trying to control something, anything, because she can't control her body into conceiving the child she longs for. I rub my hand over the pocket of my oversized jeans, feeling the outline of the flask containing the money oil potion. Leoti would object if she knew I was planning to 'help' her out with the spell. But I have to do something. It's my fault she's working so hard, stress ruling her days, letting her health flounder. After the bone reading, I told Leoti she would have a little girl, but I couldn't tell her it wouldn't be Rubin's child. My spirit guide didn't give me the how, who, and when. And even if she did, I don't know that I would have shared the information with Leoti. Some things should just be left to fate, and sometimes, fate falls hard.

"I can't date, Leoti, because my coupling has been set."

"What? When did this happen? Who is he? How long have you been dating?" Cake forgotten, Leoti rushes over to the table to sit with me.

"We don't date. You know that." I say, delaying the conversation, resting my arms on the table, hands clasping.

"I did not know that. What does that even mean, you don't date? Then how all of a sudden are you getting married, or coupled, or whatever it is?"

Breaking away from Leoti's concerned gaze, I look at my

hands. "It means I don't have a choice in the matter. There's no need to date when it's been arranged." I feel her eyes watching me as I stumble through the confession. "And it has. Been arranged. For a long time now, evidently. Papa only told me last night."

"Well, who is he? Look at me, Ama. You do know him, right?"

I meet Leoti's eyes and answer. "Elan Darach." The breath I've been pushing deep into my lungs escapes. "And yes, I know him. Everyone knows everyone in The Community. He's an apprentice, working to be a healer. He's twenty-eight years old, the son of Elder Mack Darach, and he has slept with half the women in The Community."

"Oh, Ama." My sister starts carefully, her tone barely above a whisper. She clutches her chest. "How do you feel about this?"

"Does it matter?"

Leoti reaches to take my hands. "Of course, it matters. This is your life. Who you share it with should be your choice."

"That's not how it works in The Community, not if you've been chosen to be an elder anyway."

"Why have you never told me this before?"

"I didn't know." I shrug, thinking on how many of the details about my life in The Community I've neglected to follow up on, childishly believing Papa had my best interests at heart.

"How could you not know? Haven't there been multiple couplings in The Community before?" Leoti leans back into the chair, folding her arms across her chest.

"Of course there have." I lean back in my chair and mirror my twin's actions. "But the unions have been between The Community's regular members, not elder prospects."

"Ama, this is not what you want."

"No, but I don't have a choice."

"Yes. You. Do." Leoti pulls her spine straight, grasps the edges of the tabletop, knuckles whitening. "You tell Daddy no. Tell him this is not the man you want to spend the rest of your life with. This is horseshit, Ama."

"I can't tell Papa that."

"And why not? Daddy is fifty-one years old. He has lived and continues to live his life the way he wants. Why should he deny you the same? It's not fair, Ama."

"You think I don't know that, Leoti? Look, who is going to choose to love me anyway? With this thing on my face? I'm not exactly beautiful, Leoti." I run a palm over my forehead, feeling sweat build on my brow and wonder if Leoti has left an oven heating.

"Well, thanks a lot, Ama. In case you forgot, we are identical twins."

"You know what I'm saying. We may be identical in looks, but you don't have to live with this mark on your face. Papa can claim all the day long that this stain makes me special, chosen, what the hell have you. But you and I both know it's a deformity, regardless of whether or not it gives me some supernatural gift of sight and healing. Besides that, if I tell Papa, 'no, I won't couple with this guy,' it'll be the same as cutting myself out of The Community of becoming chief elder. And then where would I go?"

"Here. With me. Rubin wouldn't care one bit if you lived with us. He wants the best for you, too, Ama. He's your brother-in-law. Rubin considers you a sister. You must know he doesn't have high regard for The Community. We could help you get established. You could work here with me until you decide what you want to do."

"What would I do, Leoti? There's not much calling for conjure work in Waynesville."

"Healing. Lots of people are looking for natural remedies. I can't tell you the number of requests I've had from some of Mama's old customers. All those herbal remedies she made. They worked, and people still want them."

"So why don't you do it? You know all her remedies. You still have her recipe book, right? All you would have to do is get the garden out back going again." I may not have been our mother's biggest fan, but Mama's herb garden was something I always envied, even plucked from if I couldn't find a particular herb one of the elders had requested for a potion.

"Right now, I'm so busy trying to get the baking side of the business going again, I can't take on herbal potions too. But you could. You should, Ama. You know all the remedies far better than I do."

The phone rings. Leoti stands, hurrying behind the counter to answer it.

"Yanni's Bakery," I hear her say to the caller at the other end. She listens for a moment and answers. "Yes, Mrs. Whitmore, I'm putting the finishing touches on it right now." She pauses. "Thirty minutes. Yes, ma'am. I'll have it all set for you to pick up. See you soon."

Leoti replaces the receiver into the cradle. She looks over at me. "I've got to finish this cake, but we're not done with this conversation."

Leoti heads to the back of the bakery and picks up her piping bag. I stand and go about performing the task I came here to do. Before long, Leoti will be much too busy to be hounding me about leaving The Community, even if I might want her to.

ESME

NOVEMBER

Why didn't I just stop by Mama's bakery and pick up some cookies? I twist the knob on the old oven to preheat the temperature to three-hundred-fifty degrees. *Because you didn't want to hear her harp about how much time you spend with your church family.* I open up the fridge, digging to the back where I hid the cookie dough I prepped last night after getting Jay into bed. Though I'll never match the accuracy of my mother's hand, I work to get the dough onto the baking sheets in evenly proportioned balls.

Crashing noises resonate from the living room; Jay yells vroom, vroom over the high volume of voices on the television. I throw the spoons into the bowl of cookie dough, hurrying around the corner to see him sprawled out in the center of the room. *Didn't I ask him...? I know I did.*

"Jay, I asked you to take that race car track to your room thirty minutes ago."

"And I told you I wasn't done playing with it."

"Now, Jay." I kneel in front of him, pulling apart the pieces of track, placing them in the box. "My bible study group will be here any minute."

"So what." Jay snatches the box from my hand. "It's just a

bunch of old broads talking about God. Why do you have to do this every week anyway?" He asks, slamming the racetrack pieces into the container.

"Because it makes us feel closer to Jesus when we talk about God and study His word." I hand over more pieces of the track. "Please don't slam your toys like that. You'll break them."

"I wish Dad was here."

"Well, he's not. You're stuck with me tonight." And we've been stuck together way too much lately for either of us to do the other any good.

Jay's suspension after cutting the little girl's hair resulted in me having to take unplanned time off from work to stay home with him, tutoring him through the assignments from school. It's a wonder Jay's not permanently locked away in his room and that I myself have any hair left. *I shouldn't have thought that; forgive me, Lord.* That poor little girl, the chill creeps over my flesh as it does each time I think of her. I should be thankful the school didn't decide to expel Jay and that the girl's parents were Christians who believed in forgiveness. Still, their beliefs didn't keep them from having their child moved to another classroom, and I can't blame them.

Jay is not the only one wishing Kirby was home. I've found myself thinking the very same thing on many occasions of late. I could use my husband's help around here, but I understand. In the past month, even more of Kirby's longtime colleagues have been let go. We're lucky Kirby still has his job, especially right now with the holidays upon us.

I pass over a toy car for Jay to add to the box. "Now, take those things to your room. Wash up when you're done and come to the kitchen. Your dinner is ready."

Pushing up from the floor, I run my hand over the coffee table and the television console, brushing away as much of the dust as possible. The fireplace is set and ready to light should any of the ladies get cold. Underneath the edge of the sofa, I spy a stray toy car. I grab it and toss it into the cabinet under the console. I hurry into the kitchen and pull Jay's meal from the microwave, peeling off the plastic film and stirring the contents to cool as Jay rounds the corner.

"Awesome," he says, dragging a finger through the remaining cookie dough. "Why didn't you tell me you made cookies?"

"Get your finger out of there. That's got raw eggs in it."

Jay slurps his finger, a loud popping sound escapes as he pulls it from his mouth. Before I can stop him, he digs inside the bowl, pulling out another mound of the dough.

"Jay, I said NO. You're going to ruin your appetite. You can have a cookie after they're baked."

"I don't want one after they're baked." Sitting on the stool at the counter, Jay sucks the dough away, inspecting the contents of the meal in front of him. "What is this crap?"

"Your dinner. Please watch your language."

"What? Crap? Crap is not a bad word. It's better than saying shit."

"Jay!"

"Whatever." He runs his fork through the pulled pork, swirling in the macaroni with the meat. "Haha, now it looks like shit."

I don't have the energy or the time for this battle. "Please just eat. You can watch television in my room when you're done," I tell him, spooning out dough to fill the baking sheet. "Unless you'd like to sit in and listen to our bible study tonight." Though if I'm honest with myself, I don't want Jay sitting with my group. It's the best night of the week for me, easing my nerves, taking my mind away from all that is wrong in my world right now. But, it is a lesson that would do Jay some good.

"I don't want to sit with your stupid group." Jay stuffs an oversized forkful of the mixed food into his mouth and adds, "They all look like witchy old hags, and they smell funny."

"Jay, your words are very hurtful. You should think before you speak, and that's exactly what tonight's lesson is about."

Our study for this week is out of the Book of James—

tempering the tongue. 'Let every man be swift to hear, slow to speak, slow to wrath: For the wrath of man worketh not the righteousness of God,' James 1:19. This scripture has been particularly interesting to me. The power of the tongue and learning to hold it, to think before you speak, a lesson we all learn as children yet quickly forget. A lesson so many would benefit from if only they would heed the wisdom. This week, I have been more conscientious about listening to others, hearing their words, and responding with kindness.

Jay doesn't respond to my last comment as he continues to shovel the food into his mouth, and I don't push the subject. I need Jay to finish up and settle down before the women arrive.

There are five of us in our group: Margie, Florence, Patsy, Debra, and me. We've been meeting once a week for two years now. We gather at six, all chipping in with a covered dish. After the blessing of the meal, we eat and catch up on the week's happenings. By seven, we begin with a prayer for our enlightenment, then work into the lesson and worship before wrapping up our time together around half past eight. Our routine is practiced and easy. Though when it's my turn to host, it inevitably tends to go awry in some way or another.

I'm the only member of our group in the midst of child-rearing. Therefore, when it's my week to host (and even otherwise if Kirby is on the road), Jay is present for our meetings. When Jay was younger, my bible study group was women nearer my age—only a few years into our marriages, our kids all going through the same stages. We would work the meetings around our children; the kids played together while the moms discussed the chosen scripture. But as Jay got older and the 'accidents' became more frequent, I extracted myself from that group and signed on with the older women—their children grown, a couple of the women grandmothers. Instead of all the "have you tried this"(es) and "you should do that"(s) followed by the "we need to get home early tonight"(s), I now hear a lot of "bless your heart"(s). And that's fine by me; sarcastic or not, I can use every single blessing offered.

"I'm done. Hello? Esme. Are you deaf?" I pull my hands from the sudsy dishwater, using the towel to dry them as I move to stand across from Jay, seated at the counter.

"What?"

"I told you I was done. I want my cookie now."

"They're still in the oven. Give them just a few more minutes."

Jay jumps from the stool, heading for the refrigerator and yanking open the door. He reaches inside and pulls out the bowl of remaining dough. I grab his hand before the finger plunges inside.

"I said no, and I meant no." I tug the bowl from his grip with my other hand, extending my arm, keeping the dough away from his reach.

"Get your hands off me, bitch." Jay jerks out of my hold and quickly grabs my arm, punching it with his fist.

"Jay, I am over your mouth. You will sit and join bible study tonight so you can learn to tame your tongue," I command, already dreading the thought, thinking of how unfair the demand is on the other women.

"That's what you're studying? Taming your tongue. Give me a break. All y'all do is waggle them. I'm not listening to that shit." Jay stomps out of the kitchen and down the hall toward our bedrooms.

Feeling the sting of Jay's blow, I inspect the mark my son has left, a familiar red whelp forming, a bruise sure to follow as usual. I throw my head back, clutch the bowl of dough to my middle. Looking at the ceiling above, I pray for strength and God's wisdom.

* * *

"MARGIE, what did you find most enlightening in the study?"

"James 3:7 and 8. 'For every kind of beasts, and of birds, and of serpents, and of things in the sea, is tamed, and hath been tamed of mankind: But the tongue can no man tame; it is an unruly evil, full of deadly poison.' It's so true, isn't it? I mean, we use all our energy trying to tame our pets, our husbands, our children, our hair, but do we ever think to take power over our own words?"

Debra pipes in her thoughts on the scripture. "But sometimes it's not what you say, it's how the other person processes the meaning of your words. For example, I say, 'Margie, I love your dress. It looks so comfortable and unconstricted.' And you might hear something entirely different than the true compliment it was meant to be. In your mind, I may as well have said I can tell you are gaining weight because of all the big loose dresses you've been wearing lately."

"Well, you certainly wouldn't have to worry about me taking that statement out of context," Margie replies. "I can't gain a pound no matter how hard I try. But I understand your point, Debra. You don't know what's going through someone else's mind, or perhaps what's going on in their day that would lead them to process your words into another translation."

"Are we ever to be able to control our tongues then? We can't possibly know what goes through someone else's mind or how they take our words. So how will we ever know we've said something that is hurtful?" Patsy asks.

Margie answers. "I think the key here is in the first passage of the scripture. 'Let every man be swift to hear, slow to speak, slow to wrath.' We have to listen, to think before we speak, and not be so quick to be hurt by another's words. If we don't understand the words they are trying to convey, perhaps we should be asking more questions, taking more time to listen. Because it's jumping to conclusions, brooding with anger, brewing resentment, that's when we end up harboring ill feelings that starts the snowball effect of injustices, be it our own or another's."

"I probably shouldn't say this," Florence begins tentatively, "given I'm supposed to be learning to control my mouth, but we're in a safe space here. Right?" We all nod, encouraging Florence to continue. "I just feel like we have some members in our church who claim to be so holy, so devout, they're the best Christians around, but then they'll say something about someone. You know, something hurtful. And, well, I just think your mouth reveals what's truly in your heart."

As we all mull over Florence's insight, a comfortable hush falls over the room as it often does when we concentrate on a lesson. But something is not quite right. It's too quiet—and not for the first time this evening, I wonder what Jay is up to. I should check on him, I know, but so much of our group's time together is stolen by me slipping away to check on my son.

"You're right, Florence," Margie agrees. "And isn't that exactly what James 1:26 is telling us? 'If any man among you seem to be religious, and bridleth not his tongue, but deceiveth his own heart, this man's religion is vain.' It's like that old expression, 'holier than thou.' A person who claims to be superior in their morality and piety is saying they aren't willing to take the time to know what's in another person's mind and heart."

"Perhaps when we hear a fellow member of the congregation speak in such a manner, we should gently remind them of the passage," Patsy suggests.

"Well, be careful how you deliver the message. Be sure to tame your tongue," Debra jokes.

"You've been awfully quiet tonight, Esme. No thoughts on tonight's study?" Margie asks.

"I read the scripture early in the week and have given great concentration to the words. Listening to you all tonight and drawing upon your insights has been so fulfilling. I find myself sitting here wishing there was some way for me to share this lesson with those I love."

"Well, of course you can," Patsy assures me.

"I don't know," I counter. "There are some who don't seem to listen to anything, much less want my words of ministry."

"You sweet girl," Debra claims. "I know times are hard right now, but it does get easier."

Heads around the room nod in agreement. These women know. They understood, all too clearly, the undertones of my statement. They've witnessed my son's actions, his temperament, heard his hateful rhetoric.

"They grow up, Esme. And when they do, they finally realize their mama knew a thing a two," Florence offers.

"My daughter, Ruth, called me just last night to tell me about the trials she's having with my granddaughter," Margie begins. "Her exact words were, 'I remember you being my age, wondering why you always looked so tired, why you seemed so grumpy all the time.' And just like I told Ruth, I'm telling you, Esme, motherhood is the most exhausting time of your life."

"It's true. We've all been there, Esme. It will get better," Patsy promises.

* * *

Standing at my front door, I wave, bidding goodnight to the women, claiming I can't wait for our next meet up after Thanksgiving. And I can't. It seems so far off, although we're only skipping the one week to be with our families, and then we'll start back up on our next study. Arms folded over my chest for warmth, I watch them safely situate into their vehicles, wait to see them pull away. The support and wisdom I garner from the group is not something I am willing to give up, even though my own mother resents all the time I give to the women. Maybe it's just my own misgivings; maybe I'm embarrassed for Mama to know what a terrible mother I've turned out to be.

As the last car eases down the street, I turn and slowly push the door closed, clicking the deadbolt into place. Walking through the living room, I fluff cushions, pick up coffee mugs, and start for the kitchen.

A soft rap sounds from the front door. Through the peephole, I see Debra shivering. Shifting the cups to one hand, I unlock the bolt with the other and swing open the door.

"What's wrong? Come in. Is there a problem with your car?"

"No. I just realized I forgot my purse. I had my car keys in my coat pocket—walked out with my bible and casserole dish, didn't even think about grabbing my purse. I went to pull out my phone to let Jim know I was on the way home and realized my handbag wasn't on the seat next to me."

"At least you didn't get too far down the road. Did you set it on the counter?"

"I'm pretty sure I did," Debra says, following me into the kitchen where the women are in the habit of placing their bags.

Other than the half-eaten tray of cookies, the countertop is empty. "I was almost certain this is where I left it." Debra's forehead wrinkles with concern.

"Maybe you placed it on one of the chairs around the table," I try.

We walk to the table and begin pulling out each chair. I bend to look underneath the tabletop. Nothing. I slide a chair back into place, raking over where else to search. My eyes roam to the corner of the kitchen where Jay's backpack and our coats hang on the hooks by the bench seat at the back door.

"Could you have put it by the back door?" I ask, walking in that direction.

"I don't think I would have, but I guess you never know."

Behind the bulky outwear, I see the contents of Debra's handbag spilled out onto the floor. My stomach knots with the understanding of what must have transpired while we all gathered in the living room. *Jay, what have you done now?* I kneel, retrieving the empty purse from beneath the bench, and pass it to Debra.

I offer the only thing I can think to say. "Debra, I'm so sorry."

"I'm sure it's my own silly fault," she replies. "I probably set it too close to the edge of the bench, and the whole thing just spilled out," Debra says, though we both know the truth.

We work without further words to collect her things, get them back inside her purse. All items retrieved, we push ourselves to stand and retrace our steps to the front door.

"I really am sorry about that, Debra," I say again. There are no other words. Debra's privacy has been violated by my son. His actions a reflection of my parenting, I accept full responsibility. All I can do now is hope nothing is missing from her bag, though I know it is doubtful.

Debra reaches for my hand and squeezes it reassuringly. "I won't be at church this weekend. You have a good Thanksgiving, Esme." She steps away and moves down the front steps toward her car.

"Be safe going home," I call as she slides inside.

Closing the door, I walk to Jay's room to check he is in bed. I know he needs to be disciplined for his actions, and yet I am willing him to be asleep.

Standing over Jay's sleeping form, I watch him breathe, thinking he looks nothing like the son I know. He seems so peaceful, so solemn, so harmless, and wholesome. Guilt nestles in. I didn't even say goodnight, left him to find his way to bed, disregarded the rituals of bedtime. *Did he brush his teeth? Did he say his prayers?* Selfishly, I just wanted a break, and because of it, one of my dear friends has suffered a loss of privacy—possibly more knowing my son the way I do. I hold for a moment, trying to reconcile my feelings, then slip out of his room.

In the kitchen, I work to clear the countertops. Leftovers stored and crumbs brushed away, I flip out the lights and tread the hallway to ready for bed.

At the threshold of my bedroom, I see the bed covers a wreck, wallowed upon and untucked; pillows scattered. *He left you in peace with your bible study group, Esme.*

I know he did, and I am grateful, but it was at Debra's expense. I pull the bedspread straight and grab the pillow at the end of the bed, unearthing my laptop. Tension grips my lower back, working upward. I've asked him time and again not to use the work-issued computer. Our family computer in the kitchen is at his disposal, but the laptop is off-limits.

I plop onto the end of the bed and lift the screen to find it locked. Maybe there is hope after all; maybe Jay wasn't able to unlock it. I key in the password and find a search engine open. I think back on my actions earlier in the day. Before I left work, I closed all the open applications and shut down the system. How did he get my password? *Because you use the same password for everything, Esme.*

I work the trackpad to open the history, checking to see what Jay has been searching while unsupervised. Clicking it reveals the history has been wiped clean. Jay could have searched anything and everything. I don't have the parental controls set on this computer.

Exasperation and desperation mingle, settling the familiar fatigue heavy atop my shoulders. I'm going to have to confront him about rummaging through Debra's purse, disobeying my instructions about the laptop. I'll have to take away his cars and his computer privileges as punishment for his actions tonight. Another confrontation I don't have the energy to pursue.

I push the sleeve of my sweater up to view the purpling bruise on my arm, lightly touching it with the pad of my finger, pain pulsing in reminder of what happens during a confrontation.

Sliding the sleeve back down, I search my mind for a password I will easily recall. Decision made, I close out the internet browser to bring up the desktop screen.

Grotesque images flood the screen from corner to corner, all the file folders on my desktop gone. I lift the computer, holding it close, focusing on what I am seeing. Image after image, pasted together, is a collage of severed tongues. Some appear to be human, others look to be from animals. Some sliced neatly through, others jagged, torn, ripped. Some slick with saliva, some dry, shriveled. All are bloody and veiny and deeply disturbing. *What has he done?* Nausea rolls in the pit of my belly while my throat quivers in a threatening gag.

I drop the laptop to my knees, punching at the buttons, desperate to erase the images. Dizzy and disoriented, I realize my breathing is shallow and fast. I close my eyes and draw deeply through my mouth. I scroll to the top corner of the screen and click on the sleep mode to bring up my screen saver. The same images wallpaper the screen, the only difference is an added message. Overlaying the gruesome photos in uppercase bold letters, it delivers Jay's intention. "THIS IS HOW YOU TAME A TONGUE."

MEREL

NOVEMBER

The weather outside is bleak and dismal. The rain coming in sideways delivers strong pinging blows to my classroom windows. Keeping time with the howling wind, my mind whirls, going over the scheduled events for the day ahead, twisting into the memories of my dreams from last night's fitful sleep.

The weather forecasters predict the storms will continue throughout the school day. I'll have to be conscious of speaking louder than what I am accustomed for the students to hear anything I say, as well as Principal Garber, who is scheduled to be here midmorning for my evaluation.

Last month, I completed the first of the three formal observations required of a new teacher. This time around, I should be more comfortable with the process. However, I was fortunate during my first evaluation—Jay was not in attendance for the forty-five-minute lesson. I don't assume to be so lucky today, but I sure would appreciate another reprieve.

As far as the lesson goes, I'm prepared. All weekend, I sat at my kitchen counter, putting together the necessary paperwork required for the process. And though I've run through a number of scenarios Jay might pull while I'm under evaluation, only the devil himself knows what Jay has lined up for me today.

A knock sounds from outside my classroom door. I stand from the desk and walk to the door, eyes focusing on the small rectangular window, blinking away the blur of exhaustion, looking for some clue as to who else is at school this early in the morning. Outside the window, the hallway is still dark—the lights not scheduled to blaze into operation for another half hour. The knock sounds again as I near the entryway.

"Who's there?"

No answer, I place my hand on the handle, slowly pulling the heft of it toward me. "Hello?" I try again.

The light spilling through my open door floods the hallway outside my classroom. I scan both directions of the empty, dark corridor. Behind me, another knock. I close the door and turn, staring through the open blinds covering my windows. The wind and rain continue.

I return to stand behind my desk. *You can't blame this on the storm. You've been hearing a knock for days.* Knocking, nightmares, time lost to thoughts I can't recall. I tell myself it's exhaustion, the long hours of work, and the high demand of the parents and administration, but I know it's him. He's getting to me. *No. You're letting him get to you.*

"Just stop it," I call out to the empty room, dropping into the chair behind the desk, focusing my attention on the paperwork in front of me.

Thunder booms outside the window, startling me. I look toward the door through the window. The hallway is lit, teachers move up and down the corridor preparing for the arrival of students. I glance at my watch. Forty-five minutes gone. I've lost time. Again.

Dorothy sticks her head around the office door. "Good grief, this rain," she exclaims, heading to where I sit. "I hope the kids can make it through the front door this morning. They're bound to be soaking wet by the time their little butts hit the desks."

I stare at my teammate, my only confidant of late, trying to make out where the last hour went. "I know," I start, attempting to keep the confusion from marking my face, "I'm so glad I traded my bus duty this week for next week."

"That's right. You were supposed to be on duty. Why are you trading off on a three-day school week?"

"My second formal observation is today," I tell her, searching the desk for my lesson plan. *I just had it.* Forty-five minutes ago. The shuffling effort grows manic. The thump in my chest rings through to my ears.

"I forgot about that. What lesson are you teaching?"

Lifting my planner from the desk, I find the detailed plan underneath. "Science." A sigh of relief makes the one word explanation sound breathy.

"Classifying insects?"

Dorothy and I plan our lessons together weekly. We split two sets of twins between our classrooms and decided at the beginning of the school year teaching the same lessons and assigning the same homework would be easier on their parents and save the two of us from inquiries as to why one child is learning something different than the other. "Yep. I'm just hoping I can keep my little pest under control."

"Jay."

"That's the one." I clear away the desktop—hiding the planner in the side drawer, tossing all pens, pencils, and paperclips into another drawer, swiping at the edges to clear any dust that might be present.

"You can't get Cassandra to do one of her sessions with him during that time?"

Cassandra is our school's behavioral intervention specialist and my left hand these last few weeks—counseling Jay on his behavior, taking him out of the classroom, giving me a much-needed break from his antics. "Oh, don't think I haven't thought of that already. Cassandra's out all week. Her sister's getting married this coming weekend. She took off early for the holiday to help out with the last minute details."

Dorothy watches as I crouch to the floor, picking up stray bits of paper from the carpet around my desk. "I could pull him in with my class if you like."

"I can't tell you how much I would love to say yes to that offer, but Principal Garber would catch on, and I don't think it would look good for my review," I lament, tossing the paper remnants into the trash. "It's the equivalent of saying, 'I can't handle my students.'"

"You're probably right," she agrees. Dorothy places her hand on my shoulder. "Hey, are you okay?"

"I'm fine. Just haven't been sleeping very well."

"You give any more thought to joining my family for Thanksgiving? We'd love to have you at our table."

Dorothy means well, and while I appreciate her extending the offer, I can't accept it. As it is, I lean on her too much, have let myself grow too close to her. I know what happens to people I care about, and I'd hate to see something bad happen to such a good person. So, I tell Dorothy the prepared and practiced excuse, what I know she wants to hear. "I'm actually considering taking the long weekend to visit my aunt and uncle, but thank you for the offer."

"I'm so glad you changed your mind. It's good to be with family during the holidays. But, Merel," Dorothy pauses to take my hand, "whatever you decide to do with the time off, get some rest."

Averting my eyes from her concerned gaze, I wonder if she knows I've been untruthful, if she doesn't believe me. *Of course, she knows. You're a liar.*

"I will," I promise, meaning it, pulling from her grasp, readying for the drenched little bodies due outside my door any minute.

* * *

THE CRINKLING OF PLASTIC PACKAGES, the crunching and smacking of the students as they munch through their snacks while finishing up a handwriting assignment fill the space of the room. Outside, the rain has let up a bit, no more booming thunder and bright lightning to compete with for the time being. From the corner of my eye, I see Jay approaching my desk. He can't possibly have finished the assignment yet. I meet his gaze, noting he holds his right hand behind his back.

"I have something for you."

I lay my arms atop the desk, tilt my head to the side, studying him, waiting for him to continue. Most children would read the look on my face and proceed, but not Jay. He waits for my response, more likely my reaction.

"Have you already finished your handwriting?" I ask.

"Almost," he states, pulling his hand into view and passing over a pen. "I want to give this to you."

I reach to take the pen, inspecting the writing utensil in my hold, a beautiful silver pen adorned with gold tips. The engraving reads Cross. I've heard of Cross pens but never held one before.

I lift my eyes to meet Jay's. "Where did you get this?" It's not uncommon for the children to bring me gifts now and again, their faces beaming with pride and expectation. Not Jay. He wears the same deadpan look I'm finally starting to accept without my flesh prickling in chills.

"One of my mom's friends gave it to me," he says flatly, no inflection behind the words, no hint of truth or lie.

"This is an expensive pen, Jay. Maybe your mom's friend made a mistake by giving it to you."

"No."

"Well, if your mom's friend gave it to you, why are you giving it to me?"

"Because I want you to have it. You can use it."

I glance at the clock on the far wall. Ten minutes is all I have left before my scheduled observation. "I can't take this pen, Jay," I tell him, passing it back.

Jay holds his arms firmly to the sides of his body. "I said I want you to have it." His eyes bore into my own.

I feel the tension taking hold of me. I can't do this right now. Principal Garber will be at my door any minute, and I will not have her witness a confrontation. "Okay, thank you," I concede, thinking of emailing Jay's mother later and letting her know I am in possession of the pen. If she wants it back, she can handle her son.

I lay the pen to the side of my desk, clear away the unfinished grading, and inform the children it's time to clean up.

* * *

THE KNOCK I hear at my door is not a fabrication of my imagination this time—the noise draws the attention of the students, their heads and bodies swiveling to see who has made the request for entry. The door opens, and Principal Garber steps through the threshold, speaking to the children, instructing them to pretend she isn't in the room; she's simply visiting them to see what they are learning.

I take her cue. "Well, you're in luck this morning, Principal Garber. We are just about to start a lesson on classifying insects."

"Oh, how interesting," she claims, situating herself behind my desk, placing the lesson plan I left there onto her clipboard.

"I d-don't like bugs," says Amelia with confidence, determined as always not to give her self-assurance over to the speech disorder.

"I k-kill b-bugs," Jay mimics Amelia.

I ignore Jay's deplorable behavior and instead address the class. "Let's not speak out of turn. Remember to raise your hands if there is something you would like to add to our discussion, please."

In response, hands shoot up across the room.

"But let's wait for our comments on how we feel about insects until the end of our lesson." The waggling fingers drop to desktops, and I continue. "First, let's make a list of some common insects."

I call on various students, listing each response on the whiteboard as they name the bugs they come across in their daily lives. Principal Garber observes from her post, recording notes for my evaluation.

List made, we add characteristics to each insect: wings, hard shells, stinging, leg counts. I move to the KWL chart (Knows, Wants to know, Learned) using the students' input to fill in the K-W sections of the chart, then begin the sorting of the insects into different groups before introducing the new vocabulary. We take time to practice the terms. The lesson is progressing smoothly—no interference from Jay, the children engaged and interested in the subject matter. I explain the next portion of the lesson is for them to practice what they have learned, reaching to grab the assignment they are to complete as groups.

Ollie's hand rises.

"Ollie," I acknowledge, eager to hear what the painfully shy child has to contribute.

"I'm allergic to bees," he informs us. This is the first time Ollie has shared with the class. I can't recall seeing him raise his hand to offer an answer, although each time I call on Ollie, he immediately spouts off the correct response to the posed question.

Not wanting to stifle his new willingness to contribute, I veer off plan. "What happens if you get stung by a bee, Ollie?" I ask him, seeing the opportunity to share how dangerous allergic reactions can be for kids and adults.

"I have to use my EpiPen, or I can go into anaphylactic shock." Ollie's words spur confused looks on the faces of his classmates.

Caroline's hand shoots up in response. "I have to use that pen too, but not for bees. I'm allergic to nuts."

I glance at the far side of the room for Principal Garber's reaction to the turn of events. She scribbles in a looping fashion on the paper in front of her, appearing to have difficulties with her pen.

Deciding to continue with a teachable moment, I look back at the students and address the group. "Allergies can be small, say maybe a rash that can be itchy or a runny nose, and that can be annoying. But some allergies can be severe, so bad that they can cause people to stop breathing." The children focus intently. "If someone like Ollie suffers a bee sting, or like Caroline eats something with nuts in it, or like me gets stung by fire ants, then that person needs a special kind of shot with a special kind of pen."

"What happens when you get stung by fire ants?" Jay asks out of turn.

"The same thing that happens to Ollie and Caroline," I answer.

Three of us in the room require these pens. Evaluation or not, this is a good time to teach the students about what to do for someone if such a dire situation occurs.

"Let's talk about anaphylactic shock, because it can be very scary—both for the person who is suffering from the shock and the person who is witnessing it." I think back to my first episode, remembering the terror in my aunt's eyes, the fear I felt thinking I was going to die, how I almost did. "It is important that you all understand what happens so that if you see someone who needs an EpiPen injection, you can get a grown-up right away.

"When people with severe allergies go into anaphylactic shock, they get dizzy, their vision blurs, they might faint or look like they're choking. Sometimes people wheeze because they have a hard time breathing; they could stop breathing."

"If they can't breathe, does it kill them?" Luke asks.

"Yes, it can, Luke. That's why it's so important that you all understand it's an EMERGENCY situation. You MUST get help for them right away. Ollie, Caroline, and I all carry EpiPens just in case of an emergency, but sometimes we aren't able to get to our pens."

"And if you can't use the pen, you die?" Jay asks.

I look at Jay, eyes void of any compassion. "Yes," I answer.

"Speaking of pens," Principal Garber reroutes, "my writing pen seems to be out of ink. May I use your pen, Ms. S?" Principal Garber holds up the Cross pen for my view.

"Yes, of course," I nod, taking the signal to continue with my lesson. "And now, you all have pencils that need to be working on this assignment." I hold up the stack of papers as evidence, then begin passing them out to the students as I deliver instructions for completing the task.

From the back of the room, Principal Garber gasps, drawing my attention. She holds the Cross pen above her clipboard, ink dripping onto the papers secured to the board. Her left sleeve splattered with black ink stains, she states to no one specifically, "I guess this isn't my day for pens."

My focus swivels to Jay. He sits at his desk, an unreadable expression on his face, his eyes following Principal Garber as she rushes to the sink on the other side of the room.

AMA

DECEMBER 1979

deep draw of the December air, cold and dry, finds its way to my lungs. Hands shoved into the lined pockets of the long denim coat, I pull it tighter around my body as I trek farther into the forest—The Community's van at least a mile behind me now. The workers still have another hour left on the job in Sylva. The township is about twenty-five miles from The Community, so to save on fuel, I must stay close by for the duration of their project. I've told Papa I don't mind doing the odd jobs alongside The Community workers to pass the time, but he insists the labors they perform are too menial for a future elder, that I should use these moments for my own reflection.

After dropping the crew at their destination, I completed the errand list as instructed. The tasks dull and repetitive, the locals skeptical and wary of our kind.

On my last stop at the feed store, Mr. Peters, the owner, was in full-on asshole form today. Stooped frame, a long, gray, and dirty beard hanging from his sallow face, the old man's bellow could be heard throughout the establishment. The man is condescending to everyone. For a long time, I thought his disdain saved for the members of The Community, but the man has no respect for anyone, as far as I can tell. Hidden from his view, the air thick with smells of seed and leather, I saw what he did. I heard the way he spoke to the young boy he employs. I saw the man shove the kid, slap away the boy's hand, humiliate him in front of everyone present. The kid can't be more than fourteen, lanky and thin, greasy hair falling over his lowered eyes. The old man continued booming at the cowering boy as he walked away to attend to a customer standing at the register. I followed and took my place in line—listened, waited, fumed.

"And what is it you need today?" The old goat barked at me as the customer in front of me finished his transaction and hurried to exit the store.

I looked into his rheumy yellow eyes, took my time answering. Silently, I repeated the words I've heard Elder Bard use while conjuring. *Laho jabi gowa.* I let the tips of my fingers brush his hand as I slapped the money on the counter and answered, "Three bags of chicken feed."

The old man's focus bored mine as I continued the silent chant, *laho jabi gowa*, words he would never understand even if they met his ears. When I finally broke the gaze, his hand jerked the money from my hold. The old man shook his head and yelled to the boy to load the feed into the van.

Now, I worry about what I've done. But why should I? The old man spews his misery on everyone he comes in contact with, and besides, he's already sick. He'll probably be dead before the chaos curse has time to take hold of him. Not to mention that according to Papa, my capability to conjure has not yet formed. Papa says I need to focus on healing for the time being. Learn to make the oils, to prepare the waters, Papa tells me.

I've done all that hundreds and hundreds of times. How many damn times do I need to prepare oil and water to be considered proficient in the task? And, I'm sick of toting around the workers, running the errands for The Community. If I am meant to be an elder, then just let me move forward. Give me the opportunity to learn, to grow, to make use of my gifts.

Papa is wrong. I am ready to move forward with my lessons in conjure. Leoti's baking business is booming for the first time since Mama died. Leoti claims the holiday season finally picked up, but I know the money spell I cast worked.

Leoti asked me to come and work with her, to help her out with all orders she needs to fill. Papa was adamant in his refusal of allowing me to work in the bakery, though, and I had to relay to Leoti the ridiculous excuse of having too much responsibility to fulfill in The Community. Leoti's disappointment and doubt clearly marked her face. Both Papa and Leoti knew as well as I did that the excuse was bullshit.

Now, here I am, strolling through the woods, while Leoti slings cake batter and Papa conspires with the elders about whether to move ahead with my coupling ceremony to Elan Darach or postpone as Elan has requested. Elan's first child is due late summer next year, and out of respect for the mother, he wants to wait until the baby is born before he unites with me. If I had my way, the mother of Elan's child would have Elan all to herself. I want nothing to do with Elan Darach or his baby-making tool. Papa doesn't care what I want, though, and doesn't want to hear it either.

Underneath my foot, I feel the snap of something brittle, the break too hard to be a twig. The noise drags me from my thoughts. I lift my foot and back away from the spot, squatting for a better view. I dig through the decaying leaves, finding the carcass of a raccoon. Fingering through the bones, I find a few still intact and stuff them into my pockets, thinking later to cleanse them, bless them, and add them to my bone reading collection.

I continue toward the stream. The water flows steadily over the smooth stones, too early in the season to freeze yet. The icy water stings my fingers as I wash away the debris from my hands, then cup them and bring the cold water to my lips. I drop to sit, looking to the sky. The gray haze above so thick it leaves little room for light to filter through. From my pocket, I pull out the pocket knife and clean underneath my nails to kill time before I head back to the van, while I *reflect* on the injustices I must accept.

* * *

THE NINE COMMUNITY members file into the van. Ray tells me Mrs. Weaver wants them back next week to finish up the work on her barn. I slip the transmission into drive and slowly weave back up the dirt road to make my way toward the tiny town of Sylva, already dreading the trip next week, wondering what I'll have to *reflect* on then. I brake to make the right turn onto Sylva's main thoroughfare before continuing onto the highway. In the distance, I see several vehicles now fill the parking spaces outside the feed store I visited earlier.

"Wonder what's going on there?"

Janice sits in the front passenger seat next to me. "Mrs. Weaver said her scanner went berserk earlier," she replies. "Something about needing medical at the farm supply store ASAP. And you know Mrs. Weaver, well I guess you don't, but anyway, that woman hears something like that, she has to have the whole story. So Mrs. Weaver got on the party line to get her 'gossip,' as she calls it."

I wait, knowing Janice likes to spread a word around as well and will give me the full details without me having to ask her for them.

"So evidently, the kid who loads feed for the store walked in around noon to find Mr. Peters slumped over the register."

My eyes focused on the road ahead, I recall how sickly the old man looked earlier in the day, think of the silent curse that ran over my tongue as I stared into his ugly yellow eyes. "So, did Mrs. Weaver say if they got him to the hospital?" I ask Janice.

"Didn't need to," Janice says. "He was dead when medical got there." She shakes her head. "And right here at the holidays."

DECEMBER

My eyes fly open to the black of night. I throw an arm over Kirby's side of the bed, searching to curl up next to him, use his body heat to keep me warm. A cold pillow is all I find.

In the dark, my mind whirls with all that needs to be accomplished in the next two days. Jay has been specific with his gift list this year, and I've yet to complete my shopping. Kirby won't be home until late afternoon on Christmas Eve. Reluctantly, I've enlisted Mama's help. There's no one else to watch Jay while I finish the errands. If only I could trust my son to behave. Mama says she can handle him, but I'm not so certain. The temper tantrum he threw tonight was almost more than I could cope with. I had to punish him, though. Jay was downright hateful, vindictive, vengeful with our neighbor—the horrible scene on looping replay in my head.

Jay jumped from the car the moment I pulled to a stop in our driveway after work today. As he was tearing off toward the front door, I called to Jay, asking him to check the mail. Stepping out of the car, I saw Mr. Beverly taking his afternoon exercise stroll up the sidewalk and shouted a hello in his direction. As the older man threw up his hand to wave, Jay ran right into him. I hurried over to check on Mr. Beverly, make sure Jay apologized, just in time to hear Mr. Beverly tell Jay he should be more careful, look where he is going. I saw the look come over my son, the look I know all too well, the look that made me fear what might come out of Jay's mouth. But Jay never said a word; instead, he yanked the older man's walker out from under him. It took all my strength to hold Mr. Beverly upright until he could regain his balance. Mr. Beverly could have been seriously injured. As punishment for his abominable action, I ordered Jay to his room, no dessert, no television, or electronics for the evening.

A heavy sigh gives way to a yawn. I turn to lay on my side, closing eyes, and pulling the covers to my chin, trying to clear my mind, at least summon something more pleasant to think on. A strange sound floats through the stilled quiet. A chill inches up my spine. It's not the frigid air of late December cooling my blood. It's a feeling I'm not alone, that someone is in my bedroom.

Slowly, I lift the lids of my eyes, adjusting my vision in the darkness once more. I look toward the window on the right side of the room. The moonlight is faint, but enough shines through that I can see no one in direct sight. Still, the sense of being watched is strong. I twist to look over my shoulder and see him, standing motionless at the edge of my bed.

Rolling to my back, careful not to startle him in case he's sleepwalking, I search the outline of his frame, look for some clue he's awake. He holds a long dark rope of some sort taught between his hands.

I lift, placing the weight of my upper body on elbows and whisper, "Jay."

"I missed my favorite show tonight, you bitch," he says, slow and measured.

"What?" I shake my head, attempt to make sense of what he is saying. "Jay, it's late—go back to bed."

"I'm sick of doing what you want me to do."

Jay releases one end of the rope, swinging at his side. A flash of silver catches my eye. Prongs dangle at the end of the rope. It is the extension cord from the lamp in Jay's bedroom. He begins to wrap the other end of the cord around his right hand. Suddenly, I understand his intentions.

"Jay!"

Frantic, I scoot to the middle of the bed. Jay raises his arm, taking it back behind his body. The motion of his arm slings the cord forward. The lash lands across the top of my body. Pain sears through my upper arm. Jay lifts his arm again and brings the cord dangerously close to my face. The strikes come fast and hard. My thoughts and senses muddle in pain. I hold my arms over my head to shield myself and feel the burn spread over my left breast, the thin nightgown providing little padding against the impact of his blows.

I clamber across the mattress, falling over the edge of the bed, away from Jay's wrath. On hands and knees, I scramble to stand but fall to knees again as the prongs from the cord thrash into my back.

"Jay, stop," I scream. The cord strikes again and again.

I manage to stand, dashing for the door, tripping as my foot catches the corner of the bed. I land hard, unable to break the fall, and feel the blow to my left eye as my brow bone hits the base of the dresser. Jay takes advantage of my misfortune, swinging again.

Knuckles holding my weight, I awkwardly push myself up, grab the frame of the bed. On knees, I use the bed to stable myself. I stand, ready to fight off the next blow, to force some sense into my son. But he's done with me.

Jay walks out of the bedroom, the cord dangling from his grip as his free hand slams the door behind him.

* * *

IN THE LIGHT OF DAY, the bruising looks worse than it appeared in my bathroom this morning. The rearview mirror reflects the pitiful attempt of a cover-up—makeup, caked over the swelling and color circling my left eye, looks like something a circus clown might apply before hitting the big top. I swivel the mirror back to the center of the windshield, lean back into the headrest, and ready myself for all inquiries ahead. At least the turtleneck and sweater hide the welts, though the clothing can't mask the pain or embarrassment I feel.

Across the church parking lot, Art and Gloria exit their car. Gloria spots me and waves. I hold up a finger to indicate I'll be in for service in a moment, and they walk ahead, disappearing through the wide double doors. I need another moment without Jay. I sent him inside under strict instruction to go straight to his Sunday school class, and while I hope he followed the command, I don't have the energy to check on him just yet.

The phone inside my purse rings. I dig through the bag, pulling it out to see Kirby is calling.

"Hey."

"Morning, hon," my husband starts. "How you feelin'?"

Locked inside my bedroom last night, I called Kirby after I tended to the bloody lashes on my body, iced my eye. I knew it was late, that he had to work early, but I had to talk to him, had to tell him what happened. I wanted him to come home. I wanted him to hold me, help me.

Tears well. I choke back the lump in my throat. "Like I've been flogged." I use my fingertip to dry the corners of my eyes.

"I'm so sorry, honey."

I want to tell him it's okay, it's not his fault; but the truth is, unjust as it might be, I do put some of the blame on him. If Kirby were home more often, he could help me with Jay, handle the tantrums, the yelling, the hitting. But we both know that can't happen right now. We're fortunate Kirby still has a job, given all the layoffs his company has served to other drivers. Kirby can't give them an excuse to let him go too.

"Esme?"

"Yeah, I'm here. Sitting in the car outside of the church, practicing the lies I'm going to have to tell everyone inside God's house."

"What are you going to say?"

"That I was headed down into the basement. My hands were full. I don't know... with maybe Christmas gifts I was hiding or something. That I thought I could make it without flipping on the light—that I fell down the stairs."

Kirby doesn't reply. *He thinks it's a poor explanation; he thinks it's sinful to lie.*

"I hate lying to our church family, Kirby, but what else can I say?" Having our friends think I'm a bad parent is one thing, having them think Jay is a thug is another. If Kirby has a better excuse, now is the time to help me come up with one.

"Kirby, please. Please say something. Please don't make me feel like a heathen. I don't know how much more I can take, but I certainly can't go on without your support." Tears fall freely, cutting a trail through the heavy makeup.

"Esme, honey. I support you one hundred percent. It is our son I can't... What do we do with him? I'm ready to lock him up, Esme. Jay can't keep doing this to you. I wish I were there, and then I think—well, I don't know what I'd do to him if I saw you like this. Maybe it's better I'm not there. I feel helpless, Esme. I can't protect you like I should."

"I keep thinking about Philippians 2:3 'Let nothing be done through selfish ambition or conceit, but in lowliness of mind let each esteem others better than himself.' Do you think I'm not putting Jay's best interests first? That maybe I'm so concerned about what everyone else is going to think of me as a mother, I don't see the good in Jay—I'm not giving Jay the opportunity to be who he is because of my own ambition and conceit?"

"Esme, all you do is put Jay's best interest first. It's not right, him hitting on you, his belligerent attitude."

As we sit in thought, I glance at my watch.

"Kirby, I have to go. I didn't want to walk into church too early, but I also don't want to walk in after preacher starts his sermon either. Every head in the house will turn to see who has shown up late."

"I know. I understand. Hey, I'll be home tomorrow, Esme. I'll try and call you later, but I've got a long ride ahead. If I don't talk to you before you go to bed tonight, please remember to lock the bedroom door. Okay?"

"I will. Be careful on the road, sweetie. I love you."

"I love you too. I'll be there in time for Christmas Eve with your parents tomorrow night. I promise."

"Can't wait."

* * *

MANEUVERING THE CAR THROUGH TOWN, I dart in and out of parking spaces, dash through stores, collect the last of the Christmas gifts on my list. I dropped Jay off at my parents' house this morning. Mama said she had some orders she needed to finish at the bakery and would be taking Jay to work with her. I feel so guilty. Mama working on Christmas Eve. Daddy at home, still under the weather. Me leaving Jay in their care with the mood he's been in lately.

As I wait in the long line at the toy store for check out, Kirby calls. In the chaos of the crowd, I barely make out that he is dropping off the truck and completing the paperwork from his last haul. We disconnect so he can get finished with work, and I can make this last purchase.

Holding in line behind two teenage girls buying a gag gift for a friend, I think back to when Kirby and I were their age. Life was so much easier. Always together every moment possible, no worries other than when we would be able to see each other next. Kirby's been gone over a week, and I can't wait for him to get home. Knowing I'll see him soon, coupled with the fact I'm getting my to-do list accomplished, lends me hope. The holiday is ahead, promises of celebration and memories to be made are around the corner. I feel lighter than I have in weeks. The

Christmas spirit might finally be finding its way into my head and heart.

I grab my bag as the cashier places the last of my items inside and hurry out to the parking lot. One final stop at the grocery store and the errands will be done. With any luck, I'll be home before Kirby steps through the front door.

My phone rings as I slam the trunk closed. The display tells me my father is calling.

"Hey, Daddy. Everything okay?"

"Well, Esme, not really." Daddy sounds tired. His battle with atrial fibrillation has been a stressful struggle for both of my parents. Since July, Daddy has undergone three different procedures to try and correct his irregular heartbeat, but none have proven successful.

"What's wrong? Are you okay? Is Jay okay?"

"I'm fine, Jay's fine, but your mama's not doing so great."

My stomach sinks at the declaration. Mama's been under so much pressure with the bakery and taking care of Daddy, and now I've gone and left her with Jay.

"What's wrong with Mama? I'm pulling out of the toy store parking lot right now. I can wait to go to the grocery store until Kirby gets home," I ramble, head swiveling back and forth as I reverse the car out of the tight parking space. "Kirby should be home soon. I'll have plenty of time to get groceries later. I'll be right there."

"Don't go to the house. We're not there."

"Where are you?" Brake pedal pressed firmly to the floorboard, I hold the car at the exit of the store's lot. Behind me, horns blare, urging me to move forward. I turn right and drive along slowly, waiting for Daddy to tell me where to find them.

"We're at the hospital. I had to drive your mama to the emergency room."

"I'm on my way." I disconnect, tossing the phone to the passenger's seat.

My mind spins with questions and worry. *What's happened to*

Mama? Where is Jay? Is he with them? Is Daddy strong enough to handle the stress of the situation? What is the situation?

I whip into the hospital parking lot and find a space near the emergency room. Rushing from the car, I race through the sliding doors of the ER and see them, Daddy, Jay, and Mama, situated in the corner near the television. Jay focuses on the screen overhead, his blank stare eerily reminiscent of when the two of us sat in the very same spot waiting to hear about the condition of the little boy Jay injured on the playground. Daddy sits with his hands on his knees, spine pulled straight. Mama's head hangs low, eyes staring into her lap. She looks pale, older.

I hurry over and take the empty chair next to Mama. "Hey, what's going on?"

Mama gives a weak smile and turns to Daddy. "Hon, why don't you and Jay take a walk outside? Get a little fresh air."

Daddy nods, stands, then looks at Jay, motioning with his head for Jay to follow. Jay stands without further coaxing, a true blessing. I can't think of the last time he didn't give me pushback on any directive.

I watch the pair walk through the exit door then turn to Mama.

"That eye looks plumb awful, Esme."

"I know, Mama, but it's feeling better. Now, tell me what happened."

"Jay and I were at the bakery. I could tell he was getting antsy, but I had a couple of orders I had to finish up, and then I also had to finish off the cupcakes I was making for our get together tonight. I told Jay he could take some home with him to leave for Santa if he wanted."

"Jay doesn't believe in Santa anymore," I tell her, worrying over what comes next in this story. "It's a new development," I add, mumbling.

"Yeah, he told me as much. Said he didn't want to leave cupcakes for a fake fat man. That you and his daddy would end up eating them. 'And why should they eat MY cupcakes,' he yelled at me."

"I told you, Jay has been a handful lately. I don't know what to do with him anymore," I admit, lowering my eyes, defeat, failure, and guilt chasing out the hope I felt earlier.

I see it, then. Under the long sleeve of Mama's thick cardigan, I catch sight of her wrist, red and swollen, blue and black streaking through. "Oh, Mama. That looks terrible."

"I'm pretty sure it's broken," she says, holding out her arm, pulling her sleeve back. "I can't move it."

"What did he do?"

"I finished up my chores at the bakery, told Jay we were ready to load up and head home to check on Pawpaw. He just kept going on and on about those damn cupcakes. I should have just let him have one, but I was holding my ground, trying to teach him to have a little patience.

"We pulled into the driveway, and he's still carrying on. I went to the trunk to pull out the box of cupcakes, and Jay walked up behind me. He said to me, 'I'm getting one of those fucking cupcakes.' Where did he learn such language, Esme? I know you and Kirby don't use that word."

"I don't know, Mama. School? The internet? I try to monitor his activity."

"I asked him. I had one hand on my hip, one on the lip of the trunk, and I said, 'Little boys who use that word aren't allowed to eat my cupcakes. And where did you learn such a word anyway?' Jay looked at me with those eyes. Pure evil in them, Esme. He screamed, 'None of your fucking business, you old bag.' And then, with all his might, he slammed the trunk on my wrist."

MEREL

DECEMBER

The endless knocking—as if someone is demanding entry but is never there—grows louder and more persistent with each passing day. The memories spilling, tumbling over the barrier I thought solidly constructed. As soon as Thanksgiving break was over, I began the countdown to the winter holidays. It was all I could do to get through a school day. Time. I told myself I just needed some time off to recuperate, to get some sleep, to get my head straight again. But now, four days into the winter holiday break and I'm desperate for a reprieve from all the empty hours.

Through the drawn shades on my living room window, the light of the sun is starting to fade away. I wait anxiously for nightfall, for this day to pass. When Christmas is over, the holidays long gone, I can start fresh in the new year, pack away all my memories and move forward.

Lounging on the sofa, phone in hand, good intentions deferred, I pick at the pilling on my overly worn pajamas. I should change, put on something nicer for the holiday. But, why bother? I've no plans to see anyone, for anyone to see me. The only place I ever go other than school is the grocery store, and it is closed.

The phone in my hand feels warm. I stare at the screen, two

hours gone by since I picked it up to hit the contact phone link for Letty and Shu, a long memorized landline number that stares back at me reproachfully. I've avoided the obligation far longer than acceptable. It has been five months since I left. Calls screened, voicemails deleted, texts ignored. Today is Christmas, and not calling, not reaching out to them, is not an option. I owe them more, but I'm not ready for that. The very least I can do is make the call.

My finger presses the blue link. I click on the speaker button.

Ringing.

"Hello," she says tentatively.

"Merry Christmas." The greeting I put forth hardly conveys the intended sentiment.

"Merry Christmas to you, too."

Silence.

I watch the seconds tick by on the phone screen.

Breaking the quiet, "How are you guys?"

"We're doing well. How are you? Been thinking about you, wondering how things are going for you." A hint of hostility? Condescension?

Disappointment. She's disappointed in me. I've done nothing but give her good reason to be. But she is not without her own faults. We both know that.

I tuck the animosity away for the sake of the holiday and answer her question instead. "Super busy. The job is more strenuous than I thought it would be—always on my feet, paperwork that never seems to end."

"How's the school? You said second grade, right?"

"Yeah, second grade. The school is great. I have a great teammate; her name is Dorothy. You two would probably hit it off. She reminds me a lot of you actually. And the kids are so sweet. They call me their school mom, give me hugs, bring me gifts."

"That's wonderful, honey. I'm glad to hear you're enjoying your work. How's your health? You holding up okay?"

"It's all good. I'm fine."

"You don't sound fine."

I can see the two of them. Shu and Letty lounged back in their matching recliners, in the same house they've shared for the last forty years. That's all I ever wanted. To be like them. To marry the love of my life and spend the rest of my days with him, but I ruined all that.

Letty's familiar voice slices away my thoughts. "I can hear it..." she pauses. "Merel, I know when you're lying to me."

"It's just the holidays. They bring back lots of memories."

Letty holds.

"And, the first year as a teacher takes a toll. All the evaluations. Trying to establish routines." I pause, then add, "And I have this one little boy in my class who is quite challenging. Always stirring up trouble."

"Merel, why don't you come visit? I know you've got some time off. We'd love to see you."

"I can't, Letty. It's too hard, especially this time of year. I just need some time alone, that's all."

"Well, for the record, I don't think being alone is healthy for you."

The line goes quiet again. I don't want to address her concerns. I have enough of my own. Instead, I change the subject to the only safe topic I can think of at the moment. "Thank you for sending Poppy."

While I appreciated Letty's nostalgic thoughtfulness, I've given little thought to the doll since I received him. The doll was simply the first thing that came to mind. Though, come to think of it, I haven't seen the doll since I tossed him aside the day I received him. Was it Halloween? He must be here somewhere. I make a note to look for him after I get off the phone.

"Poppy?"

"You know, the felt doll."

Letty is silent.

"Handmade. Looks like a little gingerbread boy."

"The doll?" Letty asks.

"Yeah, you sent him to me a couple of months ago."

"I," Letty starts, then holds as if she's in thought. "The one with the red heart?"

"Yes, that one. Do you remember who gave me Poppy?"

"Merel, I haven't seen or even thought about that doll in years."

"But no one else knew about Poppy. You don't remember sending me the package? It arrived on Halloween."

"I didn't send you that doll, Merel. Like I said, I haven't seen it or thought about it since you were a little girl."

I'm not crazy. He was in my hands. The knocking may only be in my head, but I touched, felt, held Poppy. It was real.

"Merel," Letty begins.

I cut Letty off before she can continue. "Tell Shu hello for me, will you? I need to go." I've fulfilled the obligation. I made the call. I've wished them a happy holiday.

I press the disconnect button, and she's gone.

JAUNUARY

Two weeks into the new year, my routines resumed and the glorious respite from the winter weather of January, I feel better than I have in months. It helps, too, that work has been so busy I've had little time to give to the memories that plagued me over the holidays.

Second grade has switched recess times with fourth grade due to their special science labs this week. Instead of the regularly scheduled mid-morning time outside, we now have the last slot of the day, the school bell only minutes away. The students now run off their energy and the day's stress in the late afternoon sun. Our second-grade teaching foursome sits on the bench while we watch our kids enjoy their playtime.

The weather has been brilliant this week, and I am trying to soak up every ounce of vitamin D offered before the storms roll back in next week as forecasted by the local weather reporters. I listen in on the conversation being held amongst my team but have little to contribute, or should I say, anything I want to contribute. Dorothy chimes in as Ben and Alicia bemoan the trials of their homeroom parents, speaking as if the parents' issues were their own tribulations to bear. The PTA's recent decision to have all room parents work together at grade level is the current uproar among the competitive parents. The ruling has been set forth so that no one classroom has grander or more elaborate celebrations than another. Not that I don't have an opinion on the matter, mine just happens not to align with the beliefs of my second-grade teammates. These parents are obnoxious in their attempts to outdo one another. They should realize the children are the ones who suffer from their silly competitions to one-up each other for nothing other than bragging rights.

Leaving the three of them to their discussion, I watch the cluster of little girls at the far corner of the field. On a small patch of brown grass, they sit in a circle braiding one another's hair, oblivious to the cold dirt under their bottoms. Witnessing their innocence, my chest swells, knowing all too soon their lives will take a very different twist and that some of those same little girls will turn on each other. Boys, makeup, cars, clubs, their parents' status in the community—all of it will tear them apart in the years ahead.

"What did you do, Merel?" Alicia asks, chasing away my cynical thoughts.

"I'm sorry, Alicia. What did you say? My mind was somewhere else."

"I'm having a terrible time potty training Conner. What did you do with your son?"

"Oh." I drift back into a time I'd rather not visit, searching my memory bank for the days of another life. "Cheerios."

"Cheerios?"

"You toss one or two into the toilet, potty, wherever, so they float, and then have him try to aim at them. Sink them. Boys love games."

"I love that! I'm going to try it," Alicia says.

Dorothy seizes the opening. "How is your son, Merel? Have you heard from him?"

Heat rises from my chest, rushing up my neck. After all these months of working together so closely, I know Dorothy has seen through me, that she knows my truths and untruths regardless of whether she knows the details. And she most certainly knows if I haven't trusted *her* with the facts of my past, I'm not going to share them with the group.

"No, I haven't. He's on a military mission that keeps him from outside contact." I stare, unblinking into Dorothy's watching, searching eyes.

Alicia says, "That must be so hard."

"Maybe soon," Dorothy offers in truce.

I accept. "Maybe soon."

"Ms. S," Libby yells as she runs toward our group.

"What's up, Libby?"

"Ollie found a frog, and Jay says it's poisonous." Libby shuffles her weight between feet, hands flying in motion as she tries to convey the situation. "And Ollie told him it wasn't poisonous. And then Jay said it was and that Ollie was stupid and that the frog should die."

Libby, at my heels, I hurry over to the group of children circled around Ollie and Jay. I push through the students to get to the bickering pair and see Jay yank the frog from Ollie's protective grasp.

"Jay," I shout.

Jay runs out the other side of the circling children. Begging, crying, Ollie shoves his way through the crowd to follow Jay.

Struggling to get to the scene of confrontation, I see Jay slam the frog to the ground. Ollie wails, falling to the ground as Jay brings his foot up and stomps down on the poor defenseless creature. The children scream in protest and disgust. I arrive to see Jay lift his foot, inspecting the bottom of his shoe.

Dorothy, Ben, and Alicia have joined the group. Students disturbed by Jay's wicked actions, empathetic to Ollie's tragedy, gather around their teachers for comfort in a group hug.

Pulling Ollie up and into my arms, I shield his eyes, walking him away from the gruesome scene.

"He wasn't poisonous, Ms. S. He had a cross on his back. A spring peeper frog," Ollie manages to relay between sobs.

"Oh, sweetie. I'm sorry."

Ollie tries to pull from me. "We can't just leave him here, Ms. S. I have to bury him."

I stoop, taking his shoulders, turning him to face me. "Ollie, honey, the bell is going to ring any moment, and we have to get you packed up to go home. But I promise you, I will take care of him."

I turn to my teammates. "Do you all mind taking my class in and getting them packed up?"

Ben and Alicia immediately begin the process of relaying instructions as Dorothy tells me, "Tony has a shovel. He'll help you out. Don't worry about the kids. We've got them."

The mood turned somber, the teachers collectively give the signal that it is time to line up by raising one arm into the air. The students begin to shuffle into straight lines in front of their teachers, preparing to march inside and pack for the trip home.

I hurry to find Tony before the kids in after-school care take to the playground.

* * *

ENTERING OUR SHARED OFFICE, Dorothy asks, "You okay?"

From my seat at the desk, I look at her, nodding, knowing the tremble in my throat will give way if I speak.

Dorothy pulls out the chair from under her desk and sits. "He's too much for you, Merel."

She's right, but what am I going to say? To do? Jay's kindergarten teacher dealt with him. His first-grade teacher got through her year with Jay. I'm supposed to knock on Principal Garber's door and announce I can't handle this child. That's not going to happen. Somehow, I have to find the strength to carry on until the first week of June—six more months.

I draw a deep breath, pushing down the quiver. "He's a lot to deal with," I admit, but do not concede.

"I know you're worried about this being your first year, but if you asked for him to be transferred to one of the other second grade classrooms, I honestly don't think Jeanine would give it a second thought; she knows what that child has put you through. Not that I doubt your abilities as a professional, Merel, but the rest of us have a bit more experience than you do, that's all. The first year is hard on all teachers, but then to top it off with a student as challenging as Jay...."

The fact Dorothy calls Principal Garber by her first name and makes the suggestion Jay be transferred out of my class leads me to wonder what private conversations have been held on my behalf. I will not give up. I will not allow this child to take away my dream, my happiness, my sanity. One way or another, I will see this year through, and with Jay's badass sitting in one of my classroom desks.

"I'm so certain the three of you would love to draw straws for my problem kid. I'm not going to do that to any of you. I plan on having a long career here at this school, and I need to keep you all as friends and partners. I can assure you, me putting Jay off on any one of you would create some ill will towards me."

I ignore the knocking I hear at my classroom door. Dorothy watches me, question marking her features.

"What?"

"Someone's knocking at your door."

"Oh."

I stand to answer it just as Holly, one of the fifth-grade teachers, pops her head inside the office.

"Merel, one of your kiddos missed their daycare van. I've called the daycare to let them know, and they said they'd send the van back once the driver arrives at the daycare."

Holly reads my confusion. "I'm sorry; I'd sit with him until the van returns, but my baby has an appointment with the pediatrician in thirty minutes. I'm going to be late as it is."

"It's okay, Holly. I understand. I have some work I need to finish anyway. I'm going to be here for a bit. Who is it?"

"He said his name is Jay. You want me to get him settled in for you?"

"No, I've got this. You go on. Take care of your baby."

Holly makes her exit. I look at Dorothy, throwing my hands into the air.

"You want me to take him? He can wait with me," Dorothy offers.

"No. I'll handle him. Besides, at some point, I have to address his actions on the playground this afternoon."

"I'm not going to tell you what to do, but it would probably be best for the behavior specialist to handle that. Cassandra is emotionally removed from the situation, and you are far too close."

I nod, taking time to consider her advice, decide she's right.

I step out of the office to find Jay behind my classroom desk. The drawer in the middle of the desk open, Jay riffling through my things.

"Jay, that is my desk, and I'd appreciate it if you left *my* things alone."

"I was just shutting the drawer for you. It was open." His face portrays pure innocence, but I know better. I'm not fooled by Jay's act. "Your phone is in there. Someone might take it."

"Go have a seat at the reading table while you wait for the daycare van to come back." I struggle to keep my voice even, the vision of the stunt he pulled earlier still fresh behind my eyes; moreover, Ollie's precious face screwed with anguish and heartbreak.

I want to shake Jay, ask him, 'Why would you do something so awful?' Dorothy's right. I'm too close to this, too emotional to address Jay's abhorrent behavior.

"I can sit at my desk."

Jay has already proven he's bold enough to go through my desk. I'm not going to allow him to go through his classmates' things. "No. We have already put up the chairs so Mr. Tony can sweep later."

Jay lugs his backpack across the room, tosses it onto the horse-shoe reading table, and plops down on one of the chairs. I take a seat behind my desk where I can keep an eye on him. The stack of grading I need to do in front of me, I take out a pen and get started.

Jay pulls the zipper of the backpack. I look through my lashes. Jay opens the mouth of the satchel, peeking inside. Refusing to play along, I keep my attention focused on the paperwork in front of me.

I glance at the clock across the room. Ten minutes have passed with Jay lifting and peeking, lifting and peeking, no doubt trying to get my attention. We continue in silence.

A loud, painful grating noise cuts through the quiet room as Jay scoots the chair away from the table. Hand cramping from the tight grip I keep on my pen, I continue grading the students' papers. *How far away is this daycare located?*

From across the room, Jay says, "The zipper on my backpack is stuck."

"Perhaps if you stop pulling it back and forth...," I mumble, not bothering to meet his cold gaze.

"Will you fix it for me?"

I sigh, fold my arms over the papers on my desk. "Fine. Bring it over; let me see it."

Jay pulls his backpack from the table, dragging it to the edge of my desk. He stands beside my chair and lifts the bag for me to take. I pull the bag onto my lap to view the problem. There seems to be some sort of cloth object in the compartment of the bag that has been caught inside the teeth of the zipper.

"Ms. S," the voice booms from the intercom at the other side of the room.

I look at the box and call, "Yes."

"The driver of the daycare van is here for Jay."

"Thank you. We'll be right there," I announce.

I tug once more at the zipper, and it gives way. Reaching inside the backpack to push the cloth item deeper inside, my hand touches a familiar form. I pull it from the bag. A doll. The doll looks like Poppy. The felt body, hand-stitched in dark thread. Button eyes sewn with Xs at the pupils. A red heart. My breath catches under the lump forming deep in my chest. *Is this my doll? Is this Poppy?*

"Where did you get this doll, Jay?"

Jay snatches the doll from my hold and yanks his backpack to the floor. He shoves the doll inside and zips the compartment. "It's mine. Someone gave it to me."

I hurry to follow Jay as he rushes to the door and makes for the hallway.

AMA

JANUARY 1980

Inside Leoti's and Rubin's bedroom, I sit behind the small vanity table littered with makeup, lotions, and perfumes. Leoti stands behind me, working the brush through my hair. The mirror in front of me reflects our dual features, side by side the exactness uncanny. I've given in to her pleas and allowed her to apply makeup to my face. The mark is still visible but somehow more pleasant to the eye now that some of my other facial features have been played up. I watch Leoti's reflection, her diligent attention to the task at hand, careful not to jerk my hair as she untangles the knots, her gentle spirit visible. She's not capable of killing anyone, unlike me.

The old man's death weighs on me. Supposedly, the liver disease finally took him, but still, I wonder. Did I finish him off? The silent curse that ran over my tongue as I stared deep into the old man's putrid soul loops on repeat in my mind. *Laho jabi gowa.* Am I really capable of killing someone with words? With thoughts? It's never occurred to me before, the power of the conjurers. I knew what they did but hadn't considered the consequences. Is that what I want? Who I am? I've spoken to no one about the curse I laid on the old man. Conjures are to be placed with a pure heart, with intent for betterment. Is there someone out there who is better off now the old man is dead? I think of the boy who worked alongside the old man. Is the boy's life better? Have his days improved now the old man is no longer around to berate him, to shove him, to slap him?

"What's wrong?" My sister asks. She uses the mirror to lock in on my eyes, Leoti's squinting with concern. "You don't like the makeup?"

"It's different," I admit. "My skin feels weird. You know, like it can't breathe."

"You'll get used to it," she laughs, her worry slipping away. "I assume you didn't tell Daddy what we're doing tonight."

I give a slight shake of my head.

"So, what did you tell him this time?" She asks. The question sizzles with accusation, as if I am in the habit of lying to Papa. I don't lie—not really. Although lately, I've told him more untruths than truths. Papa wants me to live my life one way, and Leoti wants me to choose to live her way, but I don't know what I want. At least, Leoti wants the decision to be mine. Papa doesn't believe there's a choice to be made. Leoti and I will be twenty-two in a few months. Leoti is married to a man she loves, a man she chose to spend her life with. She has a career she's passionate about and plans for her future, while I still live as if I am a child. Going through my days, doing what I'm told, fetching this and picking up that.

I pick at my cuticles, pull at a hangnail. "He thinks I'm staying in the woods tonight."

"It's the middle of January, Ama. He bought that?"

"Course. Why wouldn't he? I do it all the time."

"Stay outside? In those woods? By yourself? Un-huh. Nope. Not me." I glance up at the mirror to see Leoti shaking her head emphatically. "I wouldn't stay out there by myself if it was the middle of the day, the middle of summer, much less at night in the dead of winter."

"It's peaceful. The rustle of the leaves, the song of the wind, the stars, the roar of the fire." The thought leads me to question my decision about what I'm doing here, what I've agreed to.

"It's not safe, Ama."

I return Leoti's glare via the mirror. "Thought you quit believing in the boogie man a long time ago."

"There's plenty more in those woods to be scared of. You never know what kind of varmints you're going to come across in the middle of the night," Leoti claims. Her facial expression reminds me of one our mother used to make.

I don't bother to debate the point. We may look alike, but we're two completely different people when it comes to how we find solace.

"I'm not going to have any hair left on my head if you keep brushing. Aren't you almost done?"

"Yeah, but I still wish you'd let me curl it."

Dragging the brush forward, Leoti reverses the direction she combs. Long dark hair falls over my face, blocking my vision.

Through the curtain of hair covering my eyes, I answer, "No. Absolutely not. I agreed to the makeup."

Leoti drags her forefinger along the left side of my scalp, styling my hair out of its usual center part. The extra hair falling over the right side of my face helps conceal the stained cheek. With both the makeup and the hair, I have to look hard at my reflection to see the familiar mark.

"I know, and you look so pretty." She lays the brush aside, hands on hips, determination on her face. "Clothes? Let's check out the closet."

Leoti turns and pads across the room. I stand and follow.

"Where are we going, exactly?" I ask, watching her fling through the hanging garments. Leoti has been after me to try living in her world—just for a day—the proposition, the most current attempt at drawing me out of The Community.

The harassment to move in with her and Rubin, to help out with the bakery, get the herbal remedies portion of the business running again, has become a never-ending, ever-nagging topic my sister has continued to press upon me these last two months. She's finally worn me down. I agreed to do one night in hopes it would get her off my back. But if I'm honest, the curiosity about what it might be like to live as a commoner drove me to say yes. One night. That's all I am committing to right now. I'm not saying I'm willing to leave The Community. I'm not agreeing to tell Papa I don't want to be chief elder. It's an evening out, and it's not as if a few hours are going to sway me to step away from our way of life.

"Rubin is taking us to Roy's Burger Palace and Bar."

"The joint on two-seventy-six?"

"Yep. Have you been there?"

"Sure. All the time," I exaggerate, the words dripping with sarcasm. "Are you kidding me? Papa would have a shit fit. The only money we spend with the commoners is on necessities we can't gather or harvest. Burgers and beer aren't necessities."

"Well, tonight they are. They're sustenance, and you're going to see how the other side lives." Leoti hands over a pair of embroidered denim jeans and a sweater. "And I have a feeling you might just like it."

* * *

STEPPING inside the self-proclaimed *palace* of burgers, I halt behind Leoti to take in the surroundings. The room is dimly lit by neon signs that line the walls giving off a red glow through the haze of cigarette smoke. The smoke mingles with the smells of grease, beer, and bleach. Booths line the left side of the perimeter, with a few tables set up near the back. The middle of the room is clear of furnishings, delegated for dancing presumably, as four couples swirl and twirl to a twangy tune coming from some unknown source. Leoti tugs on my wrist, pointing to an open table on the left. I follow her and Rubin over to the booth and scoot into the bench across from them. Rubin pulls menus from a stack at the edge of the table and passes them around.

"Thanks," I mutter, certain he didn't hear me over the music and noise of the crowd.

I glance at the menu, not sure I'm even hungry anymore. Leoti and Rubin share a conversation I can't make out, but figure it must be about their dinner choices as they point to one another's menus.

Leoti leans across the table, raising her voice to carry over the racket. "I'm going to go order. What do you want?" She points to the menu for emphasis.

"A plain burger. I don't see one on here, though."

"Got it. I'll be right back." She slides out of the booth and heads to the bar.

Rubin gathers the menus and places them back where he found them. I look at the dance floor. Holding onto beer and cigarettes, women and men move their bodies in time with the music.

Rubin places his arms on the table, leaning his body forward. "Leoti says you haven't been here before."

I shake my head.

Rubin is not the guy I would ever have imagined Leoti to marry. A dark-haired, Jewish lawyer, thin to the point of bony. The two of them are close in height, but when Leoti teases up her hair, she appears a good inch taller than her husband. They both seem enamored with one another, though and determined to make their marriage work. Their union cost Rubin his family, all of them appalled by the fact he eloped with a mixed-race girl outside their faith-based religion.

"They have great burgers," Rubin says. "I think you'll like this place."

I nod, looking toward the ceiling, then back to the dance floor.

"Leoti sure is happy to get you out on the town with us."

I'm comfortable enough around Rubin. He's a likable guy, and he loves my sister, but small talk, fluff talk, making conversation, whatever the hell they call it, is not something that comes naturally to me.

"Yeah," I say, digging my fingers inside the tight collar of the sweater, pulling it away from my neck, trying to stretch out the fabric a bit.

Here I sit across from Rubin, wearing Leoti's clothes, makeup applied by Leoti's hand. An outsider might look at me and think I was trying to take over my sister's life. I don't want Leoti's life. I don't want Leoti's husband. I just want to see what it would be like to walk in her shoes. And here I am, literally wearing her shoes.

"So you're thinking about leaving The Community?"

Rubin's question catches me off guard. What all has Leoti told him, I wonder.

Saving me from having to answer Rubin's inquiry, Leoti returns, her hands wrapped around three mugs. She places them on the table, sliding one my way. I pick up the glass, inspecting the contents. Holding the mug to my nose, I sniff over the foam. The scent reminds me of walking through the forest, coming up on an area a skunk has previously sprayed. Above the rim of the glass, I watch Leoti lift her mug and swig, dabbing at her upper lip. I follow her example. Not bad.

"What do you think?" Leoti asks me. She looks at Rubin to explain. "Ama's never had beer before."

"Really?" Rubin asks me.

"The Community doesn't allow alcohol," Leoti tells him.

Rubin looks my way. "Why not? Is it a religious thing?"

"I don't know why," I shrug. "I've never asked." I lift the mug and sip again.

"I think she likes it," Leoti says through a teasing grin.

I look away from her and see a man with orange-red hair striding purposefully toward our table.

"Hey, Rubin. Leoti. Haven't seen you two out in a while."

"Hey there, John," Rubin calls out. "Yeah, I know. Been doing a lot of traveling lately. Haven't had a chance to do much of anything but work. We decided to get out tonight and take Leoti's sister out with us." Rubin gestures my way.

The man twists toward my side of the table and sticks out his hand. "Hey there, I'm John."

"Ama," I say and take his hand.

"So you're Leoti's twin sister," he says, sliding into the booth beside me. John runs a hand up his forehead, the sweat he pushes away spikes the bright hair into points above his pale eyebrows. "I was beginning to think your sister was yanking my chain about you." He looks at Leoti. "You two are identical. Crazy."

"Told you," Leoti laughs. "Where's Mary Kate tonight?"

"She's home with the baby. One of my frat brothers was driving through on his way to Greenville and stopped to visit. She shooed the two of us out of the house. Said we'd keep the baby up all night with our hooting and hollering."

"How is little George?" Leoti inquires.

John lays his arms on the table and clasps his hands. "Doing great. Growing like a weed."

"You just remember, I am available to babysit anytime you guys feel like a night out."

"We may take you up on that offer real soon," John says, swiveling his head quickly. "Tommy," he calls out, signaling another man over.

The man approaches and stands at the end of the booth. In a collective, practically synchronized manner, we all lift our necks to view his face.

"This is my friend, Thomas Fordham. Thomas, this is Rubin and Leoti Shulman. Rubin and I do a lot of work together. Oh, and this is Leoti's sister." John turns to address me. "I'm sorry. Say your name for me again."

"Ama."

"Leoti's sister, Ama," he politely relays.

"Nice to meet you, Thomas," Rubin says, inviting the man to have a seat.

John scoots closer to me as I position myself flush with the wall to make room for the three of us on the bench seat.

"So you guys work together?" Thomas asks Rubin.

"Not exactly," Rubin explains. "I do quite a bit of work for John's company, though."

"Rubin's contract law," John tells Thomas.

"Gotcha," Thomas says, settling back into the bench.

A woman appears table side, her arms stacked in baskets. Leoti directs her as to who ordered what as the woman places the food in front of us.

"We'll let you guys eat," John says, motioning for Thomas to scoot out.

Mouth full, Rubin holds up a palm signaling them to stop. "No, it's fine. Stay put," he tells them, swallowing behind his napkin.

"You sure?" John asks.

"Of course. This place is hopping tonight. You'll not find another table—lucky we got this one."

"Great man, thanks," John says, swiping his brow dry again. "We're going to go order a couple of those burgers. I'll grab another round of drinks for the table."

* * *

THOUGH I SAY LITTLE, because really, what do I have to offer to the conversation, I do enjoy the friendly camaraderie amongst the group. Sipping from my beer mug, which never seems to empty, I listen to their banter. The tension I felt earlier in the evening eases. My whole body relaxes, but skepticism manages to jerk me back into reality from time to time.

Across the table, I see Leoti drain the last of her beer and proclaim the current song to be one of her favorites. She shouts to me. "Come dance with me."

Before I can bat down the command, the men are scooting out of the booth to make way for my exit. Not wanting to make a scene, I slide out, deciding I will plead the need for a bathroom visit. Leoti, however, knows me too well and tugs me onto the dance floor with her.

"Leoti, I don't know how."

"Just do what I do," she directs, taking my hands.

My head feels light, music fills my ears, limbs loosen, and then I am dancing with my sister. As inhibitions fade, I decide this is fun. Leoti laughs, throwing her head back as we dance. I mimic her moves on the crowded dance floor. We bump into other bodies, unbothered when they bump back, apologies unnecessary, and I feel free.

The beat of the music slows. Rubin appears next to us, pulling Leoti into his arms. I back away and start for the table. Thomas stands from the booth and leans down to my ear, asking if I will dance with him. I hesitantly agree, searching the dance floor for Leoti, watching to see how she moves with Rubin. Thomas eases me closer to him, placing one hand low on my back, gently taking my hand into his. Following Leoti's example, I lift my other hand to Thomas's shoulder. I feel the warmth of his breath on my neck as Thomas asks me questions. He wants to know about me, about who I am, what I like to do. I am oddly at ease providing answers and even elaborating on his queries. Thomas is comfortable, unassuming, and I find myself leaning into him, letting him hold me closer. A strange heat floods my body as we sway together and share details about ourselves with one another.

Leoti and Rubin drift closer to us. My sister looks at me and smiles. I see her head snap in the other direction as John taps Rubin's shoulder. Leoti relays John's message to Thomas and me. John has ordered another round; we should go sit with him, she says. Leoti tells us she feels bad his wife isn't here, that Mary Kate had to stay with the baby.

Thomas and I break apart and head to the table. John slides in first, leaving me in the middle seat between him and Thomas. Thinking over the events of the evening, I sip from my beer while the four of them talk. I feel my head grow heavy with thoughts and confusion. I excuse myself, telling the group I'm going to step outside for some fresh air. Thomas asks to accompany. I nod, and we head to the door.

Outside, the night is cold and clear. Stars sprinkle the sky. I remember I'm supposed to be under them, in the woods, sitting and staring into the flames of the fire. Papa would be furious with my actions tonight, consider them an act of personal betrayal. I fold my arms across my body at the thought.

"You cold?" Thomas asks.

"No. I'm used to this weather. I like it." I push my foot over the gravel of the parking lot, rolling the stones under the borrowed shoe.

Thomas stuffs his hands deep into the pockets of his pants. "You know, y'all might be identical, but I don't think you're like your sister."

"No," I clip, biting back my tongue, continuing to walk toward the edge of the parking lot, pace quickening. No, I'm not as pretty as Leoti. I'm not as nice as Leoti. I'm not as sweet and carefree and loving and trusting as Leoti.

"I didn't mean that in a bad way," Thomas says, racing up behind me. "You two just seem to be two different kinds of people."

"We are," I snip. "Leoti's a lot nicer than me. People like her."

"I like you."

I stop, turn, and angle up at him, looking for the meaning of his words on his face.

"I want to kiss you," Thomas says.

I search Thomas's eyes. He means it. I want him to kiss me, I decide. I nod, and he leans down. His lips meet mine, soft and warm. The heat of Thomas's tongue finds mine. In that kiss, I think of Elan, of what he does with the other women in The Community, of the baby he has on the way, and I pull Thomas closer.

"Do you want to sit in my car?" He whispers.

"Yes."

* * *

I ZIP UP THE JEANS, tug my sweater back into place. Thomas sits next to me, quiet. The windows of the car fogged over with our breath, we can't even pretend to stare out at nothing because we're so engrossed by something outside, avoid the inevitable conversation. And so, he starts.

"You okay?" Thomas asks.

"Yeah."

It's over. I've done it. Leoti can no longer taunt me about the virgin thing. I'm still not sure why people make such a fuss about it, though. It's just sex. Leoti says it makes you feel closer to a person, that your whole body aches for more of that person. Maybe it does for her. I don't know why she would lie to me about something like that, but I didn't have those feelings.

"Can I tell you something?" Thomas asks, his tone barely above a whisper.

I nod.

"I've never done this before."

I search his face for the lie, for the truth.

"I mean, I've done some things," Thomas stumbles on, "but not this. And I don't want you to think I don't like you, 'cause I think you're a really nice person."

I turn away from him, feeling the heat of anger boiling up inside me. Am I mad at him? At me? I didn't feel anything special, so why should I be so disappointed that he didn't either? Because I wanted him to like me, regardless of my feelings about him. I wanted to know that I could make a man, any man, feel something for me.

"It's okay, Thomas. I wanted to do this. Not to please you but for me. I'm not going to beg you to marry me. I'm already engaged to someone." I blurt out. I don't want to hear him tell me I'm not good enough, that I'm not his type, whatever the hell it is he wants to get off his chest to make himself feel better.

"Really?" He twists to sit sideways behind the steering wheel. "You're getting married?"

"What? I'm not the marrying type?"

"No. I mean, yes. Yes, you're the marrying type. But why did you do it? Why would you do this with me if you're getting married?"

"Because I wanted to. Because I'd never done this before." I want him to stop looking at me, studying me, judging me. "Because it is an arranged marriage. Because the asshole I'm to marry is already having a baby with someone else." I meet his stare. "Happy? Conscious clear now?" I move to leave.

Thomas grabs my wrist. "Don't go."

I pull from his grasp and sit with my hands in my lap, leaning back into the headrest. The effects of the beer slowly fading, the realization of what has happened grows clearer.

"I'm sorry about this guy. You deserve better than that."

"And how do you know, Thomas? You don't know me. And why would you care? What? Are you going to make regular stops through Waynesville during your travels for a quick lay?"

"No. Wait. Hang on. So, Leoti and Rubin, was their marriage arranged too?"

"No."

"Then why you? Why are you being forced to marry some creep?"

"Because that's what my father wants."

"Christ, Ama. It's 1980. Who gives a shit what your father wants? You don't have to marry someone just because daddy says so. What does your mother say? Is she backing this arrangement?"

"My mother is dead, and even when she was alive, she didn't give a damn about what happened to me."

"I don't get it. You and Leoti are identical twins. Leoti got to choose who she married, but you can't?"

"It's not for you to *get*. And why would you even care to? Just forget it. You had your fun. I got what I needed to do out of the way, and now it's over."

"This is so screwed up." Thomas slouches into the seat. "I would never have pegged you to be a girl who could be easily manipulated."

"Manipulated? Me? No. I have responsibilities bigger than you could ever comprehend."

"That's not how I see it. You're going to marry some guy you don't seem to like, much less love, a guy who seemingly doesn't want you, considering he's impregnated some other woman. Shit, you just gave away your virginity to a stranger rather than the man you're set to marry."

"I don't need you to lecture me about how I conduct myself. Look, let's just move on; you got what you wanted."

"Not really." Thomas releases a heavy sigh.

"What's that supposed to mean?"

"Nothing. I thought maybe this would turn out differently. That's all."

"Well. Sorry, I wasn't good enough for you. Maybe you'll have better luck the next time."

"That's not what I meant. Look, I'm sorry."

"For what? I already told you I wanted to do this."

"I wanted to do it too, but not for the reasons you think."

"We both know you thought I'd be an easy lay. You do some smooth talking, pretend like you're interested—the ugly girl will give it up."

"You're not ugly, and it's not all about you, Ama. Look, I feel like I owe you an explanation."

"You don't owe me jack shit. I wouldn't take anything from you if you did owe me."

"Will you stop for a sec? Just let me get this out."

I sit. I wait. What the hell am I doing? What the hell have I done? And why am I sitting here waiting to be more humiliated than I already am?

Groping for the door handle, I twist in the seat, ready to spring from the car.

"I wanted to try sex with a woman. I thought maybe it might

cure me, might curb my desires. For men." His words tumble out, mix together. I'm not sure I've heard him correctly.

I release the handle and turn back to face him. "What?"

"I like men. I wish I didn't. I thought maybe... maybe if I had sex with a woman, it would change my mind."

"So, when you said you had never done this before, it wasn't that you were a virgin too, it was because you'd never slept with a woman?"

"Yeah."

"You sick, selfish, son-of-a-bitch. You used me."

"You used me too."

My eyes burn, sting with tears. I will not show weakness. I may have made one of the biggest mistakes of my life, but now I know. I know the common world is all Papa says it is. These people are greedy, using one another for their own benefit without thought for another. At least, I felt something for Thomas or thought I felt something for him. I trusted him, let myself open up to him. Shame, betrayal, humiliation, disgust— surge through me, mixing, swirling, flaming.

I grab the door handle and push out. The frigid January air floods the car.

Thomas grabs my hand again, holding me inside. "Come on, Ama. Wait. Don't go like this."

"Why? You afraid I'm gonna tell your buddy?"

"Please don't do that. Ama, I'm sorry. Just, please. Please don't tell John."

I turn to Thomas, grabbing hold of the hand that restrains me. Holding it tight inside both of my own hands, I lock his gaze and speak. "*Dogotsi gha gola ahia sanu. Odali gha gola ugano.*"

"What the hell? What did you say?"

"May all your days and relationships be plagued by misfortune and heartbreak, Thomas Fordham." I drop his hand and twist to step outside. One last time, I look Thomas in the eyes.

"Do me a favor. Tell my sister I went home."

ESME

FEBRUARY

The wood floors are cold beneath my feet. The thermostat isn't programmed to kick up for another hour yet. I pull the tie of the robe tighter around the middle of my body to help take the edge off the chill. We can't afford to heat the house any extra hours of the day right now. Kirby worries hourly about the status of his job. Will tomorrow be the day they hand him his exit papers, or maybe today? I wish I could ease some of the pressure he feels, but the only thing I can do is manage the mundane of our day-to-day lives, make sure he doesn't have to worry about what is going on at home while he's on the road.

I flip on the light in the kitchen and go through the motions of making a pot of coffee. Leaning against the countertop, I wait for the brewing cycle to complete, watching the clock on the microwave tick off the first minutes of the five o'clock hour. I push myself to stand and pull open the cabinet housing the coffee mugs.

How can it only be Tuesday? My body feels as if it should be rounding out the week, not trying to get into the groove of the work-week grind. The bout of flu that has run through the daycare has not helped matters. Somehow Jay has managed to stay healthy, but I can't say the same for myself. The aches, the pains, the chills, and the sweats—the intimate relationship I developed with our bathroom and refuse to discuss with anyone. Fortunately, the virus seems to have run its course, though the exhaustion is still settled deep in my bones. I need to rest, but there isn't time for that.

Valentine's is mere days away, and somehow I've been roped into helping the room mother of Jay's classroom with the celebration this year. Evidently, said room mother, has gotten word that Jay's grandmother owns Yanni's Bakery, and therefore, Yanni's legendary cupcakes would be the 'very best treat' for the class party.

Mama has already done so much for me. Running in and out of this germ-infested house to check on me, bringing me soup, looking after Jay so Kirby doesn't have to take time off work. I hate the thought of asking Mama for another favor.

Moreover, I hate the thought of having to spend any kind of time inside those school walls. Walking through the doors of that school wraps my body in anxiety, like tightly wound cellophane around the middle of a thick-waisted woman hoping to lose body fat. The eyes of Jay's teachers, both past and present, searing my skin. The looks on their faces as they assess my inadequacies with their burning, judgmental glares. If I could make their jobs easier, God knows I would. But what can I do? Me, his own mother, who checks to make sure her bedroom door is locked before turning in for the night.

I can't think of all that now. The house is a wreck. My bible study group meets here on Thursday. Wednesday, I have to be at work early, and that night is the weekly fellowship dinner and service at church. I've only got today to get this place back in order.

Coffee in hand, I pad into the laundry room and throw a load of clothes into the washer. *Do not forget to put those in the dryer before you leave the house this morning.* In the living room, I begin folding the blankets of last night's lounging session. *What I would give to be back on the sofa for a bit.* The carpet in the room needs to have the vacuum run over it, but I don't want to do that just yet. No need to wake Jay too early. *I'll never get my list of chores complete if he gets up now.* If I put lunches together first and clean up the kitchen, I can make the bed, jump in the shower, and get myself dressed, then finish off the rest of the list after he wakes.

I head back to the kitchen to refill my coffee.

* * *

OUTSIDE OUR FRONT DOOR, the cold air slaps my cheeks and stings my eyes. Mrs. Beverly waves from her front yard, her blue bathrobe hanging open and fluttering in the breeze. I look around her yard and home for signs of Mr. Beverly, wondering if something is wrong, if maybe she needs help. *Surely, she wouldn't be out here in this weather wearing only her night clothes if everything was okay.* Mr. Beverly is nowhere to be seen. *Perhaps he's still in bed?*

"Jay, go get in the car. I'll be right there. I need to check on Mrs. Beverly. Something doesn't seem right."

"What? She seems all right to me. Crazy old bat in her bathrobe."

"Just get in the car." I watch him huff away and slam himself inside the car before walking over to our neighbor's yard.

"Good morning, Mrs. Beverly," I call out, crossing the invisible property line between our homes. "How are you today?" A high-pitched squeal seems to be coming from the area where Mrs. Beverly stands.

As she turns to greet me, I see she holds a shoe box in both hands. "Hello there, Esme. I'm doing fine, and you?"

"I'm well. It sure is cold out here this morning, though. You must be freezing. You need something warmer on your body. You'll catch a terrible cold in this weather."

"I'm fine, dear. No need to fuss over me. It's these little ones I'm concerned about." Mrs. Beverly holds out the box for me to view.

I step closer, peeking inside the box. Four tiny, bald baby squirrels nestle close together.

"These sweet babies seem to have fallen out of their mama's nest," Mrs. Beverly relays.

"Isn't it early for babies to be born?"

"Maybe a bit early, but we had a mild beginning to the winter, so mama and daddy probably got an early start on the season." She laughs, looks down at the babies, then back at me. "I walked out to get our paper this morning, and there they were on the ground under the tree."

My chin to the sky, I search the tree limbs and spy a nest high above in the upper branches of the leafless maple.

I look back at Mrs. Beverly, staring into the box. "So what are you going to do? You can't possibly get them back up there."

"Well, in the past, I've just made them a nice little nest box," she waves her hand over the shoe box as if performing a magic trick, "and set it where the mama can find them and get them back into her nest. Figure I'll collect some twigs and leaves, get them settled, then leave the box next to the tree for their mama."

A car door slams behind me. Suddenly, Jay is at my side to inspect what is going on.

"Good morning, Jay," Mrs. Beverly says.

Jay offers little in return. "Hey. What's that?" He points to the box of squealing babies.

"Baby squirrels. See how tiny they are." Mrs. Beverly holds the box to Jay's eye level.

"Yeah. Why do you have them?" Jay asks brusquely. *It's high time for another discussion on respecting elders.*

Mrs. Beverly seems unbothered by Jay's snarky tone. "Sometimes babies fall out of their nest, especially if the wind is strong like it was last night."

"You gonna eat 'em?"

"No." Mrs. Beverly appears taken aback by the question. She pulls the box closer to her and continues. "Why, I'm going to keep them safe in this little box until their mama can come back and get them. They're still too young to be on their own yet."

"Well, good luck with your project Mrs. Beverly. You've got a good heart," I say, offering her a warm smile. "Now, go put on a coat before you go looking for nest materials."

She smiles, clutching the box protectively. "I'll do that, dear."

I look at Jay. "Jay, we need to get a move on, or you're going to be late for school." He slugs back toward the car. I look to Mrs. Beverly. "Have a good day, Mrs. Beverly. Take care of yourself."

"See you soon, dear."

* * *

DINNER DISHES dry and back in the cabinets, I look out the kitchen window, trying to recall what it was I intended to do next. The dark of night outside doesn't trigger any memories but rather a tired ache at the base of my spine. Time change can't come soon enough for me. I need more hours in my day, but some extra daylight would at least be helpful.

I lean over the kitchen counter and notice the mail isn't in its usual spot.

I call to Jay in the living room. "Jay, where did you put the mail?"

"What mail?"

I walk around the counter and through the door to the living room, trying to save the little voice I have left, my throat raw and swollen. My weak immune system seems to have been unable to stave off the cold I most certainly feel coming on.

"The mail I asked you to grab for me earlier. It's not on the kitchen counter."

"I didn't do it."

I lean over the back of the sofa, looking at where Jay sits on the floor, the television on in front of him. "You didn't get the mail? Why not?"

Jay stares at his lap, unbothered to look at me as he says, "I didn't feel like it. Get it yourself."

That feeling washes over me. The one that sounds warning alarms in the back of my head. Something is not right with this situation. Jay isn't focused on the television. Instead, he stares at the object in his hands, and whatever it is, Jay obviously doesn't want me to see it. With his back to me, I check the areas surrounding him, looking for clues as to why I can't shake the uncomfortable sensation gripping my shoulders. *Uh-huh.* The handle of my kitchen scissors pokes out from underneath his crisscrossed legs. Jay didn't get them tucked in far enough. *But, what is he doing with my scissors?*

And, what else is hiding from me?

I push myself back to standing and hesitantly step around the sofa. In order to get a better look, I make my way to stand in front of the fireplace, pretending to warm myself from the heat it emits. In Jay's lap is a small brown doll. Though I can't make out any other details, the doll seems familiar somehow.

"Jay, what have you got there?" I ask, my voice barely above a whisper.

"Some kind of old doll," he answers, keeping his focus on the object.

"Where did you get it?"

"It's mine," he screams.

"I never said it wasn't, Jay. I asked you where you got it—and there's no need for you to raise your voice."

Jay raises his eyes to meet mine. "I found it." The menacing glare chills me through despite the heat from the fire behind me.

I rub my upper arms to ease the gripping tension that has taken hold. "Where did you find it?" I ask, slow and careful, trying to withhold any hint of accusation.

Jay looks down at the doll then back up at me. "Grandma's house."

Maybe that's why I thought I recognized the doll. My shoulders ease, and the breath I've been holding slowly leaves my lungs. I'll ask my mother about it later, find out if she gave Jay the doll while I was in bed with the flu. The task still remains, however, of getting those scissors away from him. I proceed with caution.

"Oh, okay," I say, hoping to deflect an episode. "Hey, are those my kitchen scissors? I've been looking all over for them." I bend quickly and jerk them from underneath his leg. "How'd they get out here?" The question, rhetorical and fake sounding even to me.

"I took them," he answers, locking the stony and vacant glare on me once more. "I thought you were going to get the mail."

"That's right. I knew I was doing something." I turn toward the front door, grab my coat, and head outside, stuffing the scissors into my coat pocket as I make my way down the porch steps.

Across the yard, I see Mr. Beverly, hunched over his front-wheeled walker, slowly shuffling down the walk toward the street. The wheels squeak with the exertion of the activity. It doesn't take me long to catch up to him. I slow my pace to match his and speak.

"Hello, Mr. Beverly. How are you this evening?"

He stops to answer. "I've been better, but why complain? Nobody likes a whiner." Mr. Beverly scoots forward again.

"I guess you're right about that. Only makes you feel worse to complain, is what I've discovered."

"Yep, yep, does indeed," he says, making it to his mailbox.

"And God doesn't give us more than we can handle, right." I step over to my box, popping open the lid. Retrieving the leaflets and envelopes, I turn to wait while he digs inside his box pulling out much of the same.

"I guess so." He shoves the mail underneath his arm to begin the shuffle back to his front door.

"Did Mrs. Beverly's little squirrels make it back into the nest?"

Mr. Beverly stops and lifts his shoulders a bit to meet my eyes. The crease in his brow deepens.

"Damnedest thing, I tell you. Martha's been watching that

box all day. Front door kept creaking open and groaning shut, waking me up just as I dozed off. No mama squirrel showed up the whole long day. Martha wouldn't even let me go out and check the mail earlier, thought I might scare off the mama. Then Martha went out to check on 'em again about an hour ago and found all of 'em dead."

"Oh no. Was it too cold for them out of the nest?"

"Nope, nothing like that. Their little heads were off their bodies. Martha thinks maybe a 'coon must have gotten to them."

"You mean, like, a raccoon bit their heads off?"

"Well, that's the thing. I didn't want to say this to Martha, but those babies looked like something had taken and cut their heads from their little bodies. Didn't look like no bite marks on them to me. 'Sides, if a 'coon had gotten to 'em, it would have eaten them, not taken their heads off and left." Mr. Beverly shakes his head. "Martha's beside herself. Says it's her fault for leaving them unprotected."

Mr. Beverly turns back to his walker, the wheels slowly roll forward again. I watch until he makes it to his front door to be sure he gets in okay.

As he reaches for the doorknob, I call to him. "Please tell Mrs. Beverly I'm praying for her."

Once Mr. Beverly is safely behind his door, I reach into my coat pocket, feeling the outline of the scissors inside. Horrific scenarios run through my mind. I've heard about disturbed children doing harm to animals, but surely Jay wouldn't do something so terrible. He has his moments, yes. But to cut the heads off baby squirrels, that's the work of someone more sinister than my son. My fingers fumble over the lip of the pocket. Reaching inside, I pull out the scissors. I turn toward the street lamp and hold them up to the light, inspecting the blades for blood or some other tale-tell sign. A deep, steamy sigh of relief exits into the cold night air. The scissors are clean.

I shove them back into my pocket and head inside to get Jay ready for bed. I open the door and look to the spot on the living room floor where I left Jay only minutes ago, but he's gone. Hanging my coat, I retrieve the scissors and think of the doll Jay tried to hide from me. I search the floor, under the table, and the sofa. He's taken it. *Why is he hiding this doll?*

I check the clock on the mantel. Seven-thirty. I place the scissors behind the clock where Jay would not think to look for them. Turning in the direction of the hallway, I open my mouth to yell to Jay and feel my throat burn at the thought of the action. Instead, I walk toward the back of the house, searching him out.

Standing inside Jay's bedroom door, I do a quick scan and find him hunched down on the other side of the bed, his head barely visible over the top of the mattress.

"This room is a wreck, Jay. I asked you to clean it earlier."

"So."

I step over and around the mess, nearing the bed. "What are you doing over there?"

"Nothing."

"Well, it's time to get in the shower."

"I'm not dirty. I don't need a shower."

"I don't care if you think you need one or not. You're going to take a shower. There are too many germs floating around this time of year. Now go."

Jay uses the edge of the bed to push himself upright and stomps past me down the hall in the direction opposite the bathroom. I throw my head back, saying a silent prayer, then follow him through the house.

In the kitchen, Jay stands at the counter, his hands thrust deep inside his backpack.

"Jay, what are you doing? I asked you to get in the shower."

"And I told you I don't need one," Jay spouts, his eyes fixed on something inside the bag.

I grab the bag from his hold. "It's not up for debate. Go. Get. In. The. Shower."

Jay yanks the bag away. "You better watch yourself. Don't. Touch. My. Shit."

He flings the bag at his side. It hits me, knocking me off balance. I right myself, watching Jay plod down the hallway toward his room.

Deciding we both need a moment to cool down, I walk in the other direction. In the laundry room, I grab the clothes I threw into the dryer earlier this morning. I carry the clean laundry to the room Kirby and I share, toss them onto the bed, and begin the process of folding and sorting. Across the way, I hear Jay in his room banging the drawers of his dresser. The slamming of the bathroom door follows.

I work to put away the clothes that belong in our room, then grab Jay's stack of clean laundry to take to his room. Before entering the hallway, I listen. The spray of the shower starts, and I ease down the hall toward the bathroom. Halting outside the door, I wait to hear the curtain pulled back and forth to be sure Jay actually gets into the shower.

I leave the door and trek down the hall to Jay's room. At the door, I stop—the mess before me appalling. *He's done nothing I've asked him today.* I don't know why I thought he would have picked up his room as I had asked after dinner or that it would somehow have miraculously occurred in the short time he was preparing for his shower. I toe around the mess to the dresser and place his clean clothes inside.

I scan the room again. *I'll do it myself. The task will be far easier than the argument that will follow if I ask again.*

I toss toys into the chest inside the closet. Pick up shoes and clothes from the floor, hanging the clean, throwing the dirty into the hamper. On the other side of Jay's bed where I found him sitting earlier, I find an empty bag of potato chips, remnants of the snack scattered along the floor. I drop to hands and knees, working to gather up the bits and pieces, sticking them back inside the empty bag. I run my hand under the bed, fingers feeling out more scraps that might attract bugs. Reaching deeper underneath the bed, my arm extended, my fingertips brush against something hard. It feels like a long piece of wood. I lean further into the edge of the bed and push my arm as far as it will physically go. I grasp the object and pull back. A ruler.

I sit with my back against the bed and examine the long, thin measuring tool. It's an older ruler—one edge wood, the other a sharp aluminum for tearing straight paper. *Where did this come from?* I've only purchased plastic rulers for Jay's school supply lists. I run my finger along the wood side marked by the tiny centimeters trying to detract my eyes from the silver edge divvied to measure inches. Some sort of dark sticky substance covers the top six inches of the ruler. Hesitantly, I use my pointer finger to touch the metal edge of the ruler. Semi-soft and a bit gooey, it feels as if it's beginning to crust.

And then I realize, it's blood.

I look up to see Jay standing next to me.

"What are you doing?" Jay's eyes, typically so cold and expressionless, blaze with a heat I've never witnessed before.

Fear and disgust and anger roll through my body, mixing and sloshing into a rage I don't understand or even know how to handle. "No, Jay. The question is, what did you do?"

"I told you not to touch my stuff."

"I was cleaning your room, Jay," I yell, ignoring the pain at the back of my throat. "Remember. I asked you to do it, and you completely disregarded my request. So, here I am, cleaning up your filth, and I find this." I wave the bloodied end of the ruler at him.

Jay watches me. The heat of his anger disappears as quickly as it came on. He holds his body stiff, frozen, expressionless, a wax figure without emotion.

"Where did you get this ruler, Jay?"

He doesn't move. He doesn't answer. He holds position, his eyes focused on me.

I lower the ruler and inhale deeply, hoping to draw in a sense of calm. The last thing I want right now is to enrage Jay while he stands over me. I don't think I have the strength to fight Jay off if he goes into one of his fits and attacks me. But I have to know. I have to know what Jay is capable of, whether I wish to know or not. Ultimately, I am responsible for his actions. I am his mother.

I stand. "Jay, did you find Mrs. Beverly's squirrels?" I ask slowly and without judgment.

"Yes."

"Did you do something to those baby squirrels, Jay?"

"I took them out of the box."

"Why?"

"I wanted to hear them cry," Jay says, his eyes blank, a green soulless void.

"Did you hurt them?"

"I squeezed it. It died."

"What about the others? Did you squeeze them too?"

"Only one other one."

My heart races. *And what about the other two?* I'm frightened, scared of what he will say, of how I will react, of what Jay will do after he tells me.

"Did you put the dead squirrels back in the box?"

"Yes. After I cut their heads off."

"And you used this ruler to do that?"

"Yes."

My eyes burn with tears. I breathe around the lump welling at the back of my throat, fear weighing down my lungs.

"And what about the other babies?"

"I cut their necks off too, but while they were still alive."

The wet heat of tears trails over my cheeks. "Why?"

"I wanted to know if they would scream," his declaration unfaltering and sedate.

MEREL

FEBRUARY

The classroom buzzes with noise and activity: students chatting happily as they work, room parents patiently aiding children, two blowdryers whirring at stations set up in the corners of the classroom to dry craft projects. Using the money collected earlier in the school year for holiday events, the room parents purchased the materials for the kids to make miniature jewelry boxes as Valentine's gifts for their parents. In addition, the room parents supplied the students with bags to decorate so they could wrap their presents.

I walk the room, oohing and awing over the children's creativity and hard work.

"Ms. S," one of my students calls for me, requesting I view what they've created.

I turn. It's Jay. My jaw tightens in response.

"Did you see my project, Ms. S?"

I stop beside Jay's desk. "I didn't."

I catch myself crossing my arms, and bring them back to my sides as I quickly glance to see where Jay's mother is located in the room. I'm actually surprised Jay's mom is helping out with the holiday celebration. She's not done much in the way of classroom volunteering and, of late, seems to be growing more at odds with me in regard to her son's behavior. While Jay's mother never responded to the message about Jay stomping a frog to death on the playground (leaving me to wonder if she even got the incident report), she tersely replied to my inquiry about the doll in Jay's backpack—firmly denying that Jay would take someone's doll as 'Jay does not play with dolls,' that I must be confusing him with another child. Though I am trying to remain tolerant and unbiased of both Jay's and his mother's conduct, my patience is waning.

"Would you like to show it to me?" My tongue pokes at the inside of my cheek as I take in a deep breath.

"Yes," he says, keeping the box from my view.

"Well, why don't you pull it out of the bag so I can take a look?" I tilt my head to the side, feigning interest, fighting an eye roll.

"Okay. But, don't tell my mom."

I watch him, my eyebrows drawing up in question.

"It's not for her," Jay explains.

"Why not?"

Jay's focus narrows. "It's not like she'd be surprised," he says, with a sarcastic edge most of my second graders haven't accomplished yet. "She's here, duh."

I ignore the disrespectful remark rather than create a scene in front of the parents roaming the classroom. "Okay. Then what are you planning to do with your box?"

Jay's never-blinking glare pierces me. "I'm going to use it to hide things."

"Let's see it then," I challenge. Jay's menacing stare-downs may be unnerving to others, but I've grown accustomed to them over the last months. It's what he's doing when I'm not watching him that unsettles me.

Jay reaches into his bag and pulls out the cardboard, heart-shaped box. Unlike his classmates, who covered their hearts in fabric, Jay has painted his box black. The instructions for the project were to fabric-cover or paint the box, then decorate the lid of the heart using the sparkly beads, sequins, and glitter glue available. Jay strategically holds his hand over the lid of the heart, careful not to display his creativity until he is ready. Jay meets my eyes to be sure I am watching his big unveiling.

Using green glitter glue, Jay has formed a single eye on the center of the lid. He cleverly left the center of the eye black to mark the pupil. Pink beads have been adhered to form a large X over the eye.

The eye immediately brings to mind my missing doll, Poppy. "Makes me think of the doll you had in your backpack." The snide remark rolls out before I have a chance to bite down on it. "Where is that doll, Jay?"

"I can't talk about it."

"Why not? Such an unusual doll—I'd like to see it again."

"I. Told. You. I. Can't. Talk. About. It." Jay's voice rises with each word he spits forth.

My gaze bounces over the room to see if we have drawn attention. Everyone remains focused on the tasks at hand. I drop the topic for now.

"Are you going to decorate your bag?"

"Nope." Jay snatches his box and stuffs it inside the bag.

Exasperated by the exchange, I leave Jay and continue my rounds. A knock sounds at the classroom door. I look in that direction, then around the room, checking to see if another head turns toward the entrance. The pounding grows louder, yet no one else seems to notice the forceful thump. It's possible, given the noise level in the room, no one else has heard. Is there someone at the door, or is this another ploy of my mind?

While the mothers continue to help the children, I edge toward the door. With each step, the knocking becomes more pronounced, forceful. I peek through the small rectangular window into the hallway outside. A few children on restroom breaks travel the corridor. Hand on the handle of the door, my eyes rove over the room to see if anyone looks my way. I ease the door open, looking in both directions of the hallway, no one nearby. The knocking continues as I shut the door, standing, holding firmly to the door handle. The lids of my eyes fall heavily as I work to shush the noise, trying to recover from the obtrusive, never-ceasing pounding in my head that has plagued me these last months.

A hand braces my shoulder. I jump in response.

"I'm so sorry. I didn't mean to startle you, Ms. S." Mitchell's mother studies with me with concern.

"Oh, no. You're fine. Just caught me off guard. I thought I heard someone at the door," I explain, regaining my composure.

"I think the children are about done. They keep asking about passing out their Valentine cards."

"Of course." I twist away from her scrutiny to survey the progress. "Once we get everything tidy, we'll be ready to do just that."

"I'll get the parents started on clean-up," she says, taking quick leave.

Projects completed, the students grow restless with nothing to keep them occupied. I hurry along the cleanup process to curb the bustle. The room parents work to collect the remaining materials, clearing away the mess of the craft. As the last desk is cleared and the projects have been safely stored, I call the class to order and convey instructions for how the next portion of the party will proceed.

One by one, I call the tables to retrieve their special Valentine mailboxes from the cubby area to place at their desks. The last group returns to their seats. And so, the chaos must begin. I pull a smile onto my face and announce it is time to deliver our Valentine's cards. Chairs scrape along the concrete floor as the students push back from their desks, eager to get started. I remind the few who have not heeded instructions to come back and push chairs under desks so as not to create a trip hazard.

When all the students are finally on task, I grab my stack of cards to begin depositing them into the children's handmade Valentine's boxes. The students are enjoying the activity. They giggle behind their toothless little smiles, announcing to me proudly when they deliver the card they have for me into the box I constructed late last night. All is going smoothly, given the commotion. Even Jay seems to be behaving. Still, I keep him in the corner of my vision. Maybe it's the presence of his mother in the room that has him exhibiting model student behavior. The thought makes me consider encouraging her to do more volunteer work inside the classroom.

I finish the delivery of my cards much faster than the students. So as not to appear standoffish and rude, I walk to the vicinity of where the room parents congregate, hoping to perhaps join their conversation. Dorothy recently explained a sure-fire way to be hired on for next year is to receive compliments from parents, which in turn spurs teacher requests from the parents of rising students. According to Dorothy, the best way to accomplish a teacher request is to remain approachable.

The parents stand at the edge of the room, perched against the wall and closed door to the shared office. They have dressed for the celebration, decked out in red and pink, flashy jewelry to complement, not a hair on their heads out of place. Now that the craft is finished, they've paired off, heads close, each set holding deeply engaging conversations from the intent looks on their faces. Clearly, I am not going to be welcomed to chit-chat, and truth be told, I don't want to be part of their conversations.

I want to go behind that door they block, close myself away in the office. I want to stretch out on the floor and close my eyes. Just for a few minutes, just close my eyes. Not sleep. In waking rest, I can control my thoughts; well, at least push them away. But the moment I drift into unconsciousness, the dreams snake in— coiling, squeezing, choking out my efforts to forget, to move on. The dreams, or rather nightmares, are vicious in their undertaking to drag me back into that time, that place.

Still, I linger, hoping to be noticed, to belong. Back in my parenting days, I was always the outsider—never quite fitting in, awkward and unsure about how to navigate the social circles and cliques of the school parents. I foolishly believed as the head of a classroom, I wouldn't have to worry over such trivialities. Yet, here I am, ever the outsider.

I dawdle around the horseshoe reading table where the room parents have laid out the party treats, scrutinizing the *fabulous* cupcakes we've been promised. I pretend not to be interested in their conversations, attempt to convey I've completely tuned them out, that all of my attention is on the students. I catch the eye of sweet, little Winston, giving him a smile and a thumbs up.

In my peripheral vision, I see Caroline's mom lean close to Jay's mother then hear her confide, "I don't know how teachers do this day in and day out. I can barely control my own child, much-less twenty-one others who don't belong to me."

"I know," Jay's mom agrees. "If it weren't for the Xanax, I don't know how I'd get through the weekends," she confesses.

Under lifting brows, my eyes widen. Now, I know her secret —how Jay's mom makes it through the day with that child.

Caroline's mom laughs at the divulgence.

"No, seriously," Jay's mom says. "I'd have popped one before coming today, but I can't find them." She touches the arm of Caroline's mother in a show of confidence. "And, I just had that prescription filled. I'm sure I'll be turning the house upside down when I get home." The two laugh conspiratorially.

The knocking begins again. With my back to the room mothers, my head down, I close my eyes to the noise. The attempts to silence it do not work.

"Would you like me to get that, Ms. S?" Caroline's mother asks above the racket of the students.

I turn, realizing the parents have heard the knock as well. I haven't imagined it this time.

"Yes, please."

Caroline's mother pulls the door open for Amelia's mom to enter. She holds firmly to the tiny blanketed bundle in her arms. I try to curb my irritation with the intrusion. During the parent meeting at the beginning of the school year, I requested parents not bring siblings to classroom celebrations, so as to foster the students' feelings of importance in that the celebrations are about them. It wasn't all about the students, though. I have my own selfish reasonings for the request. Parents expect me to call down their students, but I have zero control over their other children, not to mention the added layer of chaos siblings present.

From the other side of the room, Amelia spots her mother and baby brother. The smile on her face defuses my annoyance.

"M-Mommy! You came." Amelia rushes across the room, throwing her arms around her mother's waist.

Amelia's little brother was born in late November. The arrival of the new baby has kept Amelia's mom from having the time to volunteer inside the classroom. Before the birth of little Joey, Amelia's mom, Belle, was one of my best parent volunteers. Belle quickly became my favorite student parent, so genuine and caring with each student, so eager and committed to each child's learning. Most of the parents seem to care only about logging volunteer hours into the PTA handbook, but Belle was always earnest in her desire to help the students.

Belle hugs Amelia, offering hellos to the other mothers. She looks at me, her face apologetic. "I hope it's okay I brought Joey. I know you said no siblings at parties, but Amelia wanted to show everyone her baby brother, and I missed seeing the kids."

Suddenly, I realize how much I've missed Belle's company. Under other circumstances, we both might feel comfortable to call the other a friend. Perhaps when Amelia moves on to third grade, we will feel more at ease with the idea. "Of course. We've heard so much about this little guy, every milestone, in fact. Amelia loves to talk about him."

"I'm going to finish delivering my Valentines," Amelia tells her mother. "Then can we show Joey to my friends?" She asks Belle without a stammer; Amelia's work with the speech therapist seems to be paying off.

"Yes, sweetie," Belle says patiently, holding tight to little Joey.

The other mothers crowd around Belle, cooing over the baby,

sharing the stories of their children's baby stages. I stand to the side, letting them carry on, turning my attention to the students as they finish up with their deliveries.

As most of them return to stand at their tables, shaking their boxes, anxious to see their cards, I issue a two-minute warning.

"Does that mean we're about ready to deliver snacks?" Mitchell's mother hurries over to ask.

"Indeed. I'm going to get the students settled at their desks, and when everyone is seated, go ahead."

Mitchell's mother nods and turns to relay the game plan to the other mothers.

The students happily oblige my directions, waiting patiently for their snacks to be served. I glance at the clock. Forty minutes until dismissal. I wanted to wrap this party up right before the end of the school day, but at this rate, we'll be cutting it close.

"How were your holidays? It's been forever since I've seen you." Belle pulls me out of my thoughts.

I turn to her. "Quiet. I'm sure a lot quieter than yours," I say, nodding at the baby in her arms.

"Yes, things have been harried around our house these last couple of months."

"Mommy," Amelia calls across the classroom. "Will you come help me with my juice packet?"

Belle nods to Amelia and turns to address me. "Amelia loves her little brother, but I do feel like she's starting to compete for attention. Do you mind holding Joey for a minute?"

"Sure," I agree, reaching out to accept the baby from her.

Belle hurries over to Amelia's desk, then takes a moment to talk with the children. Amelia wants to show her mother all the cards she has in her box.

I wait for Belle's return, holding Joey, looking down at the pair of brilliant blue eyes focused so intently on me. Pulling him closer to my face, I smell the powdery sweet baby scent. His little cheeks, so rosy and full as his tiny lips form a smile. "You are a precious little thing. So small, yet so full of possibility." Memories flood my thoughts, cloud my eyes. *We had so many dreams, held so much hope. We made plans, had solid visions of the future, thought nothing could hurt us, that we knew exactly what we were doing.*

I feel a tap on my arm and look to see Amelia has come up beside me, Belle heading toward us.

"Merel, are you okay?" Belle asks.

I realize my cheeks are wet. Unable to brush away the tears, I must address the embarrassment of my emotions. "Yes, of course. I'm fine. I guess I was lost in my memories. It's been a long time since I held a baby."

Amelia tugs at her mother. "Now, Mommy. I want to show my friends Jay."

Eyes wide with confusion at Amelia's announcement, I pull the baby close to my body. "What? Belle, I don't think that's a good idea."

Belle's face falls, a frown tugging at the corners of her mouth. "You don't want Amelia to show her friends the baby?"

"No. I mean, yes. She can do that. I..." I pause to think about how to phrase my thoughts, scanning quickly to see where Jay's mother is in the room. "I don't think it's a good idea for her to let Jay see the baby," I whisper.

Belle laughs, "No, Amelia is saying she wants her friends to see Jay. She's been hung up on giving him a nickname." Belle's eyes search my face for understanding. "That's what Amelia calls Joey—J."

The baby in my arms feels heavy. His little body so hot, I feel like I'm holding a smoldering log. I quickly pass him to his mother and step aside, swiping my fingertips over my face.

Watching them walk away, I think no. No, Belle should not let Amelia do that.

AMA

OCTOBER 1980

Solace eludes me. I can no longer find it—not in my cabin, not in the woods, not in front of the flames of the fire. I cannot sit, yet lying down provides no relief and walking only brings pain. It's punishment. I feel it deep in my bones, the ache tearing at me from the inside, my midsection constricting, pulling tighter and tighter. It's punishment for losing faith in The Community, in Papa, in who I am, in where I belong.

If I could change one day in my life, it would be that day. The day I defied my father and The Community, my future husband, my legacy. What's done can't be undone. I know that. But now, I don't know what to do. Conjures, herbal remedies—nothing I've tried has worked, and now I must face what is to come.

The walls of my cabin close in around me, the air sucked from the room. I can't stay here. I need Leoti. Will she see me? We haven't spoken since the night at the Burger Palace. I gave her no explanation for leaving that night and, to this day, no reason as to why I haven't visited in all these months.

I told myself I needed time, that Leoti and I needed distance, just as Papa had been trying to tell me all along. Splitting myself between the two lifestyles had bred confusion and doubt. I had to wholly and completely immerse myself back into the only place that accepted me for who I am. So I buried myself in duties to The Community, convinced myself I didn't have the time to see Leoti even if I hadn't imposed the temporary separation.

For the first month, I felt I was growing, evolving, becoming stronger somehow. Then our birthday came 'round, the first birthday I didn't spend in the company of my sister. Even Papa questioned my actions, though he didn't press me to go and see her either. I think it made Papa happy to see my renewed commitment to The Community.

As one day carried into another, I began to worry I had waited too long. Would Leoti be angry with me? Would she push me away if I turned up to say hello, to see how she was faring?

But right now, I need her, regardless of how she will react. I wipe the perspiration from my forehead, grab my jacket from the chair beside the door, and make the trek through the woods to Waynesville, to Leoti.

* * *

Outside Leoti's front door, I question what I am doing here, if I'm doing the right thing. Leoti flings open the door, the opportunity to flee gone. She stands rigid on the other side of the screen door, glaring through narrowed eyes.

"What are you doing here?" The second entryway acts as Leoti's protective barrier.

"Can I come in?"

Leoti stands firm, unmoving, eyes hard, but I see the hurt behind them.

"Please."

"Why now, Ama? Daddy piss you off again?"

"Just let me in."

"Are you kidding me? You ran off all those months ago, and then out of the blue, turn up on my doorstep without even an apology—just a 'let me in,' like I'm the rude one?"

"There's a lot you don't know."

"Then there's a lot you didn't tell me."

Even though Leoti holds her position, I can tell she's softening. I wait, hoping I won't have to stand here much longer. The pain is building again, and I know from previous bouts I don't have much time. I may have been able to conceal my ailments in the last months, but that was mere discomfort compared to the agony I feel at the moment.

I back out of the way as the screen door creaks open, then quickly dart inside before Leoti changes her mind. In the kitchen, I wait for Leoti to secure her entryway and join me. The latch on the door clicks into place. She tentatively walks toward my direction, keeping her distance, closing herself off inside folded arms.

"What happened that night, Ama? I was worried sick, you know."

"I told that guy to tell you I went home."

"You mean Thomas?"

"Yeah, him." I refuse to utter his name ever again. Just hearing it come off Leoti's tongue makes my stomach roll.

"He told me," she states matter-of-factly, moving to lean against the kitchen counter. "So, Rubin and I rushed straight home to check on you. And guess what? You weren't here." Her face flushes with anger. "So, we waited. And waited. And still, no Ama. I made Rubin drive me up to The Community, Ama, and you know how Rubin feels about The Community. Knocked on Daddy's door. Asked him if you were there. You know what he said to me?"

Leoti waits.

I wait.

"He said, 'You're not welcome here.' Not to me. To Rubin. My father looked my husband—the man I love with all my heart —dead in the eyes and told him he wasn't welcome inside The Community. I told him, 'If Rubin isn't welcome, then neither am I.' Did he tell you any of this?"

"No."

"Unbelievable."

Leoti turns, opens a cabinet as if searching for something, then slams it shut. She walks circles in the middle of her kitchen while I stand aside and watch.

"So he never bothered to tell you I came looking for you, that I was worried about you?"

"No." I had no idea Papa had even seen Leoti that night. I only knew he hadn't mentioned her, and I hadn't even realized that until a few months had gone by.

"So you're saying Papa knew I had been with you that night?" I ask to further clarify our father's position.

"Yes," Leoti leans against the countertop again, folds her arms again.

Papa never said anything to me about that night. As far as I was concerned, Papa didn't know I had even left our land to go to town. I had told him I was going to the woods for the evening, to reflect in the flames of a ceremonial fire. Papa never questioned me about the fact I had lied to him. What else does Papa know? We haven't had much communication lately. I've stayed busy, kept to myself. Has he guessed? No one else seems to have noticed. I've kept my condition hidden pretty well. Big loose clothes. I'm barely showing. I've only eaten when necessary, hoping somehow I might starve this thing out of my body. But it's there, no intentions of going anywhere until it is good and ready.

"Did you tell Papa what we did that night?"

"No, Ama." Leoti throws her arms up and flings them back down, slapping the sides of her thighs. "Are you hearing me? That was the worst night of my life. I lost my father and my sister that night. I've been living all these months believing my whole family left me." Tears streak her face.

"I'd never abandon you, Leoti."

"But you did, Ama. You walked out of the bar and left and never looked back. Didn't bother to even tell me, and then for all I knew, you told Papa you didn't want to see me. For months, I've been going over every word said that night, every conversation that led up to that night, trying to figure out why you would do that to me. I always thought no one could come between us." She turns to the counter to rip a paper towel from the roll and dabs at her eyes, wipes her nose.

"Leoti, I'm sorry. Really, I am. I had no idea you'd feel this way or believed I would hurt you like that."

"What happened, Ama? What made you leave and not want to see me again?"

I lower my head, looking at my hands, picking at my fingertips. "I needed to find my way back."

"You did. You made it back to The Community, and then I found you, and you refused to see me."

"No, that's not what I mean." I raise my eyes to meet Leoti's. "You're not hearing me. I had been struggling with where I belonged. I didn't feel like I fit in anywhere. I thought you understood. That's why I agreed to go out with you and Rubin, to let you dress me, to meet your friends. And when I walked out of the bar, I knew I didn't belong in your world. I had to separate myself for a while. Please, Leoti. It had nothing to do with you."

Now, Leoti refuses to meet my gaze. She's struggling. She's hurt. It's all because of me. I did this to her.

"I've missed you, Leoti. More than you can imagine."

"I don't think so. I'm pretty sure I've missed you more," Leoti lifts her head, offering a crooked smile.

I return a smirk. It's a game we've played for years, a signal to end our disagreements. She's forgiven me.

"What are you wearing? Have you been to a funeral?"

"Yeah, like every day," I answer sarcastically, though it's the truth, really. Every day since I realized this thing was in me, has felt like the end of my life. If I ever get it out of me, maybe I'll finally be able to live again. "Where's Rubin?"

"At work—where he usually is on a Tuesday afternoon at three o'clock."

"Who's running the bakery?"

"The girl I hired to help me out six months ago. What's with all the questions?" Leoti asks. She turns and busies herself putting together a snack. I haven't the heart to tell her I couldn't eat right now if I were half starved to death—which is how I feel, how I am, how I look underneath this sheath.

"Just curious. I went by the bakery first, thought you'd be there. The girl said you'd left already, so I came here. I figured maybe Rubin might have been home with you, is all." I'm glad he's not, though. Better yet would be that he is out of town for the evening, but I can't inquire about his actions again. Leoti will know I am up to something, and I can't tell her. She can't ever know. No one can ever know.

Pain rips through my lower body. My pelvis feels like it is going to break apart at any moment. Head down, I pull a chair out from under the dining room table and sit. Relief does not come. I stand again and walk to the window to look out at the backyard. My face turned away from Leoti, I let the grimace I've been hiding form. The noise of Leoti pulling out glasses and plates, going through her cabinets disguises the deep breaths I draw to ride through the pain.

As I stare out the window, harnessing energy from the landscape, the contraction subsides. This view is familiar, calming. It dawns on me, it was one year ago, on an October afternoon much like this one, I sat at Leoti's dining table and performed the bone reading. I told Leoti she would be the mother of a little girl but didn't tell her my spirit guide said it wouldn't be Rubin's child. Leoti is still childless. For all I know, though, they could be in the process of adoption.

I turn, using the chair at the table for support, holding onto the high back to conceal my midsection. "How are you?" I ask, genuinely interested. I've missed my sister. Regardless of how I feel about the way she lives, where she lives, Leoti is the person I care most about in this world.

"Ama, what the hell is going on with you?"

"Far be it for me to want to know what is going on with my sister," I snip, trying to turn her attention away from me. It would kill Leoti to know I have what she wants most, a thing I only want gone, to be done with. With any grace left in this world, it will be after tonight.

"I realize it's been a while since we've seen each other, but you've never been one for polite chit-chat. Cut the bullshit. Something's going on with you."

"I haven't been feeling well." I drop my body back into the chair, able to sit once again, hiding the lump in my middle under the table.

"Are you sick?" Leoti walks to stand beside me, laying her hand across my forehead. "You're not feverish. What is it? Your stomach? Throat?" Leoti backs away from my chair. "Oh my god, it's not the flu, is it? I cannot get the flu going into the holidays. I can't run the bakery with the flu. Not that I'm trying to be insensitive. I will take care of you. I want to. But I have to keep my distance. Do you think it's the flu?"

Without realizing it, Leoti has given me the perfect out. "I'm afraid it might be, but I'm not familiar with the symptoms."

"Body aches, chills, nausea, cough, trouble breathing, vomiting, diarrhea. Do you have a headache? Is your nose running? Are you tired?"

"I guess." I fake a cough behind my hand.

"Come on. I'm putting you to bed. The guest room is all setup. I'm glad you came here. I'll take care of you. God only knows what kind of medical care you'd get in The Community," she says, a sneer on her face. "But, now, don't get offended if I have a bandana around my face when I come into your room. Nothing personal, but I am way too busy right now to get sick."

I heave myself from the chair, no need to conceal the body aches Leoti assumes are a side effect of the flu. Keeping her head turned away, Leoti takes my elbow, guiding me through the hallway.

* * *

I MAKE my way to the guest room while Leoti hurries off to collect one of her nightgowns. She insists it will be more comfortable and 'far less depressing than that black funeral getup.' As Leoti hands off the gown, I request a glass of water. She rushes off to fetch it while I quickly disrobe and change into the gown, then situate myself under the covers of the bed before she returns.

Leoti places the water glass on the nightstand then perches on the edge of the bed. The red bandana covering her nose and mouth muffles her voice.

"I'll be right in the kitchen. I'm going to get dinner started. Rubin wants pork chops tonight. Do you think you might be able to eat those? No, you can't eat those. I'll fix you something else."

"You look like you're about to rob a bank."

"If I get sick, I'll be robbing myself of business."

"I'm sorry I brought this into your house." Leoti won't get the flu from my make-believe ailments, but her heart would break if she knew what was really going on with me.

"I'm glad you want me to make you better. It makes me feel useful," she says, eyes shining with sadness. "So. Can I bring you anything else? Something else to drink besides water? Maybe some hot tea?"

"I think I just need to rest."

"Okay then, I'm going to leave you to it." Leoti pats the bed as she stands to leave. "Oh, I put some fresh towels in the bathroom in case you'd like to take a hot bath. It might help with the body aches if you feel up to it. Get some rest," she says, pulling the door closed behind her.

I lie in bed, looking at the ceiling, breathing through a contraction, contemplating how I'm going to do this by myself, what I'm going to do after it is over. I've assisted the elders during childbirth and know from experience the time is near. By my count, I've been in labor for at least twenty-four hours now. While I may know exactly what to do, the challenge will be clearing the mess of the birth away and getting the baby out of the house before anyone ever knows what's happened. If only Leoti could help me, but no, I will not put her through that. Besides, Leoti would never allow me to give up this baby. She would insist I raise it, and that is not possible even if I wanted it.

And I don't want it. It will ruin my life. It is ruining my life. I am carrying a commoner's child. A commoner who used me as if I were a laboratory rat. I want nothing to do with it. Many plans have been made on my behalf, and having the baby of a commoner would erase them, rob me of my legacy. No. No one can ever know about this child.

Pots and pans clang in the kitchen. The faint mumblings of the television filter down the hallway. It must be getting close to time for Rubin to come home from work.

Pressure builds again in the lower half of my body. I brace for the next round. My bladder aches. I roll to the side of the bed and push myself up to head for the bathroom. At the door, I hold, feeling the tightening around my middle. I wait for it to subside before I enter the hallway, to hurry along the short distance where I can close myself behind another door.

The phone rings. Leoti says hello. Pain or no pain, now is the moment I need to make the dash. Hunched and cringing, I make it inside the bathroom. Another contraction begins, bringing me to my knees. It's coming. No longer able to walk, I drop to hands and knees, crawl to the side of the tub, twist the handles, and plug the drain.

On the other side of the door, Leoti knocks. "Ama, you okay?"

"Fine," I manage to return.

"Rubin just called to say he has to work late. I'm going to run to the store to pick up some soup and saltines. Will you be all right by yourself?"

"I'm good."

"Okay, then. I'll be right back."

When I'm sure she is gone, I let out the moan I've pushed deep and crawl over the side of the tub into the warm water. The nightgown clings to my body, wet with sweat and bathwater. I feel it. It's finally making its exit.

* * *

THE LAST OF the water drains from the tub. Outside I hear the slam of a car door. Leoti is back. Or is it Rubin? I need more time. The head is out. Not much longer, and it will be over.

The urge to push.

A searing pain.

A knock at the bathroom door.

Leoti calling from the hallway.

The shoulders are out. I reach down and pull it from my body. It's ugly and blue, covered with mucus, the cord still connecting it to me. I can't touch it and lay it aside, readying for the placenta.

Leoti's knocking becomes more furious. The doorknob rattles. The door bursts open, and my sister halts, staring, mouth agape.

"Ama?"

* * *

WHILE I CLEAN up the remnants of birth, Leoti holds the baby, her face marked with concern and light and confusion. It was not supposed to happen like this. Leoti was never to know. No one was ever to know. The baby has yet to make a peep, I thought, hoped maybe, it didn't make it, didn't survive. Everything would be so much easier.

Leoti pads down the hall toward the living room. She settles into the rocking recliner, eyes never leaving the child in her arms. I follow and take a seat on the sofa across from them.

"Do you want to hold her?"

"No."

Leoti draws her gaze from the baby to look at me. "She needs to eat, Ama."

I meet Leoti's scrutiny, unable to erase the horror from my face, the statement absurd.

"You need to nurse her."

"I'm not touching it. I've waited a long time to get that thing out of my body. No way am I going to let it latch back on."

"How can you say such a thing? This is your baby, Ama. Your daughter. She's counting on you to take care of her. You're her mother."

"No, I'm not. I don't want her. I don't want anything to do with it. And if you hadn't burst through the damn door, it would already be gone."

"Gone where, Ama? Were you..."

"No," I deny. "I was going to leave it at the church down the street."

A tear slides over Leoti's cheek. "Why Ama? What happened to you? Is it the man you're supposed to couple with, Elan? Are you punishing him?"

"God, no. I haven't let that man touch me."

"Then who is the baby's father?"

"We're not having this discussion, Leoti." Slouching back on the sofa, arms folded, I stare back at my sister.

So much has gone wrong. It wasn't supposed to be this way. I should have gone to the woods as I initially planned, but I couldn't take the chance of having one of The Community members stumbling upon me giving birth to a commoner's child.

"Whatever happened to you, Ama, it's not her fault." She turns her attention to the baby stirring in her arms. As the baby settles again, Leoti looks back at me, realization crossing her face. "Does the baby have anything to do with why you haven't been around in," she pauses, her face screws up in concentration, "nine months? Ama. Does this have anything to do with that night? With Thomas?"

"I said we are not talking about this. It doesn't matter."

"Of course it matters."

The front door opens wide. Rubin steps through the threshold and looks down the hallway. "Leoti," he calls toward the kitchen, having yet to realize we are seated behind him.

"I'm right here," Leoti says, her voice barely above a whisper.

Rubin turns to view the room, taking in the sight of me first before his eyes land on Leoti holding the baby. "What's going on? Whose baby is that?"

"It's Ama's."

"No, it's not."

Rubin shakes his head, slowly approaching Leoti's chair. He looks at me. "If it's not yours, then who does it belong to?"

"Ama was raped."

"What?" Rubin's body stiffens.

The sound of Rubin's voice causes the baby to stir again.

"Shh," Leoti demands. "Ama doesn't want to talk about it, and she's having a hard time accepting the fact she is the baby's mother."

"I told you, I am not that baby's mother."

Rubin looks at me. "Are you okay?"

"Fine."

Rubin twists toward Leoti. "Is the baby okay?"

"She's perfect," Leoti answers, running her pointer finger over the baby's nose and along its cheek, smoothing its fine, dark hair with her palm.

Rubin moves to take a seat on the other end of the sofa. "Let's back up for a second." He leans forward, elbows on knees, hands clasping. "Ama was raped. By who?" Rubin looks at me.

"She won't tell me, but I have a pretty good idea," Leoti says but doesn't relay her suspicions. She looks at me, her eyes narrow, then turns her attention back to Rubin. "Ama showed up here this afternoon saying she had the flu," Leoti begins again.

"I didn't say that; you assumed that," I interject.

Leoti throws me a glare. "Fine," Leoti continues, "I assumed. But you said you weren't feeling well," she says to me, then turns her face to address Rubin. "I put her to bed in the guest room to get some rest and then ran out to the grocery store. When I returned, Ama was in our bathroom, where she had just given birth to the baby. I didn't even know she was pregnant." Leoti looks back at me. "Wait, did anyone know you were pregnant?"

"No."

"How in the hell did you hide a pregnancy?" Rubin asks.

"Look at her, Rubin," Leoti says. "She's bone thin."

"I couldn't tell anyone," I mutter.

"Let me guess, because of The Community," Rubin says, not bothering to curb his disgust.

"Rubin, can I speak with you in the kitchen for a moment?" Leoti asks.

Rubin sighs wearily, pushing off his knees to stand. Leoti eases out of the chair and walks over to my spot on the sofa, readying to hand over the child. As I prepare to protest, a knowing look sweeps across her face. She turns to walk down the hallway, holding tightly to the sleeping baby.

I hear them begin speaking in hushed tones and tiptoe down the hall, stopping at the corner to listen.

"I think she was going to hurt the baby, Rubin. I'm scared if I give Ama the baby, she'll do something terrible."

"Like what? You think she'll harm the child?"

"I don't know, Rubin. It's like I don't know her right now. Maybe she's in shock? Maybe the offense against her was so awful she blames the baby? I just have this feeling something terrible will happen to this poor little girl if I force Ama to take her."

"Then what do we do? The baby needs to be checked out by a doctor. Ama needs to be checked out by a doctor."

"Ama told me she was going to leave the baby at the church, but before she said that, she told me if I hadn't walked in on her, the baby would already be gone."

"She's your sister, Leoti. Do you really think she's capable of killing an innocent newborn?"

"Maybe we should keep the baby."

"What? Leoti, come on now. I know you want a child, but we aren't prepared for a baby. We have nothing to take care of an infant. No bottles. No diapers. No formula."

"Well, neither does Ama. We at least have the means to take care of a baby, and then maybe if we give Ama some time, she will come around. She'll realize she can't give up her own child."

I step around the corner. "I told you, I don't want that baby, Leoti. I'm not going to change my mind."

"Ama. You're eavesdropping?" Leoti holds the child to her shoulder, patting its back protectively.

"That thing is evil. I want nothing to do with it. Do you hear me?"

Rubin walks to me, taking hold of my upper arms, searching my face. "Ama, you're tired. You've been through a lot. Obviously. The birth. Hiding your pregnancy. Why don't you get some rest, and we can talk about this in the morning."

"I will never have anything to do with that child."

ESME

———

MARCH

Bone tired and mentally depleted, I toss back the covers of the bed, contemplating the crawl to slumber. I stand at the edge of the mattress, longing to see Kirby stretched out on the other side. Though I desperately yearn the rest, another night of cold, fretful sleep alone holds little appeal. I turn my gaze to the entrance of the bedroom, checking to be certain the door is secured, then twist to turn out the lamp and climb into bed. Pulling the covers to my chin, I stare into the engulfing darkness.

My nightgown, crumpled and bunched beneath me, seizes my freedom of mobility. Underneath the heft of the blankets, I tug the fabric to fall along the sides of my body, yank down the elastic sleeves caught on my elbows to grip my wrists. Kirby hates when I wear this gown, but it keeps me warm through the night when he is not here to do so, which is more often than not lately. Unfortunately, these long stretches away from home don't seem to be coming to an end anytime soon. At least he's making it home every other week, but I am missing his four days on, three days off schedule.

Back when Kirby first began driving, he would be on the road for a month, sometimes two, at a time. I expected our routine would become easier once he finished his rookie year, but then came the act of accumulating seat time. We went through some tough years while Kirby worked to gain the trust of the guys in dispatch. Once they understood they could count on Kirby to make the deliveries as scheduled, the dispatchers began assigning Kirby routes that didn't deposit him in the worst parts of unfamiliar towns or maneuvering the most congested highways. With all the years Kirby has behind the wheel to date, he should have one of the best route schedules the company has to offer.

When the company started laying off drivers, we didn't know it was streamlining in preparation for selling to the highest bidder. The announcement of a new management takeover was relayed the last week of February. Now it seems as if Kirby has to prove himself all over again. We were fortunate Kirby was able to keep his job during the transition, though. Things can always be worse. I came to that understanding many years ago.

I vividly remember the first time that revelation occurred to me. I was home cleaning the bathroom for what felt like the thousandth time in my young years—only twenty-two years old, actually.

From the day he was born, Jay has always been a handful. By the time he turned three years old, I had given up hope it would ever get easier being his mother. Kirby's schedule was so grueling during those early years, everything that needed doing around the house fell on my shoulders. My daddy had always taken care of that stuff while I was growing up—I assumed Kirby would do the same. I was inept and awkward, trying to discern a monkey wrench from a pair of pliers, learning the best way to work a plunger.

Bitterness, frustration, and loneliness swallowed me up, left me in tears most hours of my days. But it came to me, as I was cleaning the toilet early that one morning, the understanding, the revelation. God's grace was great. My child was healthy, as were Kirby and I. We had a roof over our heads and, food in our pantry, good friends to lean on. What did I have to be so unhappy about?

My life was, and is, good in comparison to so many other unfortunate souls wandering this world, be they homeless, or disabled, abused or unloved, unhealthy or hungry. From that moment on, I have understood; only I can make myself happy. So now, when life gets rough, I think of all the positives I have to be thankful for, and I smile and let God know how much I appreciate His grace.

My thoughts drift to Kirby again. *How is he? Why haven't I heard from him today?* I texted him earlier—please call, no matter the time. I need to hear your voice, know you're okay.

In a vain attempt, I roll my head side to side on the pillow beneath it, trying to loosen the knots permanently embedded at the base of my neck. Eyes wide and mind at full speed, I lie on my back, the black of night closing in around me. The darkness settles atop my chest, motioning for the lurking fear to take its place. It's the one thing I can't shake, unable to talk myself into a better mindset, to let go of the fear.

Why is this the hardest part of my day when all I've done during the long hours of wakefulness is look forward to it?

"Dear God," I begin, my voice above a whisper, "thank you for another day. A day in which I accomplished a hard day's work and had a nice conversation with my mother. Thank you for permitting me the privilege of witnessing baby Ashley's first steps, but please comfort her mother's heart, as I know it is broken to have missed the momentous occasion.

"I am so grateful for the beautiful day, for the spring season showing signs of its impending arrival. The glory of your work is nothing less than awe-inspiring. I do appreciate all of your gifts, God, but I need to ask for some of your time. Simply to talk with you, to share my troubles. Speaking them to you lifts away some of the weight I struggle to carry.

"First, I want to ask that you watch over Kirby, God. Kirby is under so much stress and working hard to support us, care for us. I pray you will keep him alert and conscientious of all the drivers he comes in contact with along his travels.

"My daddy isn't well, God. The doctor has scheduled another

ablation to try and correct Daddy's irregular heart rhythm. This will be the doctor's fourth attempt, and Mama is beside herself with worry. I pray, God, that you will guide the doctor through Daddy's procedure, steady the physician's hands and mind to finally heal my father and ease my mother's anxieties. My parents have had a difficult year plagued by illness, injury, and concern for my family and me."

The sudden ringing of my cell phone shatters the silence, the calm that was slowly settling in. I reach to the bedside table and disconnect the phone from the charger. It's Kirby.

I push myself to sit up against the headboard of the bed. "Hey, I was so worried. You okay?"

"Yeah, I'm fine. Long day. Paperwork got misplaced, couldn't find the location dispatch set for the drop—you know the drill."

"It's going to take some time for the new dispatchers to get a handle on their jobs. Hang in there, honey."

"I know. How was your day? Did you get the car out of the shop?"

"Yes. Finally. I felt like such a heel bumming rides from people at church, asking Mama to tote me around to get errands done."

"What was the final mechanic bill?"

"More than we thought. I had to pull from savings, a lot from savings."

"Can't be helped. You have to have a vehicle."

"The car problem is solved, but now we have another one, a bigger one."

"Do I ask?"

"It's time to renew the rental agreement."

"And?"

"I told you Mr. O'Leary died," I start, but Kirby cuts into my delivery.

"When? I don't remember you telling me that."

"Almost three months ago now."

"That's a shame. Liked him." Kirby goes silent. I'm sure he's taking a moment to let the loss settle, maybe saying a quick prayer.

Mr. O'Leary, the man who owns the home we've lived in all of our married years, passed away during the last days of December. I hadn't given any thought to how his passing might impact us. Honestly, I haven't had the time, and evidently, I failed to share the news of his death with Kirby as well.

"Did you attend the funeral?" Kirby asks, drawing me out of my thoughts.

"Uh, no," I stammer. "I mean, I know I should have, that it would have been the right thing to do. But. Well, I didn't want to make you feel uncomfortable in any way. I didn't want to give you any reason to doubt me."

"That was a long time ago, Esme. We've been through a lot since then, grown a lot. You have my full trust. You know that."

"We got a letter in the mail today about the renewal terms, details about the new owner." I pause. Dread swells, knowing I have to relay the next piece of information. "Mr. O'Leary left all his rental properties to his nephew."

Nathan O'Leary, Mr. O'Leary's nephew, served as his uncle's handyman for the various rental properties owned by our landlord. Mr. O'Leary was a lifelong bachelor. The fact he bequeathed everything he had to Nathan should come as no surprise to either of us, but that doesn't change the fact it is a huge problem for all parties involved now the inheritance has been realized.

Kirby's silence is loud in my ear. I want to know what is going through his head, but then again, I don't—and I don't want him to mull on the information for too long.

"Kirby?"

"Was the letter from him?"

"Yes."

"Is he kicking us out?"

"No. But he is raising the rent," I hold, then add, "thirty percent."

"Asshole."

"Kirby."

"Well, he is."

I don't say the increase has been a long time coming. Mr. O'Leary never once increased our rent during all the time we've lived in his home. Though we may well be due the additional fee after all these years, to voice the thought might lead Kirby to believe I am taking the side of the man who was at the heart of the turmoil we endured early in our marriage.

When we left my parents' home and moved in here, the neglected older home needed quite a bit of work, but we were young and determined. Kirby was convinced he'd have the time to commit to the repairs, but his job demands were all consuming. I was nineteen years old with a brand new baby and an absent husband. So, I had to call on Mr. O'Leary's handyman for the necessary repairs. Nathan and I spent a lot of time together—more time than was healthy. I own every ounce of responsibility for my transgressions. To claim the affair was conducted out of loneliness or depression would not be taking the blame for my weakness. That is what I was, weak.

Kirby and I took our problems to God. Regardless of how Kirby's parents had treated him when they learned I was pregnant out of wedlock, Kirby was still a man of faith, just as he was raised to be. My husband knew what we needed to do to get back on track with our marriage. We joined the church. Our pastor counseled us through my mistake, and I made the decision to accept Jesus into my heart.

Kirby has forgiven me, and I know I have God's forgiveness, but the hardest person to forgive is myself. Causing Kirby all that pain, making him doubt himself as a man... I can't strip away the regret of my actions.

Kirby and I often sit in silence with one another on the phone, though it is never awkward. Hearing the other breathe seems to be a sense of closeness for us both. But when that silence has the two of us reflecting on our history with Nathan O'Leary, it is not a sense of comfort.

"We can always move. Nothing says we have to stay here," I offer.

"When is our lease up? April?"

"June."

"So we have a couple of months to decide, come up with a plan," Kirby muses.

"Six weeks, actually. We have to give a thirty-day notice. We're already in the middle of March, which means we have to inform O'Leary of our intent by the first of May."

"Do you think you could find somewhere else to live in that timeframe?"

"It would be a stretch, especially with work being as crazy as it is right now. Everybody has been out sick. We're all covering for one another, but we keep passing illnesses back and forth. It's a daycare; I can't expect much else this time of year. Maybe I can look during spring break? If I can get well, I'll have some time off coming that week."

"Are you sure that's what you want to do, Esme? Move?"

"Kirby, I would move to the other side of the world to keep our marriage healthy."

"I know you're worried about me, but don't. I'll be okay. I told you, I trust you. I know how committed you are to me. We need to give some thought to what is best for Jay, though. Jay has grown up in that house, and given his behavior issues, I don't think now is such a good time to be uprooting him."

"But what about the rent increase? We're barely keeping up with our bills as it is."

"The good news is, I'm in the clear with my job. All the new drivers the company hired are rookies. They need us old guys around to train them. Most of the newbies can't make a solo haul yet."

"Does that mean you're still going to make these long trips?"

"For a bit, but there will be some extra money in my paychecks. We have to look at the bright side, Esme."

"I know. I just wish you were home more." The exertion of

whining triggers a phlegmy cough. "Sorry, honey," I apologize for the disruption.

"How are you feeling? What did the doctor say?"

"Bronchitis, but the good thing is I'm not contagious any longer. He prescribed some cough syrup and said it should clear up within the week."

"You need rest."

"There's not a lot of time for rest."

"Are you sleeping any better?"

"Not really. I have so much on my mind it's filtering into my dreams now. Last night, I had a dream about being a garbage man and getting thrown into the compactor of the truck. I woke in a panic because I'd forgotten to take the trash cans to the curb before bed. I dragged myself outside at three in the morning so it wouldn't sit by our back door for another week."

"Isn't Jay on garbage duty?"

"He is. I, however, failed to recall that he told me he didn't feel like taking the trash out, that if I wanted it done, I should do it and quit bugging the shit (sorry) out of him."

Kirby huffs. "Is he at least behaving, I mean, other than being a complete jerk to his mother?"

"If you're asking whether our son has cut the heads from any more of our neighbors' animals, then, no, Jay hasn't done that, but to say he's behaving might be offering a bit more credit than Jay is due."

"Is he staying in his room? Off the video games and TV?"

A heavy sigh rattles through my chest. "I know we agreed on the terms of his restriction, but enforcing them is harder than you think, Kirby. I hate to say it, but I'm scared. I'm frightened of my own child. What kind of mother am I that I live in fear of my kid?"

"You're not a bad mother, Esme. Jay, on the other hand, is being a bad kid."

"Jay isn't acting like a kid, though. The words that come out of his mouth, the way he glares at me, the thoughts he speaks, it's as if he is years older. And he's getting so big. Jay must have grown at least two inches over the last couple of months. He's getting stronger, Kirby. What if he doesn't grow out of this phase? What if I can't fend him off?"

"Has he come after you again?" Kirby's tone changes from concerned and supportive to fury, peppered with panic. "Did he hurt you again?"

"Nothing more than the usual," I try to calm Kirby's worries. "The regular: slapping away my hand, twisting my arm, shoving me if I'm too close."

"Why do I feel like there is something you're not telling me?"

I had not planned to get into this conversation with Kirby until he returned from this trip. Miles away from home, there isn't a thing in the world he can do about it except worry, and that worry takes his mind off the road where it needs to be focused.

"Knives are missing."

"Knives?"

"Yes, my kitchen knives. At first, I thought maybe a couple of them were in the dishwasher, so I grabbed another one to use instead. I didn't think to actually check the dishwasher, to make sure they were, in fact, in there as I thought."

"So the knives are just gone? Disappeared?"

"Yes. I have no idea where they are."

"Did you ask Jay if he knows anything about them?"

"I did," I drag in a deep breath, recalling the interaction. "Jay said he hadn't seen them lately."

"Do you believe him?"

"I don't know. I mean, I know Jay can do some awful things, but usually, when I confront him about whatever it is, he has no issues being forthright about his actions. He blurts it all out. But when Jay answered me about the knives, there was something in his voice, Kirby. Something not quite right."

"So you don't believe him?"

"Yes and no. It's just what else Jay said."

"What do you mean?"

"Well, I asked him if he knew knives were dangerous, and he said, 'Yeah, I'm not an idiot. You can kill people with knives.' It was so menacing, though. There was nothing innocent in his simple answer. It was the way he said it, looking at me with that fire in his eyes. It felt like he was threatening me, Kirby."

"And you still haven't found the knives?"

"No. They are nowhere to be found. I have one small knife left in the kitchen, and I've hidden it."

"Have you checked his room?"

"When I can get in there, I have. Since Jay has been on restriction, he's in his room most of the time. I've gone into his room while he's in the shower to search for them, but they're not there. So, maybe Jay really doesn't have them. Maybe I'm just losing my mind."

"You're locking the bedroom door at night, right?"

"I can't believe we are having this discussion. Yes," I let the answer hang, debating over whether to add more information to the statement.

"What are you not saying, Esme?"

Kirby knows me too well, and I honestly don't want to be the only owner of this issue with our child. "On a few occasions recently," I pause. *Do I lay all this on Kirby? Doesn't he have enough to worry about already?*

"Go on," he prods.

"I've been woken in the middle of the night by a noise. It sounds like someone is trying to pick the lock on the door."

"Is it Jay? Did you go to the door to check?"

"No."

"Why?"

My eyes burn with shame. "Because I'm a chicken. Because I'm scared. What if it is Jay? If it's Jay and I confront him, what will he do? He gets more powerful with each day that passes."

"That's it. When I get home, I'm putting a lock on the outside of Jay's door. We're going to start locking him in at night."

"We can't do that. We'd be treating him like a zoo animal. And what if Jay needs to go to the bathroom in the middle of the night."

"He can pee in a cup. This is bullcrap, Esme."

"Kirby. Please. I didn't mean to get you riled up over this. I'm sure it's me. I'm getting all worked up over nothing. Probably because I'm tired, and I can't get myself healthy."

"Stop making excuses, Esme. This is ridiculous, and it has to stop. We are going to have to get that boy some professional help."

"How Kirby? We already know our insurance won't cover therapy, and we can't afford to pay for it out of pocket."

"Can you at least, I don't know, maybe stay with your parents until I get this load finished up?"

"I can't do that, Kirby. In two days, Daddy has his fourth ablation. Mama is so worried about Daddy. And you know what Jay did to Mama over Christmas. I'm not going to subject my parents to Jay's tirades or the possibility of him hurting one of them again."

We talk for a few more minutes, discussing tactics to try on our son, disciplinary actions, ways for me to keep myself safe and sane. Kirby makes a spur of the moment decision that over Jay's spring break, he is going to request a couple of days off. We'll spend some time together as a family. Instead of trying to find a new place to live and creating more instability within our small unit, we'll go camping, get out into nature. Maybe that's what Jay needs. Maybe it is what we all need. Time together, an opportunity for us to all work together and have fun together and perhaps learn to trust each other.

Kirby and I say our goodnights. I roll over and reach to plug the charger back into my phone. Through the darkness, I look at the bedroom door. I throw back the covers, leave the warmth of my bed and tread across the room. Dragging the chair from the corner of the room, I wedge it under the doorknob.

MEREL

MARCH

The fluorescent bulbs flicker on and off before finally illuminating the only place I can find right now that doesn't feel claustrophobic—the only place my breathing regulates to something near normal.

"Is that you, Merel?" Dorothy calls from our shared office.

"Good morning," I call out, walking through my classroom, powering up the student computers, twisting on the decorative lamp in the reading corner.

As I circle back around and head into the office, Dorothy says, "You've made it to spring break—eight months down, two to go and these last two will fly."

"You know, it's funny. At times, I have no idea where the last eight months have gone, and at others, I find myself asking if it will ever end."

"Then you're doing just fine, 'cause that's how we all feel when this time of year rolls around."

I place my purse on the top shelf of my closet. "Did I ask you what you're doing over the break?"

"You did, but I'll tell you again. Herb and I are meeting up with the kids in Destin, Florida. Rented a big house on the beach. I can't wait to see my grand-babies."

I close the door of the closet and turn to address Dorothy seated behind the desk on her side of the office. "When do you all leave?"

"Friday morning, bright and early."

"So you're celebrating Easter in Florida?"

"Yep. Egg hunts, ham, banana pudding," Dorothy rattles off the list while logging scores into her grade book.

"I know I do not forget that I taught you how to use the grade book on your computer. I thought you said you liked that program? Said it was easy to use?"

"Oh, I do, and it is. But I like to have a hard copy. Can't trust those computers. Always some sort of glitch, or virus, or what have you."

I pull the chair from underneath my desk, shaking my head while retrieving the plan book from the shelf above to check the agenda for today's lessons.

"I know. I'm just an old dog. What can I say?" Dorothy continues with the task. "And what are your plans for the break?"

"Working. I have some things I need to do in my room while the kids are gone."

"You're room is perfect, Merel. What more could you possibly have to do? Besides, Jeanine has the school locked up tight during spring break."

My eyes widen at the revelation. "Seriously?" The news squeezes the air from my chest. *I can't spend a full week closed inside the confines of my apartment. Not now.* Shadows bleed in from the corners of my eyes, blackening the light of the room.

Though Dorothy's form is fading fast, I hear her. "Our principal has a firm policy that all staff enjoys this last vacation before the end of the school year rigor kicks in."

Dorothy disappears.

Someone calls me. "Merel? Merel. Breathe, honey. You're white as a sheet." Dorothy's instructions tremble with panic. Maybe exertion? Her feet move quickly to roll her office chair closer. Dorothy takes my hands.

I draw in a deep breath as Dorothy suggests, trying to reduce the rate of my heartbeat, attempting to match the pulse I feel in Dorothy's soft hold. The attacks being more frequent of late, the process of overcoming them has become second nature. I think it's over.

"Merel," Dorothy begins gently. "I know this time of year is difficult for you, but you can't bury yourself in work and think you'll just forget about it." Dorothy keeps me in her grip, grounding me.

Though I don't want to admit it, she's right.

Dorothy knows. I told her. Not everything, but she knows enough. When Dorothy found me passed out in the center of the classroom floor one day after the students had been dismissed, I had no other choice. She'd wanted to call an ambulance. I knew it wasn't necessary and had to share what I had been holding back. Dorothy wears the same look now as she did the day I confided in her. The undeserved pity etching the creases around her eyes, the corners of her mouth tugged downward with compassion. I look down, knowing it's wrong to accept her sympathy.

"Did you sleep last night?"

Honing in on the age spots marking Dorothy's hands, my vision slowly comes into focus. "I dozed a bit."

"You need some sleep. You need to eat. You're far too thin, Merel." Dorothy squeezes my hands for emphasis. "Use this week to take care of yourself. I think you should go home. See your family. They're there for you, no matter what it was that happened between you all." Dorothy references the betrayal. Letty and Shu, all the lies over the years.

"Maybe," I say, slipping from her hold, turning my attention back to the lesson plans.

"You know, sometimes, we build things up in our minds to be much worse than they actually are," Dorothy continues to urge.

"Sometimes," I agree, knowing my truth is far worse than Dorothy could ever fathom.

* * *

STANDING AT THE CLASSROOM ENTRANCE, mind racing with thoughts, I absently greet the students filing through the door. Libby steps inside, wrapping her arms around me with a hello. She seems taller.

At my declaration, she confirms, indeed, she is. "Daddy measured me last night. I've grown an inch and a half since the last mark," Libby exclaims with pride.

Over the last months, most of the students have celebrated birthdays, saying goodbye to seven, eager to be eight-year-olds. Very few are left to cross the milestone, and two of them will reach it during the spring holiday. Today, I will need to carve out time to recognize Nathan and Amelia, give them their special birthday moments.

For the students, with only three days of instruction, this school week is much like that of Thanksgiving. The students have a two-day reprieve before Easter which stretches into the long-anticipated spring break the following week.

Situating backpacks into cubbies, the students ready for their school day, at ease and confident in the routines we've been practicing throughout the year. As they settle behind desks to begin the morning assignment, the children chatter about impending plans upon today's dismissal, excited about the long break awaiting them.

The hallway clears out. I shut the classroom door, my eyes moving to do one last sweep of the cubby area. He is turned away from me, busy rooting around for something inside his backpack. A flash of pink catches my eye, and I realize the bag doesn't belong to him but to Caroline.

"Jay?" The one word catches in my throat. The fist inside my middle tightens its grip around my stomach as I voice his name.

Shoulders squared off to hide what is in front of him, Jay turns his head. His eyes narrow, forehead creasing.

"What are you doing?" I fold arms across the middle of my body.

"Looking for something."

"What are you looking for?"

"My snack."

"In Caroline's backpack?"

"I asked her to hold it for me when we were in bus lobby this morning." His glare doesn't waver with the lie.

"Caroline doesn't ride the bus, Jay. One of her parents always drives her to school."

I've caught him, and he knows it. Jay's deadpan stare takes me in as he decides not to bother with a comeback.

"I'll take that," I say, moving toward him, arm outstretched. Jay hands over Caroline's backpack. His hand brushes mine, the exchange searing.

I watch Jay leave the area then check through the bag to ensure the contents of Caroline's bag seem intact. Having located her snack, I zip up the backpack and return it to the hook inside the cubicle.

I move to the front of the classroom to prepare for the daily calendar lesson. Placing the star marker to highlight the current date, I stare blankly at the crossed-through days in front of me, the month of March coming to a swift close.

The fist relentlessly clutches around my stomach. Every muscle in my body tenses in response, trying to draw out the ache, fight off the pain. I struggle to resist the urge to double over. I will not frighten the children. I'm used to this. It is a yearly occurrence, one I should be able to handle by now. As winter makes its exit, this is what I must endure—the pain that physically wrenches me from the inside out.

Spring officially arrived last weekend. Seasons change, each setting forth a new set of expectations, possibilities. For most people, the spring season ushers in thoughts of renewal, rebirth, and awakenings, of hope and light. Not for me.

I believed that I had made some progress with regard to

making it through the difficult memories that accompany this time of year. The last four years while going through the rigor of obtaining my teaching degree, I was able to push back the cloaking darkness that inevitably drapes itself around me with the arrival of the season. Regardless of the fact I've endured many anniversaries of the debilitating events, worked so hard to store away the memories, as I study the calendar in front of me, my chest feels as if those terrible moments only just occurred.

I have good days. I have bad days. Days I move through without a panic attack. Days my appetite returns, and I actually remember to eat. But each time the memories, the old feelings, the pain of my past begins to slip away, it seems there's a jolt in reality —jerking me back, pushing me down, a marionette on a string.

Nevertheless, I am determined today will be a good day. My students are counting on me. It's what happens when they're on vacation for a week and a half, when I have to rely on myself, that concerns me.

ESME

—

APRIL

irby's late. I've yet to finish packing. And Jay is stomping about, fuming that he is being forced to go on some stupid camping trip during *his* spring break.

Kirby called last night to relay the rookie he's training took a curve too tightly, causing two tires on the right-hand side of the 18-wheeler to slip into a ditch. The rig had to be pulled out by a wrecking service. The incident cut several hours of road time, which is delaying Kirby's arrival. Of course, these scenarios are to be expected when training a new driver. At least no one was hurt. Still, we had not allotted time for such an incident when planning our schedule for the spring break camping trip.

When we spoke last, I suggested we cancel our plans. Kirby and I were only able to manage two days off together in the middle of the work week. The trouble of setting up a campsite for only one night seemed a bit pointless to me. But Kirby would hear nothing of it, claiming this trip is about connecting as a family. Kirby insisted he'd be home today in time for us to pull out after lunch, ensuring me we would have plenty of time to get the tent set up before nightfall. Kirby claims after a good night's sleep, we'll get up, make pancakes, then head out on our planned hike before returning home Wednesday evening.

Sure, it's easy enough for Kirby to time this out in his mind. What he doesn't allow for, is I am the one left to do the legwork, all the while Jay is on my heels being Jay. Jay says camping is boring. Jay whines that he doesn't like s'mores. Jay hates hiking. Jay defiantly disregards every directive I give him. He boisterously refuses to be a party to anything having to do with preparing for this family outing, issuing threats and tacking on derogatory names for me as he does so.

Kirby's tardiness affords me the opportunity—*look for the bright side, Esme*—to gather a few items I had completely forgotten to pack. *I mean, really, how is one to make pancakes without a spatula? Or wash up the pan without dish soap? And how could you possibly forget a roll of paper towels, Esme?*

My cell phone rings from its spot on the kitchen counter. The display informs me it is not Kirby as I was hoping but my mother.

"Hey, Mama."

"How's the trip going? You all getting close to being there?"

"We haven't left yet."

"Well, why not? You're burning daylight, Esme."

"I know, Mama. I'm waiting for Kirby to pull in."

"Good heavens, it'll be dark before you even get there. Are y'all still planning on going to the Smokies?"

"That's the plan. Kirby wants to hike the Ramsey Cascades trail."

"Where's that one?"

"Just outside Gatlinburg," I say, tossing the syrup into the food bag. "The Greenbrier entrance," I add absently as if she will know where it is located.

"Oh, good grief. I didn't realize you all were traveling that far away."

"It's only a couple of hours, Mama." I lift the lid on the cooler to make sure I remembered to pack butter.

"Well, is Jay excited?"

"Not in the least."

"I'd have thought he'd be anxious to get outdoors and run off some of that energy."

"I think that's what Kirby was hoping for. Mama, I hate to run, but I need to go. I have to get the rest of our things packed into the car before Kirby gets home so we can head out the minute he gets here."

"Okay, honey. You all have fun and be safe. Oh, and call me when you're off the trail and on your way home tomorrow. You know I'll worry if you don't."

"I will. Love you, Mama."

* * *

THE SOUND of raindrops hitting the top of the tent wakes me. Through the cushion of the sleeping bag, the dampness of the ground sends a chill up my back. I scoot closer to Kirby, snuggling in behind him, wrapping my arm tighter around his middle. My reach shortens each time I embrace Kirby. I worry over his growing heft. The unpredictable schedule he keeps, the stress of driving, and diet of greasy eateries along the highways are not good for his health. Pressing the concern aside, I breathe in his scent, allow myself to enjoy the moment of being with my husband while listening to Jay snore softly on the other side of Kirby. Kirby's late arrival yesterday left us barely enough time to check in with the park's office and set up the tent before sundown. But we're here, our small family unit resting soundly together.

Mentally, I go through the list of what all needs to be done before our hike. First, I need to get breakfast served, then put together sandwiches for the hike, and finally pack up our things while Kirby disassembles the tent and breaks down the campsite. *Did I remember to pack the jelly?*

"It's raining," Kirby whispers, pulling my arm, drawing me even closer to him.

"It was, but it's tapering off now," I whisper back, careful not to wake Jay. "You about ready for pancakes?"

"Yeah, I'll wake the boy."

I yank my arm against Kirby's chest to stop him. "Let him sleep for a bit. He's not been so nice in the early morning hours."

"Okay, your call."

We slip out of the tent and go about our chores. As breakfast nears completion, Jay crawls out of the tent, no doubt lured by the smell of food.

After our meal, we clear up the campsite and pack up the car. All is going according to plan.

Kirby stands at the driver's side door, hurrying us along. "You all ready? This hike is going to be one of the more challenging ones we've done, but you can do it. Right, Jay?" Kirby runs his fingers through his long, untamed beard—chipper, optimistic, even boyish in his excitement.

Jay mutters something incoherent, which is actually more promising than some of the other choice words he's been spouting off lately.

I settle into the passenger's seat, pulling the seatbelt over my middle, then click myself in for the ride to the trailhead.

"How long is this hike?" I ask, looking out the windshield and up at the sky. Gray and overcast, little sun makes it through the clouds, keeping the temperatures cooler than usual for this time of year.

"Four miles up, four miles back down. Elevation at right around twenty-two hundred feet."

I choke back a retort. Though I am all in for strengthening our family unit, an eight-mile hike in the dreary weather seems a bit ambitious given all the sickness I've had to overcome recently.

Kirby, the only one in the car seemingly eager to take on the physical exertion, continues. "Ramsey Cascade. This trail spits us out at the tallest waterfall in the Smoky Mountains."

"Who's Ramsey?" Jay asks from the backseat. "Some old dead guy?"

"Ramsey is the surname of the family who used to live on this land. I thought we talked last week about you doing some research on this trail?" Kirby tries to engage Jay, but Jay refuses to return comment.

The parking lot at the trailhead is empty. Kirby maneuvers the car into the space nearest the trail's starting point. We pile out of the car, grabbing backpacks, making sure we have our cell phones, that everything in the car is secure and locked up.

From the parking area, we follow a graveled road to cross a footbridge over the Middle Prong of the Little Pigeon River. The trail takes us up an old jeep road. Kirby relays this is the easiest portion of the hike.

Though we make good time on this leg of the trail (reaching the traffic circle in roughly twenty-five minutes), Jay is already in one of his surly moods. He's tired. He's hungry. He doesn't want to do this stupid hike. I ignore his complaints, listening instead to the song of the forest: the rustle of the breeze through the new growth on the trees, squirrels barking at one another, birds calling out to welcome in the spring season that's only just arrived.

Once the old road ends, the trail takes on a bleaker look in terms of difficulty. I'm no longer able to take in the sights and sounds of the forest but rather place all concentration on the path in front of me. Tree roots vein the surface of the well-worn dirt path. Jay jumps and stomps across them despite Kirby's warnings the roots are slippery from the recent rain. Farther along, rocks begin to litter the landscape. I step around them when I can, but some are unavoidable, as well as unstable.

"I think we're the only people on this trail," I say, the words breathy and broken. *I'm too young to be this out of shape.*

"Probably because it's the middle of the week, not too many people are out and about right now," Kirby muses.

"Probably because the weather sucks and nobody really likes to do dumbass hikes," Jay spouts, coming up behind Kirby, moving beyond him, and then in front of me to take the lead.

"That's enough of your mouth, Jay." Kirby's breathing is

labored, too, I notice, or maybe he's growing frustrated with Jay. That child can get the best of anyone, although admittedly, our son is taking this trip better than I anticipated.

We march in silence for the next few minutes, lost in our individual thoughts.

Jay cuts through the quiet, halting suddenly. "What is this shit?"

"Jay," I chide, coming to a full stop behind him. Kirby joins us.

"No, like seriously," Jay says, pointing to a big pile of feces at the edge of the trail.

"It's bear scat. And this is your last warning. Watch your mouth." Kirby's warning booms over the landscape.

I turn to Kirby, eyes wide. "Bear scat?" Hysteria pipes through. "As in, there has been a bear in the vicinity? And, by the looks of it, recently."

"Bears don't want anything to do with us. Let's just keep moving," Kirby orders.

Our trio continues without words. The forest grows thick with Rhododendrons. Water rushes along the side of the trail as the path leads us to a footbridge. Nothing more than a log cut smooth for hikers' use, it is narrow and rickety-looking at best. Jay uses the term sketchy, and I must agree. Voicing concerns about crossing the unstable-looking bridge laid over the rapidly-moving water, Kirby assures me if it wasn't safe, the park rangers would not allow hikers to use the crossing.

One behind the other, no room for two to walk side by side, we navigate the log. I'm careful not to look over the edge of the guardrail on my left at the big drop below, much less the wide-open side on my right.

Safely on the other side, Kirby announces, "If I remember correctly, this is the two-mile mark of the trail."

I check my watch. We've been on the trail now for almost two hours. The hike is taking longer than I anticipated.

"I need to stop for a sec, Kirby."

My body temperature has risen with the exertion. I halt, shrugging off the jacket I slipped on earlier, tying it around my waist. Kirby uses the reprieve to search the woods for walking sticks. While we wait, Jay and I sip water from the bottles I stored in my backpack.

I breathe in the perfume of nature. The scent of earth mixed with the sweet bouquet of blooming foliage. The sour odor of rotting wood where trees have fallen alongside the path. The clean, fresh smell of the river rushing along parallel with the trail. The scenery is so beautiful I pull out my cell phone to snap a picture.

"Smile, Jay." I aim the phone's camera in his direction. *Why do I bother?* Jay only has one pose, one standard expression he offers. Still, I capture the moment and think to send it to Mama. I open the text message app and attach the photo with the caption, 'hiking,' then hit send. The bar at the top of the screen moves slowly and stalls. I check the reception bars, learning I have no service.

Kirby returns with walking sticks for the three of us. "Do you have cell service?" I ask, accepting the makeshift pole from him.

Kirby pulls out his phone to check. "Nope. Doesn't surprise me, though. We are in the middle of a national park."

"We're in bumfuck Egypt," Jay says. "What did you expect?" He tromps ahead.

Kirby marches forward, grabbing Jay's upper arm, yanking him around to face his father's furious expression. "I warned you about that mouth, young man."

"You don't scare me, *old* man."

Rushing to Kirby's side, I tug the wrist of his other arm in silent plea. He releases Jay to go ahead.

"Kirby, maybe we should turn around," I whisper.

"No. Absolutely not. Besides, we're at the halfway mark. But hear me now, Esme, I'm not putting up with his crap. This has got to stop."

More obstacles to travel across and around, the traverse

continues at a slower pace. The path is mostly rock at this point, each step uneven. Concentration on foot placement eases the awkward silence. Studying the path in front of me for proper footholds, I gratefully use the walking stick Kirby gave me to maintain my balance.

Kirby's reactions to Jay's responses consume my thoughts. *Does Kirby believe I'm too easy on our son? Was he trying to tell me I hadn't done enough with Jay to curb his outbursts? Are my parenting techniques not stern enough for Kirby's approval?* If Kirby only knew half of what I really go through in a day with Jay. His taunts, his name-calling, his threats—the physical abuse that accompanies. I try to keep Kirby abreast of everything that goes on at home while he's on the road, but sometimes, it's simply too much to relay at the end of a long day.

I cease the self-doubt and forward motion to look up, taking in the next leg of this trail. Though the rocks have cleared out a bit, the elevation of the next portion is dauntingly steep.

"Anybody want a snack?" I call out, my energy dwindling, hoping for a small break before taking on the incline.

Jay eagerly agrees though Kirby is reluctant. Fishing the granola bars out of his backpack, Kirby passes them around. We find large rocks along the side of the path to sit and rest, chomping in silence, the noise of rushing water along the path making up for our lack of conversation.

We begin climbing again, saving our words as we struggle to regulate our breathing. I look up and notice the enormous trees lining the path, stretching high into the sky.

"Tulip trees," Kirby yells back to me when I call to ask him what they are.

Awed to standstill, I study the massive tree in front of me. The trunk of the tree is wide enough to fit three men Kirby's size plus four Jay's side-by-side.

Slipping out of my backpack, thinking it would be a great photo of the two of them standing in front of the old tree, I call out, "Hey guys, I want to take a picture."

They're either too far ahead or ignoring my request as they continue onward. I shove the phone into my back pocket. *Maybe on the way back...*

Trailing the boys, I glance up from the path to see they've halted. As I step closer to the pair, I understand they are assessing the best way to continue. A fast flowing stream runs across the middle of the rocky path. Rock hopping is the only option if we're to get to the other side. Kirby points out flat, smooth rocks, cautioning the surfaces will be slick and slippery.

Using the walking stick, I poke into the water, locate a solid fitting for the pole, and lean my body weight on it to step over the running water. A splash sounds behind me. I turn, seeing Jay shake the cold water from his boot.

"Now my damn feet are all wet. This sucks."

Tautly pulled lips across Kirby's face tell me he is holding back.

Under other circumstances, I might enjoy this activity—the opportunity to be outdoors, to soak in the beauty of the surroundings. But the tension between Jay and Kirby, coupled with my poor physical condition, detracts from the experience.

Just when I think we must be getting close now, we come upon another footbridge, this one even more narrow than the last one. The water rushing over the rocks below crescendos. I barely hear Kirby's words of instruction and caution. Legs weak and wobbly from the strenuous activity to get to this point, I hold tightly to the shaky guardrail, silently praying for our safety all the way across.

"That was the three-mile mark. Only one more to go," Kirby calls over his shoulder.

Rounding mile three, we climb, seemingly straight up, no clear foot-worn path to follow at this point. *How many people actually hike this portion of the trail?*

"Are you sure this is the trail, Kirby?"

"I'm sure."

The forest thickens around us, narrowing the walkway. The

terrain under our feet has turned to all rock. These rocks are slick, more treacherous. I take each step with care, concentrating, minding the ledge that falls off into the thick overgrowth of the forest. Ahead, I spot a rock staircase marking the certainty that we are on the path to the promised majestic waterfall. *It better be a good one.*

The stone steps take us higher. My knees and quadriceps push through the task of traversing the higher elevation on this portion of the hike. Water puddles in the hollowed out crevices of the ever climbing stairway. Rocks jut out from the earth beside me, making the trail even more narrow. I stumble, bending, grabbing the rock in front of me to pull myself forward. Kirby breathily asks how I'm doing. In much the same manner, I answer with a fine. *Are we getting old?*

In the distance, I hear the water again, only now realizing the noise of falling water has been absent this last portion of the expedition. *We have to be close.*

We come to a clearing marked by a trail sign and stop to catch our breath.

"Jay, do you see the sign?" I point. "I want you to read it to me."

"I'm not stupid. I can read," Jay mouths, fixing his glare on me.

"You're mother asked you to read the sign, Jay."

I appreciate Kirby's support but do not want this to escalate. "Fine, I'll read it," I concede rather than start an argument I don't have the breath for right now.

"'**Warning Closely Control Children 4 Deaths Here From Falls Please Don't Be Next**'"

Jay shakes his head, no doubt holding his tongue, which in my opinion, is a win for me. I've gotten the message across, though I'm not sure Jay will take it to heart. At the very least, it's given me a brief respite before we clear the last bit of the trail to the waterfalls. I can hear the water crashing over the rocks nearby, but we still have a cavernous trek to follow before we make it there.

Stepping around the last large boulder, the falls come into view, and what a sight it is. The marvel before me is nothing less than breathtaking. I take a moment to breathe in the energy of my surroundings, offering up a silent thank you to God for allowing me the opportunity to witness such a spectacular wonder of His creation.

The waterfall rises one hundred feet up. The water cascades over several rock ledges—loud and boisterous, offering a masterful accompaniment to nature's concerto. We step closer to the water, mindful of the wet rocks layering the landscape. The chilling spray from the falls mists my bare arms. I reach down, running my fingers through the cold water. Jay splashes through the puddles. Neither Kirby nor I bother to chastise him.

Kirby slowly approaches, pulling me into an embrace. "We made it," he says, raising his voice over the noise of the waterfall, planting a kiss on my lips. His scratchy beard tickles me. I laugh.

"We did. I confess it was looking a bit iffy for me at moments."

"Me too," he admits, still sounding winded. "It's amazing, isn't it?"

"Incredible."

Losing myself in the moment, enjoying the feel of Kirby's arms encircling me, the world around me suddenly darkens.

Kirby jerks me upright. "Esme? Esme, you okay?"

Shaking my head, vision coming into focus again, I answer. "Uh, yeah." I cling to Kirby for support, my legs trembling underneath me. "I guess I overdid it with the hike. Everything went dark for a second."

"Come over here." Kirby leads me, keeping his grasp firm. "There's a nice flat rock. Let's get you seated."

Kirby lowers me onto the huge stone, slips out of his backpack, and squats to sit beside me. Pulling my knees up, I lower my head to rest on them. Slowly, my breathing regulates.

"Jay," Kirby shouts. "Stay off of those rocks. No climbing." Kirby turns to me. "Where's your water?"

"In my pack."

"Where's your pack, babe?"

I look behind me, expecting to find my backpack hanging from my shoulders, then rove the landscape, panic moving in.

"Hey, calm down," Kirby says, quickly unzipping his bag to dig inside and pull out one of the extra water bottles. "Drink some of this."

"Kirby, where's my bag?" I ask, taking the water.

"We'll find it. Think back. When's the last time you remember having it."

I search my memory, reliving the hike, going over each moment. "At the big tree. I wanted to take a picture of you and Jay in front of the giant trunk. I took it off, set it on the ground, and called out to you guys, but you didn't answer, so I ran to catch up. I must have left it there."

"Okay, no biggie. We'll get it on our way back down."

"Mom," Jay calls, heading to where we sit. "I'm hungry."

"Mom's taking a break, bud. I'll get your sandwich," Kirby answers on my behalf.

"Kirby, the sandwiches are in my backpack."

"So, where's the food?" Jay asks, stomping up beside the two of us and looking down. "I'm starving."

"Mom left her bag back on the trail. It had the sandwiches in it. How about a granola bar?"

"I want my sandwich. We already had freaking granola bars."

"He's right, Kirby. I only packed three. We ate those earlier." I move to push myself up.

"Where are you going?"

"We'll have to head back down."

"You almost fainted on me not five minutes ago. You can't go anywhere right now. Not until I know you're okay."

"Then what the hell am I going to eat?" Jay yells.

Kirby jumps up from his spot, grabbing Jay's arm. "What did

I say about your language, you little punk? Your mother is not feeling well. Go sit yourself down. I don't want to hear another word come out of your mouth."

Jay yanks out of Kirby's grasp and rushes his father, pushing into Kirby's middle. Kirby staggers backward but catches himself before falling. I rise to stand between them, my head swimming with the sudden movement.

Kirby reaches me before my legs give way. "Sit down," he forcefully urges.

Kirby turns to address Jay, but Jay has left. He uses his walking stick to bash at trees nearby.

"Let him be, Kirby. I can't handle another blow-up right now. Please."

"Fine," Kirby says, though frustration and fury clearly mark his features. "I want you to stay right here. Don't move. I'll be back as fast as I can."

"Where are you going?" I squeak out, my voice raising an octave above normal.

"To get your pack."

"Kirby, that's at least a mile back."

"It's fine. The hike will go faster if I'm alone. You'll have some time to rest, we'll eat when I get back, and then we'll go back down."

"Take your phone," I say, rummaging through his backpack to pull it out.

"Okay, but I doubt we'll have any service. Do you have yours?"

"Yes." I reach for my back pocket, pulling out the phone, checking the screen. He's right. I have a no service message at the top of the display.

"Kirby, please be careful."

"I will. Be right back. Stay still." He orders as he takes leave.

I ensure Jay is behaving in a safe manner, then lie back on the rock, closing my eyes for a moment, letting the sound of the water soothe me.

Enjoying the moment, being at peace in nature, I break the spell to check on Jay again.

I lift upward, leaning the weight of my upper body on braced arms, scanning the area around the falls, but see no sign of Jay. Sitting fully upright, I blink away the dizziness then survey once more. My eyes widen.

Jay is scaling the rock face of the waterfalls.

Jay," I yell as loud as my voice allows. "Jay. Stop. Come back down here. That's dangerous."

Whether it is the noise of the waterfall or Jay disregarding the command, I do not know, but I am fully aware I have to stop him. I push to a stand, yelling for Jay, desperately trying to get his attention. Still, he doesn't register my pleas.

I scramble to the foot of the waterfalls, screaming for him to stop, watching as Jay continues to climb higher. The warning sign at the entrance to the falls scrolls through my mind, fueling my screams. I turn to look for Kirby, knowing full well it is too early for him to be back yet and do the only thing I can, climb after my son.

* * *

EACH MOVEMENT TAKES ME HIGHER. Arms tremble. Legs quiver. Fear of slipping, fear of Jay falling, all that keeps me moving is the adrenalin ferociously coursing through my veins. Wild, horrible scenarios racing in time with the beat of my heart, accompany the awkward clamber up the rocks. I yell, scream, for Jay to stop, my throat raw with the attempt to be heard over the gushing water spilling into the basin below.

I look above me. I'm halfway up. To my left, the water barrels over the ledge in two places. And while no water pours over the surface I climb, the rocks are wet with spray, slimy with algae and moss. Gripping the edges of the rocks, a cold ache settles into my bones. Fingers and hands cramp. I scan for Jay's whereabouts. He's near the top. *I have to reach him and somehow get the two of us down safely. If need be, we will sit up there and wait for Kirby to direct us down. Yes, that's it; that's the plan.* I keep moving upward.

A small stone trips down the rock face past me. *Did I misjudge my grip? Dislodge a piece of the falls?* I hold in panic, waiting for the rock in my grasp to give way, to crumble. Another stone follows. It bounces off the knuckles of my left hand. Tightening my grip, blocking out the pain, I resist the urge to change my grasp.

I lift my chin. Jay stands atop the falls. Even from this distance, I see the sinister look he wears as he hurls rock after rock in my direction. *Is he trying to make me lose my grip? Does he want me to fall? He is your son, Esme. He wouldn't want harm to come to you.* And though it's me consoling myself, I don't believe my own words.

I continue to climb, increasing my speed even at the risk of a hurried mistake. I'm almost at the top. The flying debris comes at me faster, harder, stone after stone—one grazes my arm, another pelts my thigh, barely do I dodge one headed for my face. I manage to make it to the top, heaving my body over the ledge, pushing up on hands and knees, the stone surface underneath me cold, wet, and slippery.

"Jay." Breathless, I pause. "Jay, why didn't you answer me?"

Jay stands near the first of the two cascades. Fast, flowing water pours over the ledge behind him. Two steps backward and Jay will be in the rush of water falling over the edge.

"Jay, you're too close to the water," my plea ragged, raspy. "Please," I beg, "Please just step away from the edge."

Silent, Jay stands rigid, arms at his side, both hands clutching rocks. Feet spread in a wide stance, Jay doesn't step forward as I request, but neither does he inch backward.

Exhausted, cold, and dizzy, the base of my neck knotted with frustration and anger. *Breathe. Clam down. Talk to him, Esme. Find out what's going on in his head.*

"Why were you throwing rocks?" I question, slow and cautious, pushing to stand upright.

Jay wordlessly holds his position.

"Were you trying to make me fall?" Half whiny, half furious, I wince at the delivery.

Still, Jay says nothing. He doesn't have to; his features speak for him. Over the years, though they may have startled me from time to time, I've grown used to Jay's menacing looks. This one is different. This look casts pure hate.

My limbs grow cold. The thump in my chest increases, the noise of it ringing through to my ears, silencing the roar of the water.

Jay moves toward me as he lifts his arm, bringing it behind his head. Using the force of his whole body, he hurls the rock in his hand. Reflexes kick in, I duck away, but the pelt makes contact with my shoulder. The pain is inconsequential as I see Jay readying to throw again. I manage to dodge the hit and stumble, my foot slipping out from under me. Somehow, I right myself and rush forward, skating haphazardly along the slimy surface.

Jay turns, hurrying toward the plunging water. I catch him before he reaches the cascade. Grabbing him from behind, I pin his arms to the sides of his body. Jay squats. His upper body slips through my hold. I quickly work to adjust my grip as Jay's leg kicks backward between mine, crooking to knock my left knee out from underneath me. I fall to the rock, my hip bone making sharp contact with the solid, unforgiving surface. Tears spring. Through the searing pain, I try to pull my leg under me and realize my other leg dangles over the edge. Fingers claw into the mucky algae, a lump of moss. There is nothing to grab hold of to pull myself forward. Using my stomach muscles, I worm forward. My legs follow, and I'm out of certain danger, pulling myself to sit, looking up into Jay's penetrating green glare, fury blazing wildly.

The tightness in my chest strangles the air desperately trying to reach my lungs. *I have to get through to him. Don't provoke him, Esme.*

"Jay, talk to me. Tell me what has made you so angry." Voice wobbly, words garbled, I wait, wondering if Jay understood my appeal.

"I don't want to talk, bitch. I don't want you here! If I didn't have such shitty aim, you wouldn't be here."

"Jay." *He can't be serious.*

Eyes blurring, I shake my head, attempt to reorder his vile words, make sense of what Jay has said. *He's just worked up. Calm him down.*

"I hate you. I hate Dad. I hate this stupid, fucking hike. You shouldn't have made me come."

Clumsy and tense, I maneuver myself to stand. I step forward, close the distance between us, reach out to him.

"Don't come any closer. I'm warning you."

"Jay, can we just talk for a minute?" *Careful. You sound hateful and exasperated.* But that's how I feel, I scream silently at myself.

"Please." I inch one step forward, again reaching out, keeping the palm of my hand open.

Jay reaches out to accept my hold.

I'm getting through.

Jay strides toward me, taking my hand, squeezing. Jay begins turning, spinning, flinging me around. The momentum builds. We're too close to the ledge.

"Jay, you're going to make me fall!"

"So."

Sliding, skidding, stumbling, I yank out of his grip, but Jay is fast. He grabs me again, fiercely tugging me to the ledge. My footing gives way, and I slip, one foot going over the side of the rock face. I hold to Jay, trying to pull myself up.

"Let go of me, you bitch." Screaming, he kicks. The toe of his boot makes contact with my cheekbone.

Terror seizes me. He's going to kill me. He's trying to push me off into the falls. *I'm going to die at the hand of my son.*

Writhing, pleading for Jay to stop, I pull and push myself up. I scurry on hands and knees to get away from him. Jay lunges after me. He slips. One half of his body hangs over the edge. I twist around, diving after him, grabbing hold of his wrist, tugging with all my strength to pull him back to safety.

Jay fights me. He's losing ground, slipping further over the side. His body dangles over the precipice.

"You cunt. You're going to regret this."

"Jay, don't say that!" Tears flow uncontrollably, hazing my vision. I can't talk myself through this.

My hands slippery from the wet rocks, the algae, the fear coursing hard and fast through me, I struggle to maintain my hold on Jay. He kicks and flails, jerks and yanks.

"You have to stop fighting me so I can pull you up," I yell. Jay's thrashing drags me forward.

"Not if I pull you over first," he threatens.

My soul quivers under Jay's piercing stare—hatred, loathing, and vengefulness reaching through to my heart and clenching mercilessly.

On my stomach, holding with all my might to keep Jay from falling, to pull him back, I search his eyes for something, anything to replace the evil emanating back at me. Arm muscles burn under the exertion, flaming in pain. Fingers cramp, threatening to seize. Drenched and cold, confused and scared, weak and dazed, I feel Jay's hands slipping away.

And then, I let go.

MEREL

APRIL

*A*ll is as it should be once more—the long spring break holiday behind me, the students busy at their desks. Feeling accomplished and thankful to have made it through the painful anniversary, I can finally breathe regularly again. Even the fist in my stomach has eased its grip.

From my desk, I watch the intensity with which the students work to complete morning assignments. They look refreshed, energized, a glow tinging their skin from recent time in the sun.

Across the room, the door pushes open. Principal Garber sticks her head inside the classroom. I rise from my desk and walk to meet her, checking the students are on task. Even from a distance, I sense something is different about her this morning. My concern grows as I near her. Normally so sure in her composure and stance, Principal Garber's shoulders slouch, her features drawn and distraught.

"I need to speak with you." Principal Garber turns to look at the students and then back at me, adding, "In your office, please."

"Of course." I run through the possible reasons she might have for calling a private conversation. *Shit, I haven't turned in attendance.*

As if to check on them, I look over my shoulder in the direction of the students, glancing at the clock. Eight-thirty. Three desks empty. Attendance is due by eight. But in my defense, today is the first day back from spring break. The oversight is an honest one.

Bubbling with information about their experiences over the holiday, the students had so many stories they wanted to share with me, and I certainly didn't want to slight any one of them. Besides, I had missed them and was genuinely interested in all they had to report. Their stories slowly lifted me from the dark place I'd been in the last week and a half. Admittedly, my interest was self-serving. So yes, I suppose I am at fault, and I prepare for whatever wrath I have coming.

I twist back to meet Principal Garber's gaze, noticing the red rimming her eyes. Something is wrong. This isn't about forgotten attendance numbers.

Principal Garber follows me as I step inside the office. She moves to close the door.

"Wait," I say with too much force. "Don't shut it all the way."

She cocks her head in question.

"It locks from the outside," I stammer. Understanding I need to be clearer in my delivery, I add, "If you pull the latch shut, the door will lock us inside the office."

Even though she is less than full force, the woman still intimidates me, and I ramble on. "We asked Tony to fix it, but he's been so busy." I let the last bit trail off.

Principal Garber nods, not pushing forth any objection or ridicule for not having brought the problem to her attention prior.

I bite my lip to halt the nervous chatter and watch her, waiting for her to begin. Wringing her hands, twisting her fingers —what is going on here?

"I have had some bad news this morning," she says. "Terrible news, actually."

My hand flies to my midsection in an effort to halt the flip-flopping motion in my stomach. I shift the weight between my feet, silently willing her to continue. To stop? I'm not sure what I want.

The principal's eyes drop to the floor. My line of sight follows. I note the carpet in the room is in need of vacuuming. Had I known we'd be conferencing in here, I certainly would have taken on the task beforehand.

"Mrs. Deacon called me earlier," she speaks softly.

"Oh?" My mind whirls, searching, processing, trying to place the last name with someone who is supposed to mean something to me. One of my students, I realize. But which one? Who? It's only been a matter of days. How can I possibly forget one of their last names?

"Yes," she says, struggling to maintain her composure, her breathing ragged.

Something is wrong. I don't want to know. I'm not going to be able to cope with whatever it is she's about to relay. I feel it deep in my bones.

I look away, checking the walls. The space seems smaller. The walls are coming together, closing in.

"Ms. Sowanoke," she says calmly as if there is nothing to fear, but she's wrong. I know this. The ringing in my ears grows louder.

She stands, watching me, blocking the door to my classroom, to my exit. I turn to the door behind me, the one that will lead me into Dorothy's classroom, but Dorothy has closed it—it's locked, no way out. I'm trapped.

"Her son," she begins.

The woman in front of me, my principal, she's speaking. I can't make out what she says. The words spill from her mouth, no coherency to them. I reach for the desktop to maintain balance.

The burning starts in the pit of my stomach, rising. Flames lap their way up my chest, into my lungs. The room spins. The walls inch toward me.

I feel my head move in a back and forth motion, disbelieving, searching.

Principal Garber speaks a garbled gibberish I can't understand.

The heat spreads, racing through my body, along my limbs. The air so thick, it's hard to breathe. Hands flying to my neck, I work to keep my throat from closing. In the corners of my vision, the darkness, like a dust storm, closes in from both sides.

And then, all is gone.

MEREL

APRIL

*I*t's too much. The thought of having to attend a child's funeral, to make the march up to the open coffin, to see his sweet little face, to see no air move through his chest. I don't think I can do it. But to not be present on this somber, solemn, sobering day has been deemed inappropriate and unacceptable by Principal Garber. Though all staff has been strongly urged, Ollie's current (as well as his past) teachers have been required to be present at today's service.

My heart is crushed. It's as if I'm reliving my own history—punishment for my past. I can't do it again. I'm not strong enough. Years, it took me *years* to get to the point I could actually conceive the possibility of thinking about the next day. Somehow though, envisioning the day laid out before me, led to looking ahead to the following week, then came a month. I still can't conceive years from now, but I don't want to either.

Last button on my blouse secure, I tuck the tail into the skirt I've chosen. The moment has arrived that I must face myself in the mirror, apply makeup, attempt to make myself look presentable. But I can't look at my image, it's not me in the reflection. It's him, staring back at me. Mocking me. Refusing to let me go.

I fall to the edge of the bed, sitting, staring at the bare walls of my bedroom. Thinking back on everything that has transpired in these last two days, playing out the conversations in my head, I am still trying to piece it all together.

Principal Garber had taken me to her office after I came around. Dorothy explained to our principal about my attacks, my past, apologizing to me later for having broken my confidence. I could hardly hold it against Dorothy. What else could she have done, given the circumstances?

Principal Garber (Jeanine) was surprisingly understanding, compassionate even, as she explained to me what had transpired.

"Mrs. Deacon went into Ollie's room to wake him for school on the Wednesday morning before the release for spring break. She found Ollie unresponsive in his bed. Ollie was in a coma for ten days. The doctors thought he was turning a corner, but in the end, he didn't make it."

"That can't be." I'd spoken the words but hadn't recognized my voice.

"I'm afraid it is. The family is devastated."

Jeanine had waited patiently for me to process what she had laid out. I stared at my lap, twisting the tissue in my hands, remembering the precious boy.

Sweet, shy little Ollie. The protector of animals. The image of him on the playground earlier in the year had reeled through my mind. I saw the tears roll over his cheeks as he watched Jay stomp the life from the frog he'd found.

"What happened?" I asked, my voice gravelly.

"Mrs. Deacon said it was an overdose," Jeanine began, then cleared her throat before continuing. "One of the last conversations she had with Ollie was at dinner the Tuesday night before spring break. Ollie had asked his mom and dad if stupid pills really worked; could they make a person smart."

"Stupid pills?" I managed to ask.

"Yes, that's what Ollie called them. Ollie explained to his parents that someone had told him about a special pill that would make him smart." Sniffling, Jeanine pulled a tissue from her jacket pocket, dabbed her nose.

"But that doesn't make sense. Ollie is... was so bright. Why would he ever have thought otherwise?"

"I don't know," she said and shook her head. "I've ushered a lot of children through their elementary years, and I can tell you, there is only a small portion of their world we as educators ever see."

"So, Ollie took these 'stupid pills?' How many did he take?"

"Mrs. Deacon didn't say exactly, but Ollie must have taken the pills before he went to sleep Tuesday night. A plastic baggie was found in the sheets of Ollie's bed. The residue in the bag matched the findings of the toxicology report. The report indicated Ollie had excessively high levels of alprazolam. Xanax."

When Jeanine had relayed the information about Ollie's cause of death, we made a plan of action. Ollie's classmates had to be told. The guidance counselor had to be briefed so grief counseling could be offered. There was little time for me to process my own sorrow; the children had to be considered. I had to be the brave face for my students and was too distraught to line up the facts.

Now, sitting on the edge of my bed, I search deeper into the recesses of my memory. Besides the fact Ollie is dead, there is something else wrong—something I am missing. It's the Xanax that's bothering me. How does a child get a hold of that much medication? And what parent would leave such a dangerous drug sitting around for a child to confiscate? Mrs. Deacon relayed to Jeanine that she wasn't and had never taken any sort of anti-depressant or anxiety medication.

I know it's there, in my head somewhere, waiting to be extracted. A conversation. Someone taking Xanax. Of course, half the parents at the school are probably taking it. Hell, I can't get through a day without my anti-depressants. I've attempted in the past to wean myself off, but each time I try, I lose traction, and the hole tries to pull me back in. I've finally come to accept I will live my life dependent on them. I know what it is to exist without them, and it's hardly an existence at all.

And then I hear it, the confession. 'If it weren't for the Xanax, I don't know how I'd get through the weekends.'

"Who said that?" I ask, my voice echoing through my apartment, no one nearby to answer except me.

Instead of a response, I hear the voice again. 'I'd have popped one before coming today, but I can't find them. And, I just had the prescription filled. I'm sure I'll be turning the house upside down when I get home.'

I stand. Walking the width of the bedroom, fingertips to my temples, I search out the answer.

I was in my classroom. The moms. They're speaking in hushed voices with one another.

"Why do I have multiple parents in the room?" I talk my way through it. Giving voice to my own answers.

"A classroom event. A party."

"What were the children doing?"

I circle the living room, pacing, focusing. Determined.

"Valentine's Day. They were passing out cards. There was a craft. Heart shaped containers for their moms. Jay shared his project with me. The green eye with the X over it. Jay wasn't going to give it his to his mother, but he didn't want her to see it either. She was there that day. Jay's mom. She was speaking to Caroline's mom. It was her. Jay's mom said it."

I stop at the kitchen counter. Jay's mom said she had misplaced her prescription. A full prescription of Xanax.

"It was Jay. That hateful, thieving child. Jay called Ollie stupid. He gave Ollie those pills."

You're really going to blame a child for killing another child?

"I know what he's capable of."

Do you?

I spot Poppy—the doll I was so certain Jay had stolen from me. Poppy is propped at the end of the countertop where I placed him earlier after finding the lost doll underneath my bed.

You misplaced that doll, and all the while, you've been blaming an innocent child.

"Jay is hardly innocent. And I searched this whole apartment, tore it apart. Poppy was nowhere to be found."

So you think Jay broke into your apartment twice? The first time to steal the doll and the second time to return the doll he stole from you?

"I know it sounds crazy, but I know Jay. He's conniving and sneaky and evil. Jay doesn't care what or who he hurts."

And Jay being absent all week, his mother's lack of response to the email you sent her about Ollie's death—how do you explain that, Merel?

"I don't know."

ESME

APRIL

When I finally come 'round, I wake with a scream that has been choking to get out for days. I find myself alone, terrified, enveloped in darkness. A steady beeping sounds nearby. Antiseptic chemicals assault my sense of smell. My vision adjusts to take in the unfamiliar room. Tubes and wires string from my body, connecting me to machines. *Why am I here?* A heavy fog clouds my memory. Fear clutches my lungs. *What happened? Where is everyone?*

A door is thrown open—light floods the room, bright and painful. Mama rushes to my side. She holds me tight while I cry, not knowing for what or why. When I have no tears left to weep, Mama brushes the hair away from my eyes and dries my face, though tears streak her own.

"I was so worried, my girl. So worried," she says, clutching me to her again.

I find my voice, hoarse and husky, and let the questions that have been running through my head spill out. Mama refuses to answer any of them until the doctor examines me, leaving me to lie in a pool of unknowing.

Doctors and nurses satisfied with my well-being, I lie in the room alone again. Mama has left to call my father while I search my memory for the last item I can register. With great speed, it comes barreling in. I remember. I recall Kirby heading back down the trail to retrieve my backpack. Jay scaling the waterfall, his hateful words and threats. Me, climbing the waterfalls, dodging the flying stones hurling toward me. And then, with a flashing force, I see him fall from my grasp—fingers uncurling and letting go. Screams sound in the distance. I have no idea they are coming from me until Mama hurries to my side once more.

My throat raw, the word comes out barely above a whisper. "Jay?"

"Oh baby," my mother soothes, and I know the answer to the question. He is gone. My son is dead—at my hand.

Darkness returns.

When I wake again, I know where I am, what I have done. My body is still, rigid, and unmoving; eyes wide and blank, but my mind travels, choosing to forget what I now know, leaving my shell behind while the world goes on around me. I hear words spoken by unfamiliar voices. The terms catatonic, depression, post-traumatic stress swim through the air, but none of the statements that flow through stick or make sense to me. It's easier to float through the ether. So, I do.

Moments of clarity arrive here and there, but I can't move or speak—arms and legs refuse to work, eyes unblinking, mouth unable to form words. From time to time, I hear voices. I think it's Mama, sometimes I believe it's Daddy, other times they belong to people who are unremarkable. Regardless of who is speaking, their words seem to travel through a long, narrow tunnel to reach me, yet fall away before I can catch them.

For how long this goes on, I don't know. Time is of no consequence to me as I remain in one position, staring into nothingness. For hours? Days?

And then, the darkness fades away. The same uncertainties return. *How did I get to this point? How did I make it off the trail to be residing in a hospital bed?* Panic grips me, threatening to drag me back into the place of un-being, and I forget to breathe. The inside of my chest feels swollen, an ache I can't and don't want to relieve. I tell myself it's not real. None of what I recall has happened, it's only a nightmare. Yet I'm awake, eyes wide and cognizant once more.

My tongue works, and I am able to speak the questions that have been thrashing, pounding to be put out for answers while my body has held them prisoner. Mama and Daddy lock gazes, some silent pact transferring between them.

Their responses reveal a reality I can not accept. They tell me Kirby is gone. Gone where I want to know.

"Is he on the road, training another rookie driver?"

No, they say, heads shaking in unison.

"Kirby and Jay are gone," Daddy says, Mama tacking on a, 'to be with God' as if this will comfort me.

I quit asking altogether. My mind locks up my body again. I don't know that my voice could even form words anymore—tongue heavy, useless. I slip away into the dank, unfeeling prison again.

Memories from childhood seep in behind my eyes, taking me back to a lake we often frequented during the summers of my youth. The sensation of floating along the surface of that still lake overtakes me now. My body holds in the laid out position—arms outstretched, eyes open to the gray-clouded sky above, ears below the surface of the water, muffling all sounds that reach me. For how long I float, I can't be certain.

Occasionally, I allow myself to hear them. They don't believe I understand, but I do—when I want to, when I think I might be able to handle the meaning of what is being said. My parents, in hushed conference, speaking about arrangements, about tragedy, about death. They argue, too. About what to do with me, what is the best way to move forward in my healing process. Daddy believes I need professional mental help, but Mama disagrees; I'm under a doctor's care. She wants me to have more time to heal myself, not go into some rigorous therapy session I won't be able to cope with just yet.

No amount of healing or therapy will ever be able to close the hole in my heart. I've lost them. My whole world, gone.

Though it doesn't seem to frequent me often, sleep is a welcome friend, the only one I wish to visit with, that is, until the woman comes. Even in my periods of semi-wakefulness, I sense her presence, always watching, waiting beyond the shadows. I remember her. My monster from childhood, ever-plaguing my dreams, twisting them into ugly, terrifying nightmares.

On rare occasions when I fully come around, experience a moment of mindfulness, finally lucid and coherent enough to put words into sentences, I tell Mama the shadow woman has returned.

"She wants to hurt me, to make me suffer."

Mama only clucks a discounting statement to my visions. "There's no one else here, Esme," or an, "Oh, honey. Let's not start that again." Her dismissals always accompanied by an urgent insistence that I need to eat as she presses food to my lips. Sometimes, I will take a bite, and at other times, I can't get my mouth to move, slipping back into myself, floating off into the horizon under the cloud covered sky.

And then the darkness takes leave again—it feels different this time, like I might be able to pull myself out of the place that holds me inside. My senses fully alert, my limbs moving, feeling stronger, I dredge up the courage to ask about Kirby.

"What happened to him?"

He was in a terrible accident, my parents say, their faces taut with concern.

When it becomes clear to them I will not accept that answer, I am finally told the truth.

"Nobody knows exactly what happened, sweetheart," Daddy starts, Mama by his side, her lips clamped, arms wrapped tightly around her middle. "Do you remember the hike, Esme?" My father asks.

"Yes," I answer, my voice strangled with grief. "Kirby, and me, and," I hold, my mind seeing my son's hate-filled eyes piercing mine, "Jay." I choke out his name.

"Your mama had been trying to reach you. You were supposed to let her know when you all got off the trail and were heading home. She called and called, knowing you had to be back at work the next day. Your mother was frantic. You know how she gets, claiming she has a sixth sense about things."

Daddy waits for my acknowledgment. I give a slight nod, a signal for him to continue.

"She called the park rangers and insisted they check on you all. Thank goodness you had given your mama the details of the trail you all were hiking. When the authorities reached the trail late that evening, they found remnants of a backpack. The rangers couldn't say for sure, but they think an animal must have been after food."

"I left my backpack next to a tree," I tell them, the memories playing out like a silent movie in my head. Mama nods, brings her hands together in a grasp, wringing, twisting.

Daddy moves to sit on the edge of my bed. "That's good, Esme. Very good. Do you remember anything else?" He asks, taking hold of my hand.

"We made it to the falls. The hike was harder than we thought it would be." My words fall forward in a sludgy, stunted fashion. "I was dizzy. I almost fainted." I stop, locking in on the memory of Kirby's face, the concern and love for me etched around his eyes. *How can he be gone? I don't know how to be without Kirby.*

"Go on," Daddy urges.

"Jay was hungry. He wanted lunch. My backpack had our lunch inside—sandwiches I had made. I told Kirby...." Closing my eyes, I swallow the knot of sorrow in the back of my throat, gulping for the few shallow breaths I can get around it. "I told Kirby I thought we should all hike back to the tree and have lunch there, but he wanted me to rest before we continued."

A tiny yelp escapes my mother's lips. Her hand flies to her mouth.

"Kirby was a good man," Daddy says. He squeezes my hand, pausing to give me a moment to process my loss again. "Do you want to continue, honey?"

I struggle with the answer, wanting, yet not wanting to know what happened or to relive it all. But I can no longer live with the questions.

"Yes."

Traveling back in time, I begin again. "Kirby left. I was sitting on a big rock. Jay was playing in the water. I laid back on the rock to close my eyes for a moment. I wanted to clear my head, make the dizziness go away. When I opened my eyes, I saw Jay climbing the rocks along the waterfall." I pause, chewing over how much of the incident I want to recall, to share. "I couldn't get his attention, so I went after him. I started climbing. At the top of the falls, we argued. Jay was mad I had followed him." I suck as much air as I can hold into my lungs, then exhale slowly. "He pushed me away, and then he slipped. I grabbed him, but I couldn't hold on." The tears slide over my face, unable to wash away the dishonesty, the lie.

We fall into silence. Daddy squeezes my hand once more, the pressure of his clutch speaking his silent reassurance. I pull away, undeserving. If he only knew what a monster I am.

"That's it," I whisper. "I don't remember anything else."

Daddy turns to look at Mama. The unspoken exchange I witness between them tells me they are questioning how much more information they should relay. But I can't stop now. I have to know.

"Kirby?" I ask, bracing myself for Daddy's answer.

"The rangers found bear tracks near the backpack."

"Oh, God. No. Kirby." I barely recognize my own voice.

"No, Esme. No. It's not what you think. There were no signs of a struggle. No attack. But the authorities aren't sure if Kirby encountered the animal, and it frightened him, or if he found the bag ripped apart and was on his way back to you and Jay. The coroner's report stated Kirby suffered a heart attack, Esme."

"But Kirby was fine. Too young to have a heart attack."

"Indications point to his poor physical health, most likely related to the stress and lifestyle conditions of his job," Daddy says.

Daddy continues to speak about the details of their funeral services, how lovely it was, something about our church family helping with the arrangements. But nothing sinks in, takes hold. All I can comprehend, fully understand, is that I am alone— nothing to anyone anymore.

The darkness begins its slow roll forward, sliding in from the corners, shutting out the rest of the world, locking me inside, where I am truly nothing.

* * *

REALITY and fantasy dance together so often now I can't trust myself to determine what is real, what is fact, what's only in my head. I don't know how many hours have gone by. I don't know if days have dawdled into weeks, weeks into months. Time means nothing to me. All I do understand is that I am stuck, a knowledge that doesn't bother me. How can my life possibly go forward now that Kirby and Jay are gone?

Caregivers arrive at my side, asking me questions, then taking leave without receiving answers. Seemingly they get what they've come for, though. I'm poked and prodded. Occasionally, they will move my limbs into other positions I hold until the time comes to position me into some other stance that suits them.

Something is different about this moment, though. While I sit here—unmoving, eyes blankly focusing on nothing as I do at all times—I understand fully what is going on around me. Mama and Daddy are in the room. They're talking with a man, a voice I don't recognize. Daddy is saying they do not know how to help me anymore. He tells the man I'm in some sort of stupor, that they can't get through to me, nor are the doctors making any progress. They want to move me, take me somewhere else.

The man asks questions. I think he's talking to me, but my tongue is thick and dry and heavy inside my mouth. When I don't respond, my parents answer on my behalf. They're giving the man my medical history, then he inquires about our family's history of mental illness.

Mama steps in front of me, stooping, searching my face. I think she's trying to get my attention. "How much does she understand about what is happening?" She asks the strange man.

"Without a proper examination, I can't say for sure," the man says. "Sometimes patients know everything going on around them, and other times, they're locked away, so to speak, and are completely unaware of what is transpiring in their midst."

"Leoti," Daddy gently says to Mama. "We have to tell him everything. We want her to come back. The doctor needs to know."

The room takes on a somber silence. Finally, Daddy breaks the quiet. "Esme is not our biological child. The circumstances were unusual."

"Esme's birth mother is my sister, my identical twin sister." The voice belongs to my mother, but my mother doesn't have any family. She was an only child raised by a single mother. Her mother, my grandmother, died before I was born.

"Our family histories would, therefore, be the same. However..." my mother says, letting the rest of the statement fall away.

Daddy finishes Mama's sentence. "We don't know for certain who the father is. What we do know is the pregnancy was unplanned and unwelcome by the birth mother."

The voices continue as my mind races through the information they have spilled forth. *My parents aren't my parents? Mama has a twin? What else have they hidden away from me?*

Nothing makes sense to me anymore, but does it even matter? The life I did have, the one I've lost was only a lie anyway.

Perhaps fantasy is reality.

LEOTI

The shadow woman had returned. It had been years since Esme had mentioned the woman. It was one of the first things Esme uttered when she finally awoke. All throughout her childhood, Esme would wake in the middle of the night terrified, screaming inconsolably that the shadow woman was nearby. Those dreams were exhaustingly reoccurring all the way up until Esme was in her early twenties.

After Esme and Kirby established their own home, Esme would tell me about the woman still continuing to steal her sleep. Once Esme and Kirby began attending their church and growing more dependent on their church family, Esme rarely, if ever, spoke about those dreams. I wasn't certain if Esme still had the nightmares or if she was simply sharing the details of them with someone else. Either way, I didn't want to bring up the subject to her. Doing so might have spurred them again, and the last thing I wanted to do was put more stress on my daughter. Esme had more problems than she could handle, in my opinion. Jay was not an easy child to raise, especially with Kirby on the road so often.

Rubin has always declared I fret too much, and maybe he's right. But with Esme slipping in and out of mindfulness, coping with the grief of losing my grandson and son-in-law, and then the re-emergence of the shadow woman, of course I was in a tizzy. I tried to excuse away the reappearance of the shadow woman, to both Esme and myself. Esme had been asleep for so long after the accidents that killed Jay and Kirby, I thought the episode must be some long dismissed night terror returning in response to all my poor girl had been through. Yet each time Esme would return to us from one of her stupors, she would tell me, "The shadow woman is watching, Mama." I just couldn't shake the feeling the woman's return was some sort of ill omen.

All throughout Esme's youth, I tried to get rid of that woman, and I was always pretty good at soothing my daughter's ailments. Esme wasn't the healthiest child, always suffering from some sickness or affliction. By the time Esme hit her teen years, my Mama's book of herbal recipes was tattered and faded. Flipping back and forth through her handwritten potions, I concocted one herbal remedy after another. As soon as the symptoms of one sickness subsided, others would take its place. Both Ama and I were the picture of health throughout childhood on into our adult lives. I often worried it was bad genes from Esme's biological father, or perhaps my child had inherited hypochondria-tic tendencies from the man.

But Esme was truly sick. The doctors were doing their best, yet nothing they had done cured my child. It was as if Esme was under some sort of trance, locked deep away inside of herself. Every day I watched over her, waiting for the rare moments she would come around. And when she did, Esme was just as lucid as the days before the terrible tragedy that put her into the state. I kept hoping each time Esme surfaced, she was going to stay. But without notable trigger or even warning, she fell back into that trance, holding whatever position she landed in for days. The doctors advised me not to bother moving her, twisting her around, that they and the nurses would do it. I worried, though, about her getting cramps, getting locked up in some twisted position for the rest of her life. This was no way for Esme to be living.

My child was far too young to be trapped into existing that way for the rest of her years.

Desperate for a solution, I sought out Ama. We'd hardly kept in touch since Esme was born. After our big fight about Rubin and I raising Esme as our own, Ama and I rarely saw one another. Ama came by the bakery to let me know when Daddy had passed on, and occasionally on our birthday, she'd make a surprise visit. We never went back to being close like we were during our youth, though. I missed my sister, but I wasn't about to give up my child for her. Ama had made it clear she'd have nothing to do with me if I didn't see things her way. That was the way she wanted it, and that's the way she got it. I could be just as stubborn as my sister.

I wasn't sure what to expect when I went to Ama but was hoping for at least a bit of empathy from the woman who had given birth to my only child. Ama was impassive, indifferent at best. She reiterated the same hateful rhetoric Ama always used in reference to Esme. Ama wanted nothing to do with her. According to Ama, whatever fate had fallen on Esme, was Esme's to endure, not mine and most certainly not Ama's.

So, I did what any mother would do for her child. I knew in my heart Ama could make Esme well again. After each visit with Esme, witnessing no progress in her situation, I would drive myself up into the woods belonging to The Community, march straight to Ama's door, and demand help. Day after day, we had the same argument until finally, Ama broke down. She stated that under no circumstance would she perform it and had little faith I would have any success with it, but nevertheless, offered up a spell I could at least try.

Try, I did. Ama was not the only one with special gifts. Daddy might have chosen Ama as his apprentice, training her to take his position as leader of that damned community, but Mama was a true healer. I've always believed Mama's healing abilities were what drew Daddy to my mother in the first place. Not that he didn't love her; I do believe he did. But Daddy's talents lay elsewhere. He was born into a family with roots stemming deep as conjurers and, according to Mama, some voodoo practices as well.

Conjuring, healing, voodoo, whatever the spell was Ama had given me, I was determined to make it work. I performed the ritual each day at sundown for two weeks, using the exact ingredients Ama had listed out, then chanted that incantation verbatim —word for ridiculous word, even if I wasn't pronouncing some of them correctly. Progress. Esme made progress. More progress than she had under doctors' care for the last year and a half. My girl was coming 'round.

The statuesque states and blank stares slowly dwindled away. Esme began talking to her physicians, taking an active role in her recovery. It seemed all my hopes and prayers had been answered. Then came her family sessions.

Rubin and I dutifully attended each requisitioned therapy session. At first, the sessions were going so well. Esme participated. Rubin and I cooperated without hesitation. And then, just when I thought I was getting my daughter back, my world fell apart.

I've no idea how Esme learned the truth, but she did. Somehow, Esme knew about my twin. While she didn't know Ama's name, Esme knew she was my sister's child. I was stunned and speechless, not knowing what to say or how to answer. Rubin handled it well, though. He was direct and honest with the few details we could offer. It wasn't enough for our daughter, though. Esme felt deceived and cheated, her whole life was a lie. How could she possibly know who she was, given the fact she had never known her whole truth? She deserved to know more, had a right to know everything.

What could I say? I wasn't about to tell my emotionally raw and fragile daughter her birth mother would have abandoned her (or worse) had I not intercepted Esme, and that while I gained a daughter, I lost my sister because of it.

Ama's warnings ringing in the back of my mind, we gave Esme what little information we could, and that was far more than I was comfortable relaying. Ama would be furious with me, but what other choice did I have? It was the specifics Esme called for, about who Ama was and where she lived, that we held onto. And though we may have been holding back information about Ama for Esme's own welfare, we honestly couldn't provide Esme with the identity of her father.

Of course, Rubin and I had discussed who he might be, throwing out alternate theories over the years, trying ourselves to surmise who was Esme's father. We only ever really came up with two likely possibilities—Thomas Fordham, the man our friend John introduced us to the night we took Ama out for burgers, or Elan Darach, the arranged fiancé Ama was supposed to couple with but somehow never went through with the ceremony. Given the information we garnered, both men seemed unlikely prospects. Ama was adamant the father was not Elan, ever steadfast that Esme's father was a commoner. And when Rubin had questioned John about Thomas Fordham, we learned he was gay.

Esme didn't accept what little we could give her. While she could understand we might not know the identity of her father, Esme was hell-bent on learning more about Ama. She'd find out the information herself, Esme proclaimed.

It was devious, I know, but Esme assumed Ama's last name was my maiden name, Sowanoke, and I didn't bother to tell her otherwise. Ama and I were his and her twins. Mama took me and gave me her last name, while Daddy took Ama and titled her with his last name, Pullen.

As Esme's strength and health returned, I hoped her acceptance of us as her rightful parents would as well. I remained hopeful that, at some point, she'd come to terms with the way things were, had always been. Esme had parents who loved her, cared for her, and would do anything for her well-being.

Grateful and thankful aren't terms that do justice for the feelings I had the night those rangers called to tell me they were bringing my daughter home. The woman they brought down from the trail, however, wasn't my Esme. Esme was gone.

AMA

OCTOBER 2012

They named her Esmerelda. Leoti called her Esme. 'Esme this, and Esme that.' I told Leoti I wanted nothing to do with that child the night it was born, and I meant it. For years, Leoti held onto the belief I would come around, be a part of the child's life in some capacity, but I never did, and I never will.

Leoti had no business taking the girl on as her own. If I had never gone to seek out Leoti that afternoon... if only I had been able to carry out my plan once that thing had left my body. But no, Leoti caught me. Leoti wanted a baby. Rubin couldn't give her a baby. Poof, a baby falls into her hands. Leoti gave no regard to my wishes, to my well-being. She didn't care the child could ruin my life.

The night it was born, I had let Leoti and Rubin believe I would rest and give the matter some thought, as Rubin had suggested. The only thing I *thought* on was an alternate plan to get the child out of my life for good. After Leoti and Rubin retired for the night, I would take the child and go through with my intentions. I should have realized once Leoti had that baby in her arms, she wouldn't put it down. I had paced their guest room, scheming, fuming, coming up with no good ideas to put into action. I had to accept Leoti was going to keep the child as her own. Fine. That was what Leoti wanted, and that was what I gave her, even though I knew the girl was cursed from the moment of her conception.

When I placed the conjure on Thomas Fordham, I had no idea I would conceive his child. *May all your days and relationships be plagued by misfortune and heartbreak, Thomas Fordham.* The curse had coursed through my body for nine long months, growing, festering, but when the girl was born, she wholly owned the curse. With any luck, the curse would handle the child before I had to deal with the ramifications of what I had done.

I had slipped out in the early hours of the morning when the three of them had settled into bed, and I didn't go back, at least not for a good length of time, that is. As always was the case, I missed Leoti, had hoped she would have recognized her error and done right by me.

In the cover of night, deep in the woods away from the ever watchful eyes of The Community members, I lay the last log onto the pyre, then douse it with the ceremonial oil. I need to remember, I need to see the scene again. I need to be certain. I call on my spirit guides to set forth the vision, to portray it in the flames—the exchange between Leoti and myself, the year 1981.

The flames lap the night sky, growing in intensity and heat. I stand at the edge of the fire and watch as my much younger self approaches Leoti's bakery.

A year gone by since the night the child was born, I hear the tinkle of the bell above the door as I watch myself step through the threshold. Leoti's head swiveled to see who entered, then immediately swung around to view the baby behind her. It bumbled happily about inside a playpen.

Leoti's spirit seemed happier than I'd ever seen, but there was something else in her eyes too. I saw it, the fear she tried to mask.

She snatched up the baby, told the girl working with her she was going to step out to visit with me—she would be back soon.

Leoti marched us out of the bakery, grasp wrapped tightly around the handle of the stroller she pushed along the sidewalk to the nearby park. Leoti directed us to a deserted bench, doled out some sort of snack for the girl, and turned to me.

"You keep disappearing."

"Yeah, well, I came back."

"Did you come back for Esme?" She asked, her eyes watery, her throat thick.

"Hell no. I told you I didn't want anything to do with it."

Leoti turned away, scanned the park.

"You named it Esme?"

"Esmerelda."

"What did you tell people?"

"Tell people?"

"Yeah, people. Neighbors, bakery customers, friends."

She drew a long breath. "A story I read in the papers once. That she was my miracle baby, I had no idea I was pregnant. I wasn't feeling very well one afternoon, and she just showed up." Leoti lowered her eyes. "It's not exactly a lie. Esme is a miracle. My miracle," she said, her voice barely audible.

"I can't believe anybody bought that load of crap. Seriously?"

"For the most part, they have. All the non-believers have come up with their own theories. I've heard the whispers throughout town. Rubin and I paid a surrogate because I couldn't have a baby. We bought a baby. Rubin impregnated his mistress, and now we are raising the child as our own. People make up their own stories." Leoti paused, drank in the sight of the child. "I know she's not mine, but I feel like she's mine."

"Cut the shit, Leoti. You believe she's yours. You've got yourself believing that ridiculous ass story you made up even if no one else does."

Leoti caught the tear falling from her chin, then ran her hand over her pant leg. "I love her so much, Ama. I know Esme is yours, that you were able to have the baby I couldn't."

"Don't say that." I slid along the bench, putting more space between us. "It is not mine. I don't want it. I never wanted it."

I watched Leoti as she broke off another bit of cracker and passed it to the child. "And, by the way, you're not the problem. Rubin is sterile. You can have a baby, he just can't give you one."

"What? How do you know that?"

"I saw it in the damned bone reading."

"Then why did you tell me I was going to have a little girl?"

"Because my spirit guide told me you would. I wasn't privy to the details. I thought maybe you'd have an affair or something."

"I would never cheat on Rubin."

"Does it even matter what I did or didn't tell you? You got a kid, and you're obviously set on keeping it."

"I promise you, Ama, Rubin and I will always love and protect Esme. We've talked about it, and we really want you to be part of Esme's life. I mean, after all, you gave her life."

"Look, Leoti. I see how happy she makes you, and maybe one day, I can accept that. But the fact you and Rubin want this child to be part of your lives does not mean I want it to be part of mine. I made myself clear the night she was born. I have no intentions of being in this child's life—not its mother, not its birth mother, not even its auntie. Nothing. If you keep this child, I'm out. She is never to know about me, about the fact you have a twin. Nothing. I mean it, Leoti. Nothing. I have too much at stake. You break this pact and the consequences will be dire."

"How can you hate her so much? She's an innocent baby. None of whatever it is that happened to you is Esme's fault."

"Yeah, you've said that already, upon which I told you it is not a conversation we are going to have."

Leoti pulled out a towel and wiped the baby's hands and face clean. "So why are you here, Ama?"

"Because I needed to know what you did with it."

Leoti leaned forward and pulled the baby from the stroller.

She sat the child on her knee so it looked at me, offered me a slob-bery smile.

"Would you like to hold her?"

I stood, took a step away, and looked out over the park. Behind me, Leoti shuffled the baby and the stroller to stand. She walked up beside me, balanced the baby on her hip with ease.

"You aren't going to take Esme away from me, are you?"

"What?" I asked, then turned to look Leoti in the eyes, see how much she really knew. It was not Leoti I saw, though, it was the child, and I turned away again.

"Please, Ama. If you don't want her, just let me be happy, let Rubin and me raise her."

Why had I come here? Deep down, I hoped I would find Leoti had gotten rid of the baby. If she truly loved me, she would have abided by my wishes the night of that baby's birth. But no, it was now clear to me, she intended to keep the child in her life even if, by doing so, she would lose me. And she would. I was done. I was tired of being everyone's second choice, Elan's, my mother's, even Papa's—The Community always came first with my father.

"I came here today to tell you Papa is sick. He's not doing well."

"Sick? What's wrong with him?"

"Do you really care, Leoti?"

"Of course I do. He's my father too."

"Well, you haven't seen him in almost two years now. That doesn't seem caring, in my opinion."

"You know why I haven't seen him. He refuses to accept my husband, the way we live, therefore, he doesn't accept me. I don't approve of how he lives, but I don't insist he change his lifestyle to be my father."

"It's lung disease."

"Oh no," she exclaimed and shifted the child to the other hip. "Has he been to the doctor? He needs to start treatment."

"You know perfectly well that is not an option he will consider."

"So what, he's just waiting to die?"

"No. We're handling it, the other healers and me."

"I love you, Ama, and I believe in your abilities, but you don't take a man's life and well-being into your hands and think you are more capable of healing him than a trained professional would be."

Not that I would admit it to Leoti, but I had mulled over the same concerns. I knew I'd not led an exemplary life, and I could handle the repercussions of my past actions, but I couldn't shoulder the responsibility of my father's death. I voiced the concerns to Papa. In doing so, I had almost jeopardized my place in The Community. In no uncertain terms, Papa condemned my lack of faith in The Community, going on to say I may not be the right one to lead The Community into the future after his passing.

"Papa is firm in his beliefs, Leoti. He has no intention of seeking help outside The Community. Doing so would be going against doctrine, a doctrine he himself authored."

"I want to see him. Maybe I can convince him. Maybe if he meets his granddaughter, he'll have the incentive to seek a doctor's advice."

"Absolutely not. There is no way you are bringing that thing around him."

"Ama. You will stop referring to Esme as a thing or an it. She is my child."

"And Papa is never to know about her."

"Why not? What makes you think I would tell him the truth? I haven't told anyone else. As far as the rest of the world is concerned, Esme is my flesh and blood."

"Papa would know. He would see it all over your face, and her face, and my face for that matter."

"And why would that be so bad? Esme is his granddaughter no matter what he saw on our faces."

"Because she's a baby I conceived with a *commoner*."

"Well, if Esme were my biological daughter, she'd have been conceived by two commoners. I don't understand the problem here, Ama."

"Are you really that daft, Leoti, or is it that you could care less about my well-being, about my future? I stand to lose everything if it gets back to Papa that I've had a child with a commoner. My life and everything I've worked for in The Community would be over."

"And that would be so bad? You've already questioned the decision to continue on there."

"I may have had doubts in the past, but those are long gone. Now, I know where I belong. The Community is the only place in this world where I am accepted and respected for who I am. I've worked all my life to become an elder. When my training is over, I will be the strongest elder ever to oversee The Community. I'm not giving it up because of her."

"I thought I knew you, Ama. I thought you wanted more out of life than day in and day out in that place, with their stupid rules."

"What makes the rules I live by any more ridiculous than the societal norms you adhere to?"

"I'm free to live my life however I choose. Nobody makes decisions for me but me."

"That place, as you call it, is the only place people don't look at me like I'm a freak. In The Community, I'm nobody's second choice, Leoti. I was chosen."

The baby's soft whimpers escalated to a full-blown crying fit. Leoti did her best to shush it, but none of her attempts seemed to work. She walked back to the stroller, dug through a bag in the bottom of the carriage, and produced a bottle. She settled herself on the bench and proceeded to feed the child. She was a natural, I gave her that, probably just the same as our mother was, but how would I know? Our mother chose Leoti, and now Leoti had chosen the child over me.

There was nothing left to say. I slipped away while Leoti tended to her child.

The flames of fire die down. I don't bother to stoke it, I've seen the conversation I evoked. Remembered clearly, the reason I've had so little contact with my sister in the years thereafter.

I signed the legal documents Rubin drew up under one stern stipulation—the girl would never know of my name or existence. Leoti and Rubin long held the agreement. As far as the girl knew, Leoti had given birth to her, and Rubin was her biological father.

The truth is out now, however. Leoti insists she has no idea how Esme learned of the secret. Leoti has informed me the girl has requested to meet me, and as I've reiterated in the past, in the present, and for the future, that will never transpire. The flames have confirmed—I made myself clear from the beginning.

I have far too much at risk for this girl/woman to ruin everything I've worked years to achieve. My appointment as chief elder will commence on my sixtieth birthday. I've put fifty-three years into obtaining the highest esteem ever held by a Community leader. And I will do whatever it takes to be certain no one takes it from me.

I had once entrusted my life to fate, but now, I control my destiny.

RISING FROM THE DARKNESS

The healing process, if you could call it healing, was long and arduous. Days and weeks stretched into months, eventually spanning almost two full years of believing I would never be able to carry out the life of a normal person again.

When I finally *truly* awoke, I no longer recognized myself. The time I had spent residing in my mind, only coming to full consciousness sporadically, had taken a toll on my body. My hair had grayed. My frame had thinned. "You're nothing but skin and bones, Esme," Mama declared. "Here, eat this," she demanded. But even though I was no longer slipping back into those long stretches of oblivion, I still had no appetite—not for food, not for companionship, not for life. I was not the same person I had once been, mentally or physically, or spiritually.

I dragged myself to the bathroom, forced myself to view the reflection in the mirror. The person who stared back at me was no longer familiar. The woman I saw in front of me had been hardened by loss, by grief, and deceit. Why had I added deception to the list of causes for the change in my physical appearance, I wondered. I understood the grief and the loss. I knew about the deaths of my son and my husband, but I could not identify the reasons I believed I had been deceived.

In therapy sessions with my doctor, we explored the reasons for this impetuous declaration—that my life was little more than a lie. It was fact I had married the love of my life; I had bore his son; I had lost them both within a matter of hours. And then, I remembered.

The recollection was disoriented, fragmented, almost as if it were a dream. But I had heard them, heard what they admitted while I was in one of my stupors, while they thought I was incoherent. I wasn't who I thought I was. My mother wasn't my mother, and my father wasn't my father. I was the product of two people I didn't know existed in the world, who both would rather not know of my existence. Perhaps that was why I no longer recognized myself?

The therapist believed it was crucial to my treatment that I confront my mother about what I thought I had heard. For the most part, she was upfront with me. My mother had a twin sister named Ama. My mother explained how they had been separated at birth yet still grew up together. I asked questions. Where does your sister live? Why have I never known about or met her? My mother declined to give me specifics, however, stating it was part of the arrangement. My mother's sister had stipulated that in order for my mother to keep me and raise me as her child, I was never to know of this woman. And who was my father? My mother claimed she had no idea of the man's identity. I worked my father for the same information, but he, too, was tight-lipped. My loving parents were in agreement; for me to know anything more than the sparse details they provided about my birth mother would be a danger to my well-being. Exactly how or what they meant by that warning, neither would elaborate. Their cagey stance, all for the sake of my safety, infuriated me.

I know my feelings were irrational. My parents weren't at fault simply because the people who conceived me wanted nothing to do with me. But as my anger and resentment grew, the grief and despair began to dissipate. The anger gave me energy and purpose, whereas the grief stole my hope and willfulness. So I let that anger grow, allowed it to fuel me, and I dwelled on their injustices.

My parents had conspired with the woman who gave me life, plotted to keep the truth from me. And even after I had learned the two were not my biological parents, they were still holding back information I believed I had the right to know. As a thirty-two-year-old woman, I deserved the long-obscured details of my parentage, no matter what they considered my emotional capacity to be. It was not their place to withhold this information from me. And if they wouldn't tell me, I would find out on my own.

I performed a search with what little information I had—a name, Ama Sowanoke. That was all I had to go on. I found nothing. There was a birth certificate on the state registry for my mother but not for her sister. I could find no property, marriage, divorce, arrest, or death records—not even a driver's license did this woman have. It was as if Ama Sowanoke was conjured in my parents' heads. Or maybe they gave me false information to again throw me off the truth.

The limited knowledge I had been able to obtain about my birth parents, coupled with the resentment-fueled energy, did little for my sense of self, though, for finding my way back to who I had been before. As my mind and body healed, the more urgent my need to evolve became apparent.

Anger did not appease the difficulty I had confronting my reflection. What I saw in the mirrored image was someone I didn't want to be. I was a widow. A mother without a child—a child I was responsible for bringing up sound, and healthy, and safe. I had failed on all accounts. I had been unfaithful to Kirby early in our marriage. My son had only made it to his twelfth birthday, and I had lied to everyone about his death. Where did I belong anymore? What place did I have in the world? How could I face those who knew me as the person I was before when I could no longer take the sight of her in the mirror?

And then it came to me. If I didn't recognize who I was, maybe others should see someone else too. The doctors and therapists were ambivalent with regard to my proclamation, but the only way it was possible for me to move forward was to create another life, a different person who was in no way related to the person I had been before.

My body had already changed. Gone were the soft curves Kirby had loved. My face was thinner, my hair longer. I would change my hair color. I would immerse myself in a different profession. I would move away from Waynesville. I would start over.

The wicked flee when no man pursueth: but the righteous are bold as a lion. Proverbs 28:1 Well, I certainly wasn't bold anymore, but I could now claim to be wicked. What was a person who killed their own child if not wicked?

Once I made the decision, my recovery progressed with amazing speed. I informed my parents of the desire to return to school, to obtain the degree I had planned on before Kirby and I married, before Jay was born. The two agreed it was a great idea. I took them up on their offer of monetary assistance but couldn't accept their emotional support.

As the days of my recovery drew nearer to completion, I realized that to truly identify as another person, I was going to have to change my name.

My parents, Leoti and Rubin Shulman, named me Esmerelda Sowanoke Shulman. Esmerelda, because my mother loved the name. Sowanoke, because it was my grandmother's maiden name. Shulman because, of course, it is my adopted family name. They called me Esme all of my life. But when I took over, I decided to use Merel.

Esme was a daughter, a wife, a mother. Merel is single, a teacher who has no family other than an aunt and an uncle. Merel calls them Letty and Shu.

I'd built two distinctly different worlds, but now those two worlds were colliding.

MEREL

APRIL 2018

Hand outstretched, long fingers curling, the shadow woman beckons. She's been coming to me in my dreams all of my life, frightening me throughout my childhood, disappearing during my young adult years, then returning after I lost Jay and Kirby. Each time she came to me in my sleep, I believed the shadow woman meant to do me harm. But during years of therapy after losing my family, I'd learned how to deal with her reoccurring presence.

Perhaps if I could finally see her face, the reign she holds over my sleep would be over. I do as the shadow woman requests, slowly moving one foot in front of another. Guided by the light of the full moon overhead, I tread over the fallen branches, through the towering trees of the forest to the clearing where the woman summons me to her.

Long uncombed hair hangs down the middle of her back. A dark shroud covers her body. Standing amid the flames, she shows no fear of the fire lapping up around her, hemming her inside the circle of long orange tongues. As I near her, I search out her features. The shadows from the fire make her appear faceless, though, and now, the fear I thought overcome rises from my middle.

I halt outside the ring of flames, repeating the mantra my therapists taught me to protect myself from panic. "No harm can come to me in my dreams."

The fire heats my skin. A bead of sweat trickles down my brow. The shadow woman is within arm's reach. Lifting her head, she motions me forward. I need to see her face—I'm so close. The woman extends her hand to me. Her fingertips brush over my wrist, along my arm. Her touch searing, I jump back before she grasps me.

My tongue thick, body slick, the panic wins out, waking me. Fear squeezes the breath from my chest. Pull in. Push out. I work my lungs until I can do so without thinking.

Sitting upright, wet bedsheets bunched inside my clutch, I reluctantly release them. Drenched in sweat, the nightshirt clings to my body. This dream was different from the ones in the past, somehow more urgent. The woman seemed almost desperate to reach me.

I throw my legs over the edge of the bed, pull the soaked shirt over my head to exchange it for a dry one, then head to the living room to spend what remains of the night hours on the sofa.

* * *

THE OFFICE IS DARK. I've beaten Dorothy to work this morning. I run through the ritual of turning on lights and booting up computers. Plopping into the chair behind my classroom desk, I wait as the computer whirrs to life, then pull up the calendar. Days laid out before me, I note how slowly the time has ticked by this month. First spring break—a long, drawn out week of keeping my mind off the anniversaries of Jay's and Kirby's deaths, followed by the return to school and learning of Ollie's death. Ollie's funeral this past weekend. Eyes welling, I move on to the next scheduled events. Dentist appointment after school today, Letty's birthday at the end of the month.

As with each one of Letty's birthdays over the last years since I learned the truth, I wonder about her twin, Ama. How does she celebrate their shared birthday? Letty will be sixty this year. What must it be like for the two of them to share sixty years' worth of history together?

I exit the calendar and click to open my school email account. My eyes immediately focus on the new message from Fiona Cooksey. Checking the date, I learn Jay's mom sent the email late Saturday evening.

Ms. Sowanoke,

Jay/Jack has been ill this past week. He will be returning to school Monday. I'm sure he has missed quite a bit of schoolwork. Please send any make-up assignments home, and I will see he completes them.

Thank you,

Fiona Cooksey

P.S. I am sorry to hear about the loss of Ollie Deacon.

Well, that answers where Jay or Jack—or whatever the hell they're calling him now—has been this last week. I rub the back of my neck, where an ache begins to creep its way up into the base of my skull. How will I ever hold my tongue with the suspicions thrashing for verification?

I look out over the classroom, inspecting the new layout. After Ollie's funeral this weekend, I came into school to change up the seating arrangement. Not only did I need the distraction of work, but I wanted to alleviate some of the students' stress over having lost a classmate. Our room will not be the same without Ollie, no matter what I do. But by placing the students into different groupings, positioning them closer together, I am hoping the new arrangement will ease them through the remainder of the school year. My students need the companionship of one another. We are all grieving. In past seating assignments, I focused on ways to keep them from socializing too much, on making sure their attention was on my lessons and not on one of their peers. The only thing I am concerned about with this seating assignment is the placement of Jay. I want to know his whereabouts at all times.

My eyes land on his desk, just feet away from mine. While I don't have proof Jay had anything to do with Ollie's overdose, I am not about to give him the opportunity to hurt another child. And though Dorothy disagrees, I still believe I have a responsibility to tell Jeanine about the conversation I overheard between Jay's and Caroline's mothers. I don't have to relay my theory to Jeanine—that Jay was the child who gave Ollie all that Xanax, bullied Ollie into taking it.

Dorothy knows of the conclusion I've drawn about Ollie's death. Wanting to check on me, she sought me out after the funeral. I told Dorothy about the conversation I overheard between the room moms, but Dorothy was unconvinced. She doesn't believe Jay could be capable of such a horrendous act and encouraged me not to say anything. Dorothy claimed I was distressed, that I had read something into the situation that simply couldn't be possible, that no child could ever be as evil as to kill another. But I knew differently. We argued.

"I realize Jay is a difficult child to handle, but for goodness sake, Merel, he's not a killer."

I couldn't blame Dorothy for thinking I was overreacting. She knew too much about my past, about my night terrors, about my parents.

"Well, he killed Ollie's frog. Or did you forget?"

"Merel, killing a frog and killing a child are two completely different things. Jay is a handful, I'll give you that. But I think you're letting your imagination get away from you on this one. Maybe you should try to have a little more compassion for Jay. I mean, given that he and your son share the same name and all. Maybe, you could try to see more of your own Jay in your student...."

"No," I had cut Dorothy off before she could finish the suggestion.

Dorothy wasn't and will never be privy to all of my history.

No one knew or will ever know of the secret slowly chewing away at me day after day. Dorothy assumes my memories are pleasant but too difficult to recall. The truth is that each time I look at Jay, I fall back into some horrible recollection of my son's childhood. Throughout the school year, each incident with Jay has dredged up the memories of my life as a mother—a life I've desperately tried to leave behind.

"I already see too much of my Jay in this Jay as it is. Every time I look into Jay's eyes, the same color, the same glare, it's like I'm seeing my son, Jay."

"And that's too much for you to handle. I've been saying it all along. Let me take him." No one could declare Dorothy Conners was a woman to give up easily. Since the day in January when Jay smashed Ollie's frog, she had been hounding me about a transfer for Jay. "We'll go to Jeanine and suggest the transfer. She'll understand, especially now she knows about what happened to your family."

I had tabled the discussion this weekend, but now I'm rethinking Dorothy's insistence. Having just experienced the anniversary of Jay's and Kirby's deaths, along with the added pressure of losing a student, probably has a lot to do with my current state of mind. I'm paranoid. That's all. All the signs are there. The feeling someone is watching my every move. Suspicious of everyone's intentions, believing the worst about others. Even the shadow woman appearing so vividly in my dream this morning seems suspect. Moving Jay out of my classroom may be exactly what I need to do for myself—maybe Dorothy is right.

As if I've summoned her through my thoughts, Dorothy pokes her head inside my classroom. "Hey there. You feeling any better today?"

The heat kicks on in the room, blasting a rush of warm air to knock off the chill of the cool morning.

"A bit," I say, standing, moving to straighten the edges of two desks to align better.

Dorothy approaches me, hesitation in her gait. "You think any more about my offer?"

"I did." I cross my arms and sigh. "Admitting it may feel like defeat, but I think you might be right. Maybe I'm not doing Jay or myself any good by insisting on finishing the school year out with him in my classroom."

"Good. I'm glad you've changed your mind. I've been worried about you all weekend. Let's go talk to Jeanine after dismissal this afternoon. We'll get her opinion and then move forward with whatever she thinks is best."

I nod. "Okay," I say, barely able to get the concession out.

"Merel," Dorothy says, reaching for my hand and squeezing, "if this is not the right thing to do, Jeanine will be the first one to tell us. But I promise you, she's not going to hold this against you. She's not as scary as you think."

I nod again, knowing that to use my voice right now might give away my feelings of failure.

"All settled then." Dorothy gives my hand another reassuring grip, her lips pressed tight in a half smile.

I suddenly recall my appointment after school. "Oh, I just remembered I have a dentist appointment right after dismissal today."

"Your crown?"

"Yeah. And the office closes early on Mondays for a weekly staff meeting."

"Well, you can't miss it. That tooth has been giving you all kinds of trouble. I'll handle Jeanine. You keep the appointment."

"Okay, but you'll be sure to let her know, I want her honest opinion on this. I am willing to do whatever is best in the situation," I say, dropping Dorothy's hand to tug my cardigan off as the temperature in the room warms.

"Oh, Merel, honey." Dorothy grabs my hand again, twisting my arm, examining. "What did you do to yourself? That's one nasty looking burn."

"I don't know. I don't remember seeing it in the shower this morning." I shrug, then add, "But I was half asleep at the time."

* * *

THE STUDENTS all deposited to their appropriate dismissal stations, I hurry back down the hallway toward my classroom. I head straight into the office, grab my purse from the closet, and gather the work I need to get done at home tonight. Digging through my bag, I search for my phone only to realize I must have left it in the top drawer of my classroom desk again and hurry out of the office to retrieve it.

Right where I left it, I pull it from the drawer. The screen is black and doesn't respond to touch. I worry the battery is dead as I hold the button waiting for it to power on. The apple appears and stalls. It's time for a new phone, but I keep putting off the expensive purchase. Cell reception inside the concrete school building limited, I walk to stand near the window, hoping to speed up the process. The screen brightens for passcode entry. I tap the numbers to unlock the phone and notice new voicemails —one from a room mom and another from my dentist's office.

Staring at the playground outside my windows, I listen as the receptionist relays the dentist has had an emergency outside the office he must attend to this afternoon. They will need to reschedule my appointment. My shoulders fall in frustration.

Perhaps it was meant to be—an intervention of fate. I might be able to catch Dorothy before she meets with Jeanine. Admittedly, a part of me wants nothing to do with this conversation, but this is my problem, not Dorothy's.

With purpose, I turn from the windows and startle, dropping my phone to the tile floor. Jay stands silently beside the office door. Backpack hanging open at his side, Jay holds his position, his blank gaze focused on me. I bend to retrieve the phone and rise, placing it on my desk, thankful the screen is still intact.

"Jay, what are you doing here?" I fold my arms across my

chest. Aware the posture is a defensive move, trying to consciously will myself to see him as I would any other child, I drop my hands to the sides of my body.

He doesn't answer, continuing to stare through me instead.

I walk toward him. "I thought I just dropped you off at car lobby."

"You did. My mom has a PTA meeting, so I'm hanging out." Jay delivers the statement in his monotone manner.

"Does your mom know where you are?"

"I told her I was coming to see you."

"You can't stay here, Jay. I have a meeting with Principal Garber."

"All those moms are boring."

I shake my head, moving to step around him.

"You're here."

"I'm sorry, Jay, but you can't be in the classroom by yourself."

"You don't like me."

His statement halts me. "Why would you say something like that, Jay?"

"Because it's true. You want to get rid of me."

"What are you talking about, Jay? What do you mean 'get rid of you?'"

"I heard you. The day Ollie's frog died, I heard you talking to Mrs. Conners in the office. I know you don't want to be my teacher anymore. You want Mrs. Conners to take me."

"You shouldn't be listening to other people's conversations. It's called eavesdropping." Blood rushes to my face. My body tenses. I can no longer hold back. "Let's talk about hearing conversations. I heard you tell Ollie he was stupid."

"So. He was," Jay says, no emotion, no compassion for the dead child.

"Did you tell him there was a stupid pill? Did you tell Ollie he could be smart if he took stupid pills?"

Jay's eyes narrow, lips clamp shut, refusing to answer my questions.

I can't do this. I've got to get both of us out of this room before I say something, do something I will regret.

"I have a meeting I need to get to." Stepping inside the office, I begin rooting through my purse. I need to find my keys so I can lock up the classroom when I leave, so Jay can't come back inside with me out of the room.

The office door slams. My head snaps to the other side of the office, checking to see if Dorothy's door is open, but it is pulled tight. She must have closed it during dismissal. With both doors shut, I'm trapped. *Be calm, don't panic.* I can't let myself slip into a claustrophobic attack right now. I pull my arm from my purse and grab the door handle. Twisting and pulling—all good intentions lost as quickly as I had summoned the words of encouragement—pushing and yelling for Jay to open the door.

Pricking sensations run up and down the length of my arm. Red fire ants scurry over my flesh, stinging, burning, injecting me with their poison. Oh my God, where did these come from? How? It must be a trick of my mind—I just dug through my purse in search of my phone not ten minutes ago. Fabrication or not, I frantically brush the fire ants from my arm, watching them fling to the floor. Panic wells and surges through my body.

My Epipen.

I dump my purse onto the desktop, pushing away the roaming ants that fall from the bag, tearing through the contents, flinging the items aside in search of my injector.

It's not here.

I turn the bag upside down again, shaking it furiously. The bag is empty. I never go anywhere without that pen.

If I can get to the nurse's office, I can use the spare one the school keeps on hand for emergencies. I have to get out of here.

I pull the curtain back from the small window that looks out into the classroom.

"Jay, open the door!" Tears fall over my cheeks. Heat spreads through my body. "Please, Jay."

Jay stares at me through the window, clutching a small glass house. A child's ant farm. He remembered. He remembered me telling the class about my allergic reaction to fire ants. Jay has done this intentionally.

I rush to the door on Dorothy's side, trying in vain to somehow open it. Pounding. Screaming. Pleading.

I feel my tongue and lips swell. The swift current of terror races through my veins. My chest tightens.

I run back to the window. Jay peers inside as if watching a show on television. "Please," I manage to get out between the sobs stealing my breath. The fight to get air down my throat becomes increasingly difficult—I feel it closing off. The room spins. I beat on the window, trying to get Jay to see the urgency of the situation, to let me out, to help.

He doesn't move. Jay stands, watching through the window as I battle for breath. He raises his hand as if to wave. My eyes follow in response, hoping desperately for some message of help.

The last thing I see is Jay holding up an Epipen. Then all goes dark.

AMA

APRIL 2018

The familiar tinkle above the bakery door announces my arrival. The display cases are full, but the shop is empty. Leoti emerges from the back room to greet the customer she expects to see at her counter. Upon seeing me, the forced smile slips from her face. Leoti says nothing as she steps forward.

"Happy birthday," I say, taking a seat at one of the cafe tables. The silent invitation to join me hangs between us.

Leoti proceeds reluctantly across the room and pulls the chair from underneath the other side of the table. "Happy birthday," she replies, though I detect little genuineness behind the sentiment. "I didn't expect to see you this year," Leoti says as she sits.

"Why do you say that?"

Leoti holds her spine straight against the back of the chair, eyes locked on mine. "The way you ran out of here last year, I didn't think you'd come 'round again."

"I had a lot of loose ends to attend to over the last months."

"Ha. Loose ends..." Leoti lets the statement, choked with sarcasm, fall away. "I guess this is a big one for you, huh—sixty, finally having achieved grand Poobah status and all."

"Chief elder, and yes, it is. I've worked hard for that fated status."

"They're throwing you some sort of celebration, I suppose."

"A ceremony. Tonight. I'd like you to come."

Leoti lowers her shaking head, "No."

"Why?"

Leoti's eyes raise to meet mine—anger, hatred, and heat whirling behind them. "You really need to ask me why?"

"You're the only family I have left, Leoti. We finally have a chance to fix what's been broken between us all these years."

Leoti turns her head to hide her filling eyes, fixing her stare on something at the other corner of the room. "When I was a little girl," she begins, pausing to swallow back her grief. "I would envision the two of us. Old ladies, sagging and wrinkled, caring for one another, best friends with a lifetime of memories together."

It's time for the two of us to reconnect. Leoti knows this. With Esmerelda gone, there is no one to come between us any longer.

"Look at us, Leoti; that's exactly what we are." I offer the crooked smile, wait for her smirk, the signal we've used throughout the years to end our disagreements. Leoti refuses to return it this time. I'm not surprised. For all we have been through together, there is even more, we have not shared. Our reunion will not be easy, but nothing ever comes easily to me. Difficult or not, I will get what I want.

Leoti leans forward, resting her arms atop the table, weariness tugging at her features. "No, we're not. We're not those two old women at all. You cut me out a long time ago, Ama. You made your choice. It was always The Community over me. I'm simply a commoner."

"And you can claim you chose me? No. You can't. Because you chose her."

"Why couldn't we have had both, Ama? Why couldn't we have supported one another's decisions throughout the years? Why did it have to be one way or the other?"

"I've come here to show you my forgiveness."

"You've forgiven me?"

"Yes, for choosing the child, for going against my wishes."

"What would you have done with her, Ama? What would you have done if I hadn't walked in on you the night Esme was born and found her on the bathroom floor?"

I shake my head. "I know who I am, and I know what I want. I control my destiny."

"Indeed you do, Ama. No matter the cost. Well, this," Leoti says, waving her hand erratically across the table separating the two of us, "this is not fixable. This is not figure-out-able. There is nothing left to salvage. I, too, know what I want, and Rubin may have advised me against telling you this...." Leoti eases back in her chair, attempts to erase the emotion from her face, acting as if the fitful moment never happened.

"Advised you against what?"

"Nothing."

I lean over the table, peering into Leoti's eyes. "What has Rubin advised you not to tell me, Leoti?"

Leoti turns her attention to the display cases across from us. "We've decided it's time to retire."

She's holding back; Leoti is not being honest with me, but I decide I will play along for the moment. "Retire? And what about the bakery?"

"I'm going to sell it. I've been approached by a potential buyer." Leoti continues to focus on the other side of the room.

"And you and Rubin are going to sit in the house all day and coddle one another?"

Leoti's chest expands with a long pull of air. She slowly twists her gaze back to meet mine. "We're selling the house."

"Why? I thought you were happy there."

"We're leaving Waynesville. "

"Where will you go?"

"I'd rather not say."

Her answers clipped, we're in one of our old 'tit for tat' modes. I break the pattern by holding out until she gives me more.

"Does it really matter where we go, Ama?"

"Of course it matters. You're my sister. I'll miss you."

"You now have everything you ever wanted. Overseeing The Community, your position as chief elder," she says, unable, unwilling to hide the sneer. "You'll be so busy you won't have time to think of me." She looks down, adding, "I hope."

"I don't have everything. I want my sister back. I want us to be like we used to be when we shared our lives with one another."

Leoti's attention snaps back to me. "You should have thought of that before you ripped my heart out. Our daughter, yes ours," she screams at me, rising from her seat, pacing the floor, hands flying back and forth. Tears stream down her face as she comes undone. "You forced me to keep Esme in the dark about how she came into this world. It's your fault Esmerelda could never forgive us. It's your fault she believed we betrayed her. It's your fault she ran away from us. Do you have any idea how it split my heart apart every single time she called me Letty? To hear her call her father Shu? Those were the nicknames Rubin and I used for one another. They weren't meant for our daughter. But because of you, your vindictiveness, your sadistic need for control, I never got the chance to hear my daughter call me mama just one more time. She's dead. She's dead at your hand. I don't care what Rubin says I should or shouldn't do. I know. I found the doll, Ama. I know you were controlling every moment of Esmerelda's life. You and your voodoo, your conjure. I haven't figured out how to convince the authorities yet, but I will."

"Don't be ridiculous, Leoti. You know as well as I do it is the student who is responsible for the girl's death."

"Ah, yes. The little boy, Jay, or Jack, or whatever he's calling himself these days—I know you were controlling him too. Esme's... Merel's teammate told me everything. I know about his doll, the very same kind of doll as Poppy. Not only have you taken my daughter's life, but that child is now sitting in a juvenile detention center because you manipulated him to do your dirty work.

And that other little boy, Ollie. I guess you had a hand in his overdose as well."

"I am not responsible for what you claim," I spit back, unable to hold composure under the barrage of my sister's accusations, her threats.

Leoti stares at me, disbelief clouding her face, grief welling in her eyes. "Mama was right. Conjurers are the devil's workers. She never wanted that life for you, but it doesn't matter to you what anyone wants, does it, Ama? All that matters to you is that you get what you want."

I can't deny her words. They are true. I learned to look out for myself a long time ago. "Believe it or not, you taught me that lesson. I learned from your example, Leoti. You took what you wanted no matter the consequences to another. I simply followed your lead."

Leoti halts, hands by her side, shoulders sagging. "Esmerelda never believed she was worthy. Not worthy of a loving marriage, of raising a responsible, well-adjusted child, of having a career she loved, of having a solid place in the world. You never gave her a chance. You saw to it she suffered all the way through her life. All because of what? Because she caused you pain for nine months and a few hours of labored childbirth?"

"The girl was cursed from the moment she was conceived, Leoti."

"You did curse her. I knew it. I told Rubin...."

"No, I didn't. She was indirectly affected."

"Indirectly? God, you really will say anything. Will you ever accept responsibility for your vile ways?"

"I placed the curse on the man—the man who used me. I didn't know I was going to conceive his child. And because the girl was part of him, she carried the curse throughout her life."

"Then why didn't you reverse it? You could have undone this. Esmerelda didn't have to suffer, and yet you let her."

"I can't reverse my own chaos spell. Another conjurer must perform the reversal."

"So why didn't you do that? Why didn't you go to one of the other elders and explain what had happened?"

"If I had asked another elder to reverse that spell, it would have been an admission of my wrongdoing. I would have had to admit I copulated with a commoner."

"So."

"Very specific plans had been laid for me, my fate since birth. If anyone found out about my transgression, I would never have made it to where I am today, to be chief elder of The Community."

Leoti holds onto the back of the chair she refuses to occupy any longer. "I'm sick of your bullshit, your fate," she screams. "No one's fate is sealed, Ama, unless, of course, you're controlling their destiny for your benefit. God, Ama. You are the most selfish person I've ever known."

"Maybe I am selfish, but no one is going to look out for me. No one is going to put me first. I take care of myself."

"And that's exactly what I'll leave you to do. I am done. But hear me now, Ama. I will have justice for my daughter." Leoti slams the chair underneath the tabletop. "I would exit with your words, *Wegwo di nede uya,* but we both know love cannot possibly be with you. You don't know how to love."

Leoti retreats to the back room. I sit for a moment, taking in the sights and smells of the bakery, knowing this will be the last time I come here.

I rise and return the chair under the table. Stepping to the door, I look above me. Reaching, I remove the bell and take it with me as I leave.

NEVER MISS A BOOK

Thank you, dear reader, for coming along on this ride. I do hope you had as much fun reading this work as I did writing it. If so, please take a moment to post a review, and by all means, tell a friend!

If you'd like more information on Fate Falls Hard and receive notifications of new releases as well as special offers on my books, please join my email list by visiting my website, Leliaapiet.com.

ABOUT THE AUTHOR

Lelia A Piet grew up in the deep south. Her passion for writing began in early childhood crafting stories for her younger sisters as they trudged through the woods of Little River Canyon. A graduate of Florida State University, Lelia left her career in education to pursue her lifelong dream as a full-time writer. When Lelia is not reading or working on her next novel, she is walking her dog or ticking off a carefully curated bucket list of travel destinations. Lelia currently resides in South Florida with her husband, always awaiting the next visit from her sons—she has so many stories to tell them....

facebook.com/LeliaAPiet

instagram.com/leliaapiet

www.ingramcontent.com/pod-product-compliance
Lightning Source LLC
Chambersburg PA
CBHW020130310726
48970CB00006B/1807